# CHRISTMAS in BAYBERRY

A small-town Christmas romance from Hallmark Publishing

## Jennifer Faye

# Chapter One

*Last week of November*
*New York, New York*

BIG LAZY SNOWFLAKES DRIFTED TOWARD the ground. Standing in front of the large glass windows of the Manhattan skyscraper, Wesley Adams had an excellent view of the late-November sky, making it seem like the city was inside a great big snow globe that someone had given a shake. Or maybe that's just how life felt right now—shaken and turned on its head.

He started walking, refusing to let the entire day go sideways on him. If he kept moving, he could meet all of his deadlines. He glanced at the black leather wristwatch with the gold face that his mother had given him when he'd graduated from college. It had been all she could afford—probably more than she could afford—and he loved both her and the watch dearly.

For a senior business advisor, there was so much work when the end of the year rolled around. Worst of all, everything needed to be done at once. For Wes, when it came to holidays or a deadline, the deadline always won out. There were always risk analyses and restructuring deals that needed to be completed ASAP. Business didn't take holidays. It was the mantra of Watson & Summers.

Wes rushed down the hallway toward his office. Even though the holiday season was upon them, the office was devoid of decorations. Not one tiny Christmas tree or so much as an ornament was to be found anywhere on the floor. There wasn't even holiday music playing over the speaker system. Mr. Summers, as he insisted on being called, thought bringing Christmas into the office would encourage employees to act as if they were on holiday instead of proceeding with business as usual. Wes didn't agree, but it wasn't his place to argue the point.

As usual, Wes was prepared to work through the entire Thanksgiving weekend. He was certain it would be the same for Christmas. Too much work and not enough time. He told himself that being in the office was the way he liked it—a chance to get ahead.

After all, he was in line for a promotion to assistant vice president. If he could land the prestigious position, it would mean more money—money he could use to rent a place for his mother here in the city, near him. As his father had passed on a few years back, Wes worried about her living all alone in Florida. It was so far away. And she didn't like to fly.

Of course, she insisted she had all of her friends, should she ever need anything, but sometimes he wondered if she was truly as happy as she let on. Or was she saying what she thought he wanted to hear?

He wouldn't put it past her. All she'd ever wanted was for him to be happy.

Right now, he had fifteen minutes to verify the projected five-year growth report and print out an income statement for his next meeting with an important client. He'd meant to get it done this morning, but one impromptu consultation had led to another. No wonder the work on his desk piled up.

"Hey, Wes," the president of the firm called out to him.

Wes stopped in front of the office door. He peered in at the older man, who had just a few gray hairs left on his head and permanent frown lines marring his face. "Hello, Mr. Summers. What do you need?"

His boss's bushy brows drew together. "Do you have the report on the Wallace account?"

"I do. It's in my office. I'll get it for you."

"No rush. As long as you have it to me by eleven."

Wes nodded. He checked his watch again. Fourteen minutes till eleven. So much for not worrying about getting the report to Mr. Summers right away. His mother had always said, *If you want something done, give it to a busy person.* Had that been some sort of prediction about his life?

After the promotion, things would slow down. He'd have staff under him to help balance out his workload. It would all get better. He just had to hang in there until the first of the year. That should be easy. Not a problem at all.

He couldn't help but smile at the world's biggest lie.

Wes stepped into the hallway, noticing Mr. Summers' assistant at her desk. "Good morning, Jan."

"Good morning, Wes." The older woman's ivory face lit up as color bloomed in her cheeks. She peered at him over her black-rimmed reading glasses. "Thank you for the Boston cream donut. I was going to save half for lunch, but one bite led to another. It was so good."

At least once a week, he made a point of stopping at the bakery on his way into the office. It was a small way to thank the people who helped him throughout the week.

"Glad you enjoyed it. How's your mother doing?"

"Better, now that her cold has passed," Jan said with a smile. "She's promising cookies and pie for Christmas. And she's making a nut roll just for you."

"You're both too good to me." He'd gotten to know Jan's mother a few years ago, when he'd volunteered to help move Jan's mother into a senior's high rise.

Jan whispered, "I've got my fingers crossed for you. It won't be long now."

He knew she was talking about the promotion. He grinned. "Thanks. I've got to run."

"Let me know if you need anything."

He greeted other co-workers but kept moving, because time was money and there was never enough of either. Still, he liked to acknowledge the friendly people he worked with every day.

"Morning Joe," he said to the mailroom guy, who was pushing a full mail cart down the hallway.

"Morning." A few years younger than Wes, Joe attended night school. He liked to say that he was working his way up through the company—starting on the ground floor. "I left those files you put a rush on in your office."

4

"Thank you. You're a lifesaver."

Joe smiled and continued pushing the loaded mail cart in the opposite direction.

*Buzz. Buzz.*

Wes stepped into his office and fished his phone out of his pocket. It was his mother. He really didn't have time to speak to her. He had the pages to print, the report to get to Mr. Summers, and he had to get back to the conference room in—he checked his watch—ten minutes.

It wasn't like his mother called all that often. She could need something important. He pressed a button and held the phone to his ear. "Hey Mom, is everything okay?"

"Of course, it is. Is that any way to greet your mother?"

He moved to his desk and perched on the edge of his chair. His hands moved rapidly over the keyboard as he entered his password. "Sorry. It's just that you don't normally call during business hours."

"I did this morning, because I need to discuss some business with you."

His finger struck the wrong key and the printer started spitting out five copies of the necessary file. He tried to stop it, but the computer froze. With a frustrated wave of his hand, he let the printer finish producing all five copies. Fortunately, the report was only three pages long.

"What business?" he asked.

"Do you remember Bayberry?"

"Bayberry the candle? Or the town in Vermont?"

"The small town."

He checked the time. He was down to nine minutes. "Of course, I remember. We lived there briefly when I was, ah, fifteen."

He envisioned his mother smiling and nodding her head. "That's right. You have a good memory. Well, I was just talking to my friend there. Do you remember Penney Taylor?"

He remembered a girl in school with the same last name. She'd been in his class, and he'd had the biggest crush on her. They'd lived in Bayberry less than a year, however, when his father had announced that they had to move because he'd landed a new job. Wes hadn't taken it well. He'd intended to ask the girl to the Candlelight Dance on Christmas Eve. He hadn't thought of her in years.

"Sorry Mom, but I don't know your friend."

"No worries, dear. You'll like her. She's the sweetest."

Why was he going to like her? He didn't have any plans to meet his mother's friend. "Mom, I don't understand, and I really have to go. Can we talk about this later?"

"My friend, Penney, owns The Bayberry Candle Company."

She said it as though it was supposed to mean something to him. "I'm not following."

He grabbed the file for Mr. Summers. Wes's gaze moved to the time on the lower right corner of his computer monitor. Five minutes and counting. He moved quickly. His elbow struck a stack of reports for his meeting. He reached out. They fell into his hands.

"My friend, she needs you to come to Bayberry and advise her on her business."

He was touched that his mother was talking him

up, but he couldn't drop everything. "Mom, I can't just leave the office." He straightened the papers. "It doesn't work like that. Right now, I have to get to an important meeting. Can we talk more later?"

"Sure. But there's something else you should know—"

"Mom, I really have to go. I promise to call you back. You can tell me all about your friend's situation this evening."

"Okay, dear. Love you."

"Love you too." He disconnected the call, grabbed the file for Mr. Summers and rushed out the door. If he hurried, he'd make it to the meeting in the nick of time.

He hoped Mr. Summers was out of his office or tied up on the phone so he could drop the file folder off and keep going.

Mr. Summers looked up and smiled. "Wes. Just the man I need to see."

Wes glanced in the office, finding Chad lounged back in one of the leather armchairs. Chad with his white-blond hair and too-bright teeth, was another senior analyst—also very eager for the assistant vice president position.

"That will be all, Chad," Mr. Summers said.

"Yes sir. You can count on me. If you need anything else—anything at all—you know where to find me." On Chad's way out the door, he paused and grinned at Wes. "Don't worry. I'll make sure all of your accounts are handled." And then he tucked his thumbs in his gray suspenders and sauntered down the hall in his designer suit and shiny shoes.

*My accounts? What?*

Chad must be confused. That was the only reasonable explanation. Although when Mr. Summers gestured for him to enter the office, Wes got a sinking feeling in the pit of his stomach.

He entered the very spacious corner office. The two outside walls were glass, giving a jaw-dropping view of the city. Right now, though, Mr. Summers had his full attention. Why did Chad think he was taking over Wes's accounts?

Wes stepped up to his boss's very large oak desk. "Here's the file you requested. Everything should be in there."

"Thank you." Mr. Summers took the folder, then gestured to the two charcoal gray chairs in front of his desk. "Take a seat."

Wes was torn between doing what the president of the company wanted or speaking up about his pending meeting. After all, Mr. Summers had the final say on who got the promotion. Wes had to stay on the man's good side, but he also had to get his work done.

Wes's mouth grew dry. He swallowed hard. "Sir, I'm expected in the conference room on the twelfth floor right now."

Mr. Summers leaned forward, resting his elbows on the large oak desk. "They can wait." His gray brows drew together in a formidable line. "This is important."

Wes had no idea why Mr. Summers was so worked up, but he couldn't help but wonder if this had something to do with the promotion. Was Chad being promoted over him?

He took a seat, perching on the edge. Then realizing he needed to appear wholeheartedly interested in what Mr. Summers said, and not ready to rush out the door at his first opportunity, Wes slid back in the chair.

Mr. Summers got to his feet. "Can I get you something to drink?"

"No, thank you."

"Well, I think I'll get something."

The man was certainly not in any rush to get this conversation over with. Maybe the promotion had been decided upon early. And if it was bad news, he didn't think Mr. Summers would waste time with pleasantries—in fact, he was quite certain of it. He wasn't one to draw out bad news.

"Sir, I want to tell you how happy I've been here at Watson & Summers for the past nine years."

"Has it been that long?"

"Yes, sir. I've learned a lot."

"That's good to hear." Mr. Summers turned with a glass of sparkling water in his hand. "I know you're up for the promotion."

"Yes, sir." He sat up straighter and smiled. "It's an amazing opportunity."

"You do know there's only one spot open and a number of strong candidates."

Wes could feel the promotion slowly slipping from his grasp. After being uprooted numerous times as a kid, moving from town to town, crisscrossing the States, he liked the thought of staying in one spot for the rest of his life. There was something to be said for putting down roots.

But if he didn't land this promotion, he was going to have to rethink his plans. Manhattan wasn't the cheapest place to live—far from it. As of right now, he didn't have a Plan B.

Mr. Summers took a drink of water. He set the glass aside. "I have a way for you to gain an edge over the competition."

Wes couldn't help but be suspicious. Mr. Summers had never showed any favoritism toward him before, so why now? Still, he shouldn't look a gift horse in the mouth.

"Thank you, sir. I appreciate this—"

Mr. Summers held up a hand to stop him. "You haven't heard the plan just yet."

Wes had a feeling there would be no chance of turning down Mr. Summers—not unless he also wanted to say goodbye to his bright future at the company. And that was not something he intended to do.

"I need you to go to Vermont."

"Vermont, sir?"

"Yes. Bayberry, Vermont, to be specific."

"Bayberry?" Wes tried to process this turn of events. First his mother, now his boss. "Have you been speaking with my mother?"

"Your mother?" Mr. Summers' forehead creased. "Why would I speak to her?"

Wes cleared his throat. "What do you have in mind, sir?"

*Chapter Two*

*First week of December*
*Bayberry, Vermont*

CHRISTMAS WAS IN THE AIR.

As Katherine Taylor strolled down Main Street, just as she did every morning, she smiled. To her friends and family, which was everyone in the small town of Bayberry, she was Kate.

*Jingle. Jingle. Jingle.*

Santa Claus rang a brass bell next to a red kettle. Large snowflakes fluttered in the air, slowly making their way to the ground. The autumn decorations had come down. Now festive red ribbons and colorful ornaments adorned street lights as well as shop windows.

Everyone passing on the sidewalk dropped some loose change in Santa's kettle. In turn, Santa paused the bell and wished everyone "Merry Christmas," followed by a hearty *ho-ho-ho*.

Kate reached to the bottom of her oversized black

leather purse, where most of her change ended up. She grabbed a handful of coins and dropped them in the kettle. She tried to guess at the identity of the person behind the Santa beard. Fred was their usual Santa, but this wasn't Fred. Whoever was behind the costume had done a really good job, because she wasn't able to put a name to the face.

"I've checked my list once and then twice," Santa said, "and it says you've been really good this year. Santa has something special in mind for you this Christmas."

Kate didn't mind playing along. "Any hints? Is it the new cell phone that just came out?"

"It's much better."

She was intrigued. She liked to believe in Christmas wishes. "What could be better than a phone that works? And doesn't keep dying because the battery is toast?"

Santa's blue eyes twinkled. "This holiday season will be extra special. You just have to keep your eyes open to the magic of the holidays and never stop believing in miracles. Ho-ho-ho."

A little boy, maybe five years old, came rushing up with some change in his hand for the kettle. His father hurried to keep up with him. Kate moved on. She had to admit that had been the strangest conversation she'd ever had with Santa. As she continued down the sidewalk, she glanced back at him. What had he meant by that cryptic message?

Tara Simms was cleaning the display window of Tara's Tasty Treats. When she saw Kate, her round face lit up, and she paused to wave. Her shoulder-length brown hair was tucked behind both ears.

Kate's smile broadened upon noticing Tara's cheery red sweater with a reindeer on the front.

The little shop had been formerly known as the Candy Emporium, but when Tara had taken it over, she'd wanted to offer treats that appealed to most everyone. With the name change, she was able to offer some treats that were diet-friendly and others made with a wholesome goodness. If you wanted a snack, Tara would have something to suit your craving.

"Good morning," Tara said. "Isn't it a beautiful day?" She nodded toward the morning sun.

"It is. It's going to be a great day." Kate's breath made a small cloud in the crisp morning air. "I can feel it in the air."

Was that the truth?

She wanted to believe Bayberry was on an upswing. She really did. After all, this was the season of hope. Her mother used to say not to trouble trouble until trouble troubled you.

But trouble was here. The Bayberry Candle Company, after which the town was named, to honor its oldest and most popular candle, was in a bind.

Her family's company was more than a hundred years old, and most of the factory's equipment hadn't been updated in Kate's lifetime. These days, the old machines broke down regularly, slowing production. Just last week, the big conveyor belt system had stopped. They'd gotten it working again, but barely. The grinding sound was worrisome. They needed to replace it as soon as possible.

However, the bank had turned them down for a loan. They still owed for the new roofs on the office and the factory, as well as for some new computers.

But Kate had a plan. She'd been working on it for a while now. And it was going to work. She refused to believe anything else.

She continued along the cleared sidewalk, enjoying how the morning sunlight twinkled off the freshly fallen snow. It was as though the sidewalks were lined with millions of little diamonds. She remembered, as a child, walking along this same sidewalk with her parents and thinking this time of the year was magical.

Even though Bayberry was the friendliest one-stoplight town, when the holidays rolled around, everyone smiled a little brighter and their steps were a little bouncier. Yes, it was definitely the most magical time of the year. That's why Kate tried to believe everything would work out for her aunt's candle company—the biggest employer in town.

Kate glanced over at the storefronts, enjoying how every business on Main Street decorated for the holidays. The Bayberry Candle Company had kept this town going through the Great Depression, wars, and every other hurdle. Because of this, everyone incorporated candles into their displays. Even the street lamps were designed to look like huge candles. If the candle company went under, people would have to move away for work. A frown pulled at her lips. The town would die—

She halted her pessimistic thoughts. That wouldn't happen. Her aunt wouldn't let that happen. And Kate was doing her part. No one knew that the local bank had turned down their loan. Her stomach knotted into a ball of tension.

There were other banks, other loans. It would all work out. It had to.

In the meantime, they couldn't let the bad news get out because, well, it was the holidays. And holidays were meant for cheer and good tidings. Not for people to worry about the future of the candle company. That could wait for the new year. And by then, maybe all would be right again.

Kate slowed as she neared the carved wooden sign with the silhouette of a coffee mug and the name Steaming Brew spelled out in bright green letters. Abby Clark owned the coffeehouse and had been one of Kate's best friends since, well, since forever.

Kate eased open the glass door, causing the brass bell above her head to jingle. The coffeehouse was small, but what it lacked in space, it made up for in decorations. Abby had painted the off-white walls with mugs, to-go cups, teacups and saucers. Attention to detail really set them off, from the tiny pink flowers on the teacups to the tendrils of rising steam. Amongst the paintings, the word "coffee" was printed in various languages.

Her petite friend, with her trendy short spiked dark brown hair, was dressed in a purple tee shirt and black apron. She'd just finished filling a coffee mug. Abby handed it off to one of the residents of Bayberry, then smiled in Kate's direction and waved her over.

"Your usual? Or would you like to try something more festive?"

Kate inspected the chalkboard menu. She noticed that it had been rewritten with colored chalk: red, green and white. Holiday flavors had been added to the usual suspects. At the top, it said Merry Christmas. And in the corner of the board, Abby had drawn holly berries and leaves.

Though all of the seasonal flavors were tempting, Kate said, "I'm in the mood for the usual."

"One of these days you might break out of your rut and want to liven things up with, say, a chai latte or maybe a hot chocolate."

Kate wrinkled her nose. "For breakfast?"

"Okay. I was just checking. Go grab a table and I'll join you. There's a lull in business today. Maybe everyone's decorating for the holidays."

"Or figuring out what to get me for Christmas." Kate sent her friend a teasing smile.

"Don't you wish." Abby grinned and shook her head.

Kate moved to their usual table. She wasn't sure when it had become "their" table for their work day chit-chat, but it had become a routine. It was something she looked forward to each morning.

Abby made her way out from behind the counter and placed a purple coffee mug in front of Kate, who breathed in the aroma and exhaled a contented sigh.

"Go ahead," Abby said. "I put an ice cube in it just the way you like." She looked at Kate expectantly.

Kate narrowed her gaze. "What are you up to?"

"Nothing. I just know you don't talk much until you've had a dose of caffeine."

"And? What is it you want to know?"

Abby's gaze moved to Kate's untouched coffee as though she wasn't going to say more until Kate had her first sip. Kate didn't need much coaxing. She'd been anticipating this cup of coffee since she'd hit the shower.

She picked up the cup and took a sip, letting it roll over her tongue before she swallowed. She did have a coffee maker at home and one at the office, but neither made coffee that tasted this good.

"Okay. What's going on?"

Abby worried her bottom lip. "You'd better take another drink."

"That serious, huh?" She sent her friend a teasing smile, but when Abby didn't return the smile, Kate's heart sank. She hurriedly gulped coffee. "Okay, tell me."

"There's a rumor going around Bayberry that..." Abby trailed off.

Kate couldn't take Abby's dragging this out any longer. If something was wrong, they all needed to pull together. It was the Bayberry way. And then she wondered if somehow news had leaked about the candle company's financial woes.

"Abby, just say it. What's wrong?"

"It's been said the white candles for the Candlelight Dance are going to be red this year."

"What?" It took Kate a second to compute what her friend was saying. There was nothing wrong?

Abby wore a mischievous grin. "That's the gossip. You know how Bayberry loves its traditions. So, is it true? Are we going red this year?"

Kate's gaze narrowed. "Are you serious?"

"Very serious. I heard it from Ester Holmes, who heard it from Mary Thompson, who heard it from—"

"Stop." Kate held up a hand in defense. She knew

just how long the gossip chain was in Bayberry. "I get the idea. And the answer is no."

Abby made a big deal of sighing and leaning back in the wooden chair as if she'd been seriously worried. "The whole town will be so relieved to hear the news."

Kate smiled and shook her head. It was always amazing what could get this small town of nine hundred and six residents excited. And then Kate mentally corrected herself. With the addition of Tucker and Jane Johnson's son, born last night, the population was now nine hundred and seven.

She took a long drink of her cooling coffee. "Now that we've brought peace back to Bayberry, it's time to move on to important matters." She reached in her purse, pulled out a stack of coupons wrapped with a rubber band, and slid them across the table. "Here are the coupons for this weekend's holiday warehouse sale. Would you mind putting them next to the register?"

"Like you have to ask." Abby scooped them up. "You know I would do anything for you." She looked them over. "Wow! Forty percent off this year."

"Yeah. It's going to be our biggest and best sale."

"With that much of a discount, I can see folks flocking to it. I know I'll be there. I'm out of votive candles and I could use some jar candles."

"You know you don't have to buy all of that just because we're friends—"

"I'm not. Trust me. I love candles in the evening, especially when I kick back with some popcorn to watch Hallmark movies."

"You're right. You're going to need a lot." Kate took a long drink, finishing her coffee. She gathered her things. "I should be going. There's a lot to do before the annual sale." She got to her feet before turning to her friend. "Do you mind if I hang an announcement in the window?"

"Go for it. But I would suggest putting it on the door so everyone who comes in will see it."

"Thanks. I will."

Kate moved to the door to hang a poster on the inside of the door, set her purse down, and withdrew a flyer and a roll of tape. Even though she was an accountant, she considered herself more of a jack-of-all-trades—pitching in where needed.

She tore off two pieces of tape and turned to the door. Just as she reached up to tape the flyer on the glass, the door swung open. Kate jerked back so quickly she lost her balance. She landed on her back-side with an *"Oompff."*

Heat swirled in her chest and rushed to her cheeks. Her gaze took in polished black dress shoes. Then navy dress pants, a black wool overcoat and then a strong jawline, straight nose and piercing blue eyes. Her heart skipped a beat.

She knew all the residents of this small town, and the handsome man staring down at her definitely wasn't a local. "Welcome to Bayberry," she managed.

"Uh...thanks." There was something familiar about him, but she couldn't place the face. He held out his hand to help her to her feet. "Sorry. I didn't see you down there when I opened the door."

She placed her hand in his warm embrace. Kate couldn't help noticing the strength and ease with which he helped her to her feet.

As she brushed off her backside, she took a closer

look at the attractive stranger. He was tall, over six feet. And he had blondish-brown hair, cropped short on the sides with longer strands on top. The cut said he was serious most of the time, but there was a little room for fun—or at least she hoped so.

Who was this mystery man? Had they met before? And why hadn't anyone mentioned such a handsome stranger?

The rattle of coffee mugs jarred her out of her trance. Embarrassed, she averted her gaze to the paper in her hand.

Remembering the stack of coupons in her jacket pocket, she pulled one out and held it out to him. "If you're staying in town this weekend, we're having a huge sale."

"Okay." He didn't even look at the coupon before stuffing it in his pocket. "Thanks. Excuse me."

She frowned as she moved aside, letting him make his way to the counter. What had him in such a rush? Her gaze followed him. There was definitely something familiar about him. But she didn't know him, did she?

As she continued to stare at his back, "All I Want for Christmas is You" came on the local radio station. Maybe he'd attended one of their guided tours at the candle shop. Or maybe he'd attended one of their annual candle sales. That had to be it—

*Jingle. Jingle.*

Kate turned around in time to see three of Bayberry's firefighters enter the shop. They each tipped their ball caps at her and exchanged greetings as they made their way to the counter.

She'd been so distracted by the handsome stranger

that she'd forgotten to hand each of them a coupon. She resisted the urge to go after them. After all, there was a large stack of coupons on the counter and she was certain Abby would hand them out.

Kate taped the flyer to the door, grabbed her purse and exited the coffee shop. This promotion was sure to be a success and generate the income her family's company needed for repairs. And come the New Year, Bayberry Candles would be in good shape. She had a good feeling about this.

He'd been away a long time.

And it appeared little had changed.

Bayberry was still the same friendly small town he remembered.

Christmas music played in the background. The Steaming Brew appeared to be a new establishment. The inside was decked out for the holidays, from multi-colored twinkle lights to the miniature Christmas trees on each table. Maybe it was the fact he'd been working too long at Watson & Summers with its ban on all things holiday, but he could've done without all the decorations. The whole season was a big marketing scheme.

Even the coffeehouse's chalkboard menu was decorated with holly and listed holiday flavors. He opted for his usual tall black coffee. As he waited, he glanced toward the door, hoping to catch another glimpse of the woman who had been his junior high crush.

Kate hadn't recognized him, just as she hadn't

noticed him back in school. It hadn't been her fault. Back then, he'd been too shy to say more than a word or two to her. Any time she'd been in his vicinity, his tongue had become stuck and his brain had refused to string two words together, much less a whole sentence.

With the passage of time, she'd only become more beautiful. He wondered if she was married. He could easily imagine that she'd had her pick of the men in Bayberry. For all he knew, she could have little ones waiting for her at home.

He wanted a family someday, but not while he was still climbing the corporate ladder. He needed to focus all of his attention on his career.

After all, Mr. Summers had practically promised him the promotion if he came to Bayberry and took on this new account. Wes had suspected there was something fishy when the business just happened to be the one owned by his mother's friend—the one she'd called him about. He still wasn't certain about Mr. Summers' angle, but it would become clear soon enough.

"Here you go." The young woman behind the counter smiled brightly as she handed over a green to-go cup. Her name tag read *Abby*. "Can I get you anything else? We have some fresh donuts."

"This is good. Thank you. How much do I owe you?"

Wes paid for his coffee and Abby handed him yet another coupon for the Bayberry Candle sale. He had to wonder about the reason behind the sale and the huge discount. He wouldn't have recommended such a generous drop in price.

He headed out through the coffee shop door and down the sidewalk. Because he'd forgotten to pack his toothbrush, he decided a stop at the Feel Better Pharmacy was in order. He vaguely remembered going there as a kid on his mother's Saturday morning shopping trips. Sure enough, there was the big red neon sign, still hanging in the window.

He opened the door and came to an abrupt halt. There stood Kate.

"Oops. Sorry." She smiled at him. Not just any smile, but a big beautiful one that warmed everything around her, including him. "It looks like we keep running into each other." She held out her hand. "Hi. I'm Kate."

His pulse picked up its pace as his mouth suddenly grew dry. *Just treat her like she's a client. Be professional. Junior high was a long, long time ago.*

He took her hand as his gaze met hers. He cleared his throat. "Nice to meet you. I'm Wesley. Wesley Adams. But only my mother calls me that." *Stop rambling.* "My friends call me Wes."

Her eyes twinkled when she smiled at him. "May I call you Wes, then?"

It took him a second to realize she'd asked him a question. After all these years, this woman still had the ability to turn his usually analytical mind into a jumbled mess.

Wes shifted his weight from one foot to the other. "Yes. Yes, you can."

"Are you visiting someone in town?"

He shook his head. "I'm here for work."

"Oh. Okay." She reached in her jacket pocket and pulled out a small slip of paper. "If you're still in town this weekend, we're having a big sale—the biggest of the year. Maybe you could stop by and pick up a Christmas present...or two."

He decided not to point out that she'd already given him one. It was simpler to just take it.

"Well, it was nice to meet you." She bestowed another dazzling smile on him. "Maybe we'll meet again soon."

"It was nice to meet you, too." But there was nowhere for him to go because she was once again blocking the doorway. "I, um, just need to grab a toothbrush."

"Oh." Her cheeks bloomed a delicate shade of pink. "Sorry. I'm in the way."

She moved to the side, but the entrance to the store was a tight squeeze. He made it past her, but not before catching the softest whiff of lavender. He couldn't resist inhaling deeply as she moved away.

He wondered how many more times they would bump into each other before he left town. Considering she was handing out Bayberry Candle Company coupons and posting flyers, he was pretty certain he hadn't seen the last of her.

## Chapter Three

*T*HEY REALLY NEEDED TO TALK.

Her aunt had been far too quiet lately.

As evening settled over Bayberry, Kate sensed something was afoot. She didn't know what her aunt planned to do about the problems at the candle company. Maybe Aunt Penney was hoping their end-of-year sale would be enough to get them through this rough patch. Kate sure hoped so.

"Penney," Kate called as she let herself into her aunt's house. The place was quiet. "Aunt Penney, are you here?"

"In the kitchen, dear."

Kate followed the voice to the large kitchen with its gas range, generous counter space, and double oven, where her aunt loved to cook and bake in equal portions. Her aunt pulled a tray of muffins from the top oven and placed it on a wire rack to cool.

Aunt Penney's salt and pepper hair was kept short. Every strand was in place. She'd worn the same straight hairstyle as far back as Kate could remember. Just as the same red-and-white gingham curtains hung by the kitchen windows and a cherry-red tea kettle sat on the stove.

Aunt Penney smiled when her gaze landed on Kate. "You're just in time."

Kate inhaled deeply as she took a seat at the island. "Mm...smells great."

"Let's just hope they taste as good as they smell. This is a new recipe I'm trying. Banana and pecan muffins."

"If they taste as good as they smell, you don't have a thing to worry about." It was well known that Aunt Penney was one of the best cooks in Bayberry.

"Thank you, dear." Her smiling face radiated her happiness.

"I baked another batch of muffins and dropped them over at Ester Holmes's. She's been feeling under the weather lately, but that doesn't keep her from gossiping." Aunt Penney shook her head. "That woman can talk a blue streak. I was there forever."

"Let me guess, you made your famous blueberry and cream cheese muffins."

"Of course. And I made sure to add the streusel topping you love. Those muffins are the best cure for what ails you."

Kate smiled. She'd heard that saying over the years, ever since her parents passed away and she'd moved to Bayberry to live with her aunt. She'd been in junior high when she'd first moved to town. It had been the worst and the best time of her life. Everyone at school had wanted to befriend her, which was exactly the opposite of what she'd expected. Coming to Bayberry had actually felt like coming home—her great-great grandparents had been the founders of the town.

Aunt Penney turned to the counter and grabbed the muffin. "I made sure to save you a blueberry muffin."

"You did?" She reached for the muffin and peeled off the paper liner. "You're the best."

"Oh." Aunt Penney waved off the compliment. "You'd say anything to get your hands on a muffin, wouldn't you?"

"I would." Kate played along. That was something else she loved about her aunt. She was light-hearted and let a lot of things roll right off her back. Kate took a bite of the muffin and moaned her approval. "They get better each time you bake them. You really are the best. The fact that you bake the most amazing muffins is just a bonus."

"Thank you." Color infused her aunt's cheeks. "I love you too, dear."

Aunt Penney started to clean off the few dishes in the sink. Sometimes Kate worried about her aunt. She'd never married, but part of that was Kate's fault. When her aunt became an overnight parent, she'd devoted every spare moment to being there for all of her niece's activities. Aunt Penney had headed up the PTA, run bake sales and even traveled with Kate's high school volleyball team as a chaperone. All the while, she'd managed the candle company. How she'd done it all still amazed Kate.

"So how was your day?" Aunt Penney asked as she hand-washed a large mixing bowl. There were certain items that she didn't put in the dishwasher.

"It was good. Although handing out coupons and

hanging flyers took all day. You know how it goes. A hello here and a how-are-you there. It adds up. And then Harry Green's pig got loose."

Aunt Penney laughed. "Buttercup gets more exercise than Harry. She's always getting loose."

"I don't know. You didn't see Harry today." Kate laughed as she pictured the older farmer in his boots and overalls chasing a squealing Buttercup down the street. "I didn't know he could run that fast. All of Main Street came to a halt as everyone waited to see who would win the race."

"Let me guess, it was Buttercup by a length."

Kate nodded. "And then some. Harry was already out of breath as he ran past the pharmacy. Then they turned the corner and I don't know what happened. Someone mentioned later that Buttercup circled back home. She probably worked up an appetite."

"Poor Harry. I'm sorry I missed it." They both chuckled.

As she took another bite, Kate recalled Santa and his cryptic message. "Do you know who's working the red kettle today?"

"It's supposed to be Sam Hansen. Why?"

Sam was tall and lanky. He had to be well over six feet tall, but this morning's Santa had been much shorter, and his cheeks had been quite plump.

"Because I ran into him this morning. When I dropped some change in the kettle, he gave me the most cryptic message. But it wasn't Sam."

Her aunt's face creased with lines. "You said you saw Santa this morning?" When Kate nodded, her mouth full of the delicious muffin, Aunt Penney said, "But Sam wasn't scheduled to work the kettle until late in the afternoon. We don't have anyone in the mornings. And only Fred has a Santa suit. It definitely wasn't him, because I spoke to him, and he was at the warehouse."

"Really?" That was odd. Very odd. And then Kate told her aunt what Santa had said to her.

Aunt Penney shrugged. "I don't know what to tell you, but I must say I'm intrigued."

"Intrigued? I highly doubt he even knows who I am, much less what my future holds."

A teasing smile came over Aunt Penney's face. "You never know. It might have been old St. Nick himself."

Kate shook her head indulgently. "And I ran into another stranger in town."

Aunt Penney turned, curiosity written all over her face. "Do tell."

"It's no big deal." Although in a town this small, a new face stood out. "I literally bumped into him twice in a matter of a few minutes. There was something familiar about him, but I couldn't put my finger on where I knew him from. Maybe he just looks like someone I know, or maybe we met once. I know it'll eventually come to me."

"You're that curious about a stranger?" Aunt Penney picked up a dish towel to dry the bowl.

"It's not like that," Kate said, even though she wasn't sure she believed her own words. "Besides, I'm sure he'll be moving on quickly."

"You're so sure of that? What if he finds he likes it here in Bayberry and decides to stay?"

Kate wasn't going to play her aunt's games. "Then I definitely wouldn't be interested."

"Ah, yes, your rule about not dating Bayberry residents."

She shouldn't have said anything. Kate finished the muffin. Aunt Penney was always encouraging her to date this person or that person. Kate did date, but it was never anyone from Bayberry. The town was just too small to get involved with someone and have it go wrong.

After all, there was only one grocery store, one pharmacy, one movie theatre. There was one of just about everything. Running into people you knew was just a fact of life in Bayberry. She didn't want to ruin the comfort and ease she felt around town.

"It's a good rule." Kate crinkled up the muffin liner. "It keeps things uncomplicated."

"Uh-huh. And it means you spend a lot of Friday nights at home curled up with a book."

Kate shrugged. "I like to read."

"I know. But you're young. You have your whole life ahead of you. You need to do more than work and read."

"I do. I was just out visiting with everyone in town today."

"Because you were passing out flyers about the sale. To my way of thinking, that's work."

"But fun work."

"Listen Kate, I've been meaning to talk to you—"
*Deck the halls...*

Kate's ringtone sounded. She withdrew her phone from her pocket, checked the caller ID, and then looked apologetically at her aunt. "I'm sorry. I need to get this."

"No problem."

Kate had been waiting to hear from Carrie. She and her friends were having trouble getting their schedules lined up in order to plan the Candlelight Dance—Bayberry's biggest event of the year.

Kate pressed the phone to her ear. "Hey, Carrie."

Carrie told her that everyone was available this evening. Kate didn't want to run out on her aunt, but if she and her friends didn't firm up some plans for the dance, there wouldn't be one. And once they all got together, they'd start talking about this and that. Before they knew it, the hour would be late.

Kate asked Carrie to hang on a second. "Aunt Penney, I'm really sorry, but Carrie, Abby and Sadie are available to talk about the dance. Would you mind if I go meet up with them?"

"Not at all." Aunt Penney smiled. "If you need any help with the planning, just let me know."

"Thanks. We will."

Kate took off out the back door, resuming the phone conversation. "I'll be over to your place as soon as I grab my binder and laptop." When Carrie offered to order pizza for everyone, Kate said, "Sounds good. See you soon."

Kate climbed the steps to her garage apartment. It was nothing fancy. In fact, Aunt Penney was horrified that Kate would want to live out here instead of in the house where she'd been living since she was fifteen. But Kate wanted her own space. The cozy apartment had one bedroom, one bathroom, a small kitchenette and a living room. Kate knew someday soon she'd have to get a bigger place, but this arrangement worked for now.

Besides, she had more important things on her

mind—like helping to make this year's holiday sale the biggest and best. Otherwise, she didn't know where Aunt Penney would come up with the funds to keep the candle company in operation.

# Chapter Four

$\mathcal{S}$OME THINGS DIDN'T CHANGE.

Like internal alarm clocks.

Wes always woke up at five a.m. to allow himself time to answer emails before he showered and headed to the office. Today, his inbox was suspiciously lacking its usual long list of unread emails. He wondered if Chad had somehow managed to intercept his business correspondence. The thought didn't sit well with Wes.

With the promotion in the balance, he had to make quick work of his project in Bayberry and get back to the main office. The longer he was away, the more time Chad would have to take over his accounts. And Wes couldn't allow that to happen.

Since Bayberry didn't have any hotels, and the closest one was more than an hour away over narrow mountain roads, he'd snagged the last available room at the Bayberry B&B. For a man who hadn't even owned a car since he lived in Manhattan, he was all right with not driving in the snow. The B&B would do just fine.

He showered and dressed in a suit and tie, then grabbed his attaché case and headed downstairs. Christmas carols played softly in the background. In the large foyer that served as a lobby stood a live pine tree decorated with white twinkle lights, red ribbon and silver ornaments. In fact, every available spot in the lobby, sitting area and dining room was decked out for the holidays. This town really loved Christmas.

"Good morning, Mr. Adams." Mrs. Murphy bestowed a big, rosy smile upon him. Her red hair was pulled up in the back. Dangling from her ears were reindeer earrings. And she wore a red jumper with a white turtleneck. "Can I get you anything? Coffee? Eggs? Toast?"

He really wasn't up for food. Even though this was his second day in Bayberry, he still hadn't gotten a feel for this project. His stomach would be tied up in a knot until he got the lay of the land. And it didn't help that he felt as if he was out of the loop concerning the promotion.

Wes smiled at his host. "Thank you. But I'm good right now."

Mrs. Murphy nodded. "Remember, we're closed for dinner. But don't worry. There's a diner in town. They stay open until eight."

"Thanks for the reminder. I have to get to work."

"The candle company, huh?"

His work was always confidential. He normally worked with very big corporations, but on special occasions he worked with smaller family-run companies like the Bayberry Candle Company. Wes was known for his discretion, but he'd never worked in a town quite as small as Bayberry. He had a feeling it was going to be much harder to keep his presence under wraps—more like impossible.

Choosing to pretend he hadn't heard her question, he said, "I hope you have a good day."

He made a hasty exit. If he had to hazard a guess, Mrs. Murphy probably knew everyone who worked at the candle company. And then his thoughts strayed to Kate. She must work at the candle company if she was hanging the flyers.

A gust of cold air rushed through the openings in his coat. A chill overtook his body. He walked a little faster. Exercise would warm him up. So would stepping inside a nice warm building. He inhaled the below-freezing air. It was certainly a wakeup call.

As he moved along the quiet side street, he recalled his school days. Most of all, he remembered Kate's sunny smile, but when she didn't think anyone was looking there was pain in her eyes. He'd always wanted to talk to her and somehow comfort her, but what does a fifteen-year-old boy know about emotions and making someone feel better?

Still, it had been her outgoing nature and lack of pretense that had initially drawn him to her. He wondered what she was like now that she was all grown up. At least she still had that same bright smile that could chase away the clouds.

The thought of running into her again appealed to him. Just the thought of her made him want to smile. The day definitely had possibilities.

Kate had worked late into the night. This morning, she was tired, but in a rush to get to the office. Her hair was pulled up in a messy bun. She ran a hand over it, trying to smooth the flyaways the blustery morning had created.

It wasn't her favorite hairstyle, but it was convenient. She just didn't have time to mess with a curling iron this morning. She'd even forgone her morning chat with Abby at the Steaming Brew and instead opted for a to-go cup. She had a lot to catch up on at work.

She'd do anything and everything to help her aunt pull off a Christmas miracle and replace some of their equipment in the new year. Because without it...well, she didn't want to contemplate how the company would survive otherwise.

The workers of the Bayberry Candle Company were like one big family. It wasn't a huge business, but Kate envisioned one day expanding their distribution from the New England area until Bayberry was a nationally recognized name.

The best part was that the employees didn't punch a time clock and then count the hours until they could leave. They had potluck lunches, birthday celebrations and work anniversaries. Kate couldn't imagine ever living or working anywhere else. Bayberry would forever be her home.

She hustled down the hall to her office. At the doorway, she came to a halt. What in the world?

There was a man seated at her desk. He had his back to her and he appeared to be sorting through a stack of papers on the credenza behind her desk.

The crime rate in Bayberry was nonexistent, unless you counted Harry's horse getting loose in the summer and stealing Mrs. Woods' apples. That man had the most ornery, headstrong animals in the county. But no human had ever broken into the candle company.

"What are you doing here?" Kate strode over to her desk.

Her hand hovered near the edge of it. The phone was within reach. The sheriff wasn't far away.

When the stranger turned around, she gasped. She recognized him as the good-looking stranger from yesterday. He certainly hadn't struck her as a criminal. After all, would a thief introduce himself before breaking in?

He certainly looked comfortable in her seat. He had papers and files spread across her desk like he'd just moved in. But this was her office, not his.

She opened her mouth to say so when he held up a finger. "I'll be with you in just a second. I just have to—"

"You'll be with me right now." Kate put her hands on her hips, waiting for an explanation.

He obviously wasn't intimidated by her outraged tone as he finished typing some numbers into the spreadsheet on the screen of his laptop. "There we go." He pressed Enter, set aside a stack of papers, and then turned his full attention to her. "Sorry about that."

"And who would you be?"

A puzzled look crossed his face as he got to his feet and held out his hand. "I'm Wes Adams."

She didn't mean his name. She remembered his name and how much of a hurry he'd been in. She wondered if he was always in such a rush. But there was one other thing she recalled from their earlier meeting—his baby blue eyes.

They were the shade of a warm sunny afternoon—the kind where you could let yourself relax and just take in the beauty of the day. And then she realized she'd been standing there staring into his eyes for a bit too long. As heat climbed to her cheeks, she glanced down at the gray tiled floor.

With effort, she shoved aside her unwanted attraction. She didn't make any move to accept his extended hand. "What are you doing at my desk? No one is supposed to be in here but me."

Wes lowered his hand. "You must be the niece."

The niece? "So, you've spoken with my aunt?"

"Yes, I have. She's the one who showed me to this office. You must have been out with your flyers and coupons."

Aunt Penney had done this? Without consulting her? Kate's lips pressed into a firm line. And then she recalled Aunt Penney mentioning she wanted to talk. Was this what she'd had on her mind last night?

The man had made a mess of her desk. There wasn't even room for her coffee or the muffin she'd snagged from Aunt Penney's kitchen. With a frustrated sigh, she headed for the doorway.

She paused and glanced at him. "I'll be back."

He flashed her a brilliant smile. "I look forward to it."

Really? She strode away. Once she spoke to Aunt Penney, this would be all cleared up.

Her aunt hadn't said so, but everyone expected when she retired that Kate would take over the candle company. After all, she was the last living Taylor. There was no one else to take over.

Unless the company was sold.

But that was never going to happen. The candle company was as much a part of her as it was a part of Bayberry, and that's how it would remain.

She marched into her aunt's office. "Why is there a stranger in—"

Her words faltered. There was no one in her aunt's office. Her aunt wasn't at home. So where was she?

Kate walked through the office, glancing in cubicles and saying good morning to everyone. No one knew where to find Aunt Penney. Kate checked the kitchen and the factory. At last, she made it to the warehouse, which was all aflutter with activity as pallets were being rearranged, making way for the annual holiday sale.

And there was Aunt Penney in the middle of everything. She was pointing this way and then that way. Employees, wearing white hard hats, were following her instructions as the forklift lifted a pallet and hauled it toward the back of the enormous building.

The sale had always been one of her aunt's pet projects. She liked to do something a little extra special each year. It wasn't just a sale. It was more like a holiday party, with baked goods and hot apple cider. Something told Kate this year would be no different.

The only thing that was different was the increased discount. That had been Kate's idea. Without a large influx of cash, they wouldn't be able to make the necessary updates. Their supply would dwindle and sales would evaporate as customers flocked to suppliers with ready inventory.

If they could draw in more people, then hopefully, they could add those people to their new email list. That way people wouldn't forget about the Bayberry Candle Company when the holidays were over. Any time customers needed a special gift, they'd go to their website or stop by their gift shop at the front of their office building.

The candle company didn't just sell wax candles. They had soy candles, custom-shaped candles, votives, lanterns, candelabras and so much more. Kate wanted to put together a comprehensive online catalog and expand their online sales. But Aunt Penney wasn't quick when it came to change. Word-of-mouth and newspaper advertisements had always been enough in the past. Traditions were deeply ingrained in the residents of Bayberry.

Kate moved to her aunt's side. "So, you didn't like the new arrangement?"

Aunt Penney shrugged. "I just thought the way we always have things would be easier for customers to find things. I hope you aren't disappointed if we keep things the same."

"You know, sometimes change is for the best." Her aunt was too stuck in her ways, Kate thought.

"I hear you, but this arrangement does flow better."

Kate nodded. "Okay. I understand."

The lines bracketing her aunt's eyes smoothed. "That's good. I guess I should have discussed the change with you since you've been helping me set up, but we've been missing each other a lot lately."

"Actually, that's why I was searching for you. Could we talk a moment?" She didn't want to have this conversation in front of everyone. "Maybe over there." She pointed to an empty part of the warehouse.

"Is something wrong?" Aunt Penney searched her face for answers. Then she turned to another employee, handed off a clipboard, and asked him to keep things moving.

When they were away from everyone else, Kate asked, "Did you forget to tell me something?"

Aunt Penney's eyes widened. "You mean the man in your office?" When Kate nodded, her aunt continued, "I'm sorry. I've just had so much on my mind lately. Sometimes I think I'd forget my head if it wasn't attached. Anyway, about him. I did attempt to warn you last night."

"I know. I'm sorry I had to run off. But I'm listening now. Who is he? And what is he doing here?"

"I've hired Mr. Adams to do some consulting. And, well, you don't actually use your office all that much—"

"I..." She was about to argue but realized her aunt was right. "I guess not."

This time of the year, Kate was usually on the go most of the day, and then she worked on her laptop at home in the evening, updating the accounting records. It wasn't the best arrangement, but when you were the niece of the owner, some allowances were made.

Aunt Penney sent her an appreciative look for not making a big deal of it. "I knew you'd understand. I appreciate your sacrifice as we have limited space. And Mr. Adams needed someplace quiet with some privacy to do his work." She paused. "Maybe you could show him around."

"You mean around the factory?"

"I guess that too, but I was thinking about around town. Help him get comfortable in Bayberry."

Kate grew worried. "How long is he staying?"

She didn't like the thought of him being in her space. She had her chair adjusted just the way she liked it. And her desktop monitor was tilted just perfectly. And now his stuff had already pushed her things out of the way. She'd even noticed that her silk flower arrangement and favorite mug had been moved to the top of the file cabinet.

"Not that long." Aunt Penney patted her arm. "He'll be out of here by Christmas. And come the New Year, you'll have your office back."

The business shut down between Christmas and New Year, letting the employees enjoy the time with their families. It was a well-earned reward for the big push leading up to Christmas.

"But that still doesn't explain what he's doing here." Kate had a sneaking suspicion she knew the answer, but she wanted her aunt to confirm it.

"Well, ah..." Her aunt's gaze didn't quite meet Kate's. "I thought it was time to bring in someone with an objective perspective and experience in these matters to give us guidance for the future."

She'd guessed right. Wes was some sort of business consultant. But what changes would he recommend? And would her aunt be okay with them?

"But we can't afford him," Kate said. "At least not at this particular moment."

"About that...I called an old friend of mine. We

keep in contact—Christmas cards, birthday cards and such. We also talk on the phone. I remembered her mentioning her son was a business advisor. And I called in a favor."

"So he's doing this for nothing?" Something about that didn't seem quite right.

"I'm paying him out of my own funds."

"You can't do that. It isn't right."

"It is right." Aunt Penney's gaze finally met hers with steely determination. "We're in a mess here, and we need some help getting out of it."

"But we have the holiday sale. It's going to be bigger and better than ever. And I'm having posters made up for the Candlelight Dance, with Bayberry Candle Company prominently displayed as the sponsor. And I've been working on our online newsletter. The number of subscribers is growing. Things will be back on track in no time." Kate hoped she sounded convincing.

Aunt Penney reached for Kate's hand and gave it a squeeze. "I hope you're right. But if not, you should get out there and spread your wings. Maybe move away. You never know what you'll like until you try it."

Move away? Was she serious? "Aunt Penney, you know I would never leave you."

"Oh, Kate. How did I get so lucky to have you in my life?" Her aunt looked at her lovingly. "But you can't stay in Bayberry for me. You have to live your own life, wherever it may lead you."

"But my life is right here."

"How do you know, if you won't even give yourself the chance to try another town or live in the city? Hang on a sec." Aunt Penney stepped forward to speak to one of the warehouse workers. "John, I think we're going to need another box of red tapers for the sale. And the green ones, too. Could you see that those are pulled?"

John nodded. "Will do. Do you need anything else?"

"Not right now. Thank you."

Once the man had moved on, Kate spoke up. "Aunt Penney, we've talked about this before. I'm not leaving Bayberry. And that's final. So it looks like you're stuck with me."

Aunt Penney arched a brow, like she did every time she didn't agree with Kate. "And what about having your own family? And don't say you don't want one. I know you do."

Kate shrugged. "When the right man comes along, he'll love Bayberry as much as I do."

"And if he doesn't?"

"Then he isn't the right man for me—"

"Hey, Penney." Fred Nicholas walked up to them. He was a jolly man with a deep, contagious laugh. He smiled at them and his blue eyes twinkled. "Hi, Kate. I saw your flyers around town. Lots of people are excited about the upcoming sale."

Fred was the kindest man. Because of his snowy white hair and matching beard, Kate had always thought he looked like Santa. She wasn't the only one. All of the kids in town called him Santa and he never corrected them. How wrong could they be when his name was Mr. Nicholas?

"Thanks, Fred," Kate said. "It's always good to hear that people are excited about the candle company. Let's hope the added discount this year will bring people from far and wide."

"Don't you worry, Kate," Fred said with a sparkle in his eyes. "This Christmas is going to be the best ever."

"Oh, Fred," Aunt Penney said, "don't be making promises you can't keep."

He turned to her aunt and the look in his eyes softened...as if she were the only woman in the world. "You just have to believe it'll all work out."

Worry churned in Kate's empty stomach. Only she and her aunt knew the trouble the company was in. But if Mr. Wesley Adams didn't know about the trouble before he arrived, he would soon enough.

"We don't have long until the sale," Aunt Penney redirected the conversation back to business. "And I need to get the setup rearranged."

"There's a lot to move," Fred said. "But we'll have things the way you want them."

"Thank you, Fred. You're the best."

His smile grew brighter at her aunt's compliments.

Fred was a lifelong resident of Bayberry and had been a fixture at the candle company for as long as Kate could remember. When something needed doing, he was the first to volunteer, whether it was the town's Santa or driving food to the sick and the shut-ins. And he was quite fond of Penney. Everyone in Bayberry knew it. Except for Aunt Penney.

Both he and Aunt Penney were easygoing and generous of heart. And with Aunt Penney's white hair, she'd make a perfect Mrs. Claus. Kate couldn't help smiling at the thought. She'd mentioned once to her aunt that if she were to give Fred a chance, they'd make a really cute couple. Aunt Penney had immediately shot down the idea, exclaiming that Fred was her employee and nothing like that could ever happen. But Kate still thought her aunt was making a mistake. Kate longed for some man to look at her the way Fred looked at her aunt.

Her aunt turned to Kate. "I have to go. But don't worry. I promise all this stuff with the company is going to work out, just maybe not like you're imagining. Maybe it'll work out even better."

Aunt Penney turned and walked away, leaving Kate to digest this information. What exactly did her aunt have in mind?

If things didn't turn around soon, people would be receiving pink slips this year in their stockings instead of bonuses. Kate prayed the email campaign she'd started online would take off. Otherwise, she had the feeling that Mr. Wesley Adams would be playing the part of Ebenezer Scrooge this Christmas.

# Chapter Five

$\mathcal{T}$HE NEXT MORNING, KATE RUSHED to get ready for work, which resulted in another time-saving messy bun. Before work started, she planned to put up the office Christmas tree. It would lighten the mood around the office. With the mechanical malfunctions of late, employees were a bit down.

The tree was where everyone placed their grab bag gifts. And then, on the last day of work before the holiday, they opened them. Some were funny, some were sweet, but no matter what, they brought a smile to everyone's face.

And though financial trouble was brewing in the background, Kate wasn't going to let it overshadow the holiday for everyone. Wearing a red and white sweater and a pair of dark jeans, she rushed to grab her red coat with the Rudolph pin on the lapel that Aunt Penney had given her for Christmas years ago. She pulled on boots, wrapped a white hand-knit scarf around her neck, and pulled on matching gloves as she rushed out the door.

The air was extra crisp that morning. Kate turned up the collar on her jacket and snuggled deeper in her coat. But as she took in the Christmas decorations in the neighbors' yards—reindeer, snowmen and other lawn ornaments—she was soon distracted from the cold.

She neared the town square and caught the time on the clock. It was ten till seven. She wouldn't have much time to decorate before work. When she neared the Steaming Brew, she hesitated. There was no way she could be in and out of there in a couple of minutes. By the looks of the line, it was going to take at least five minutes to place her order. And that was five minutes she didn't have.

With a frustrated groan, Kate kept walking. Sometimes sacrifices had to be made. But her morning coffee...ugh!

She forced a smile as she passed Bayberry residents and said good morning. She just needed her morning dose of caffeine and she'd feel more like her chipper self.

When she reached the office, she decided to grab the boxes of decorations from storage before she moved to the kitchen to start the coffee. After all, she had to pass by storage on the way in, and the kitchen was at the other side of the building.

She slipped off her coat and switched from her boots to her indoor shoes. Then she made her way to the storage room. When she opened the door, she was surprised by how much stuff had been shoved in there. Sure, she'd been in here many times over the years, but she'd never slowed down to take inventory of how many boxes had collected over the years.

The storage room wasn't that large, and fortunately, Aunt Penney had insisted that each box be marked. Kate's gaze moved from top to bottom of the first shelving unit. No Christmas boxes. She moved to the next shelves and scanned down to the bottom row. Nope, Halloween decorations. She continued to the end of the row.

She turned around to look at the next set of shelves—and there they were. She lifted them off the shelf, stacking them on the floor. There were more Christmas boxes here than she'd expected. And it was too narrow and dim in the storage room to sort through them here. She'd take them to her office. Holding two cardboard boxes, she headed out the door and hurried down the hallway, anxious to get the tree trimmed.

When she reached her office doorway, her gaze landed on the cluttered desk. This was not at all how she normally kept it. A frown pulled at her lips. She'd forgotten that she'd been temporarily evicted.

She turned and stacked the boxes in the hallway. Knowing time was ticking by, she kept moving. It took a number of trips, but finally she had moved all of the boxes next to the fresh-cut tree that had been delivered yesterday.

In the background, Christmas carols played from speakers placed throughout the building. As the lyrics to "The Twelve Days of Christmas" filled the air, Kate sang along. Absorbed in her task, she grabbed a folding chair to reach the top of the tree. Standing on it, she still couldn't reach the upper branches. She climbed down and yawned as she rushed to the janitor's room.

Kate grabbed a stepladder and headed back to the tree. Except the ladder took up a lot more space, so the boxes had to be moved once more. She set to work wrapping the tree in white lights from the top to the bottom. Usually there was more than one person decorating the tree, but this year, with the mechanical delays, everyone was rushing to get ready for the biggest sale ever.

Still, that meant Kate had to move the ladder back and forth as the tree was much too large to reach around it. She'd just gotten to the middle section when employees started to arrive. Luckily, not many people came in this direction.

"Good morning, Kate." MaryJane Harris stopped to admire the tree. She tucked her shoulder-length brown hair behind her ear. "You're started early. Could you use a hand?"

"If you don't mind, it'd make stringing the rest of the lights easier."

"Sure." MaryJane's mouth lifted at the corners. "Let me just put my things in your office—oh, wait, I forgot that guy kicked you out of your office. Can you believe him?"

"It wasn't his fault." Kate couldn't believe she was defending him.

MaryJane snorted. "Who is he, anyhow? An auditor? A tax guy?"

Not wanting to get into this with MaryJane, who was the sweetest lady, but a talker—a big talker—Kate said, "I don't know exactly what he's doing." Which was sort of true. "He's working with Aunt Penney."

MaryJane sighed as she laid her belongings over a box. "If you ask me, he's trouble."

"That's not fair. He's not here to cause problems." At least she hoped not. Kate handed her a strand of lights. "He's just here to do his job, like you and me."

"Hmph. We'll see."

Kate didn't want to talk about Wes any longer. In fact, the less she thought about him and his mission, the happier she became. "How's your Christmas shopping coming?"

It didn't take much to distract MaryJane. Her eyes lit up as she talked about her young sons. She was thrilled that she'd scored this year's hottest toy: a walking, talking, game-playing robot. In no time, the lights were on the tree. Kate plugged them in. Mary-Jane made a couple of adjustments and then stood back to admire their work.

Kate got lucky and found the blown-glass candle ornaments that had been handed down from her great-grandparents. She hung the thin gold cords on metal hooks, and carefully they placed them on the tree.

"Hey, MaryJane." Clint, who'd worked at the candle company as far back as Kate could remember, called from the end of the hall. "We have a problem with the printer again."

"I'll be right there." MaryJane hung another ornament on the tree. "Sorry. Duty calls. What would they do without me?"

"Probably not much printing."

"Exactly." MaryJane admired the tree. "I'm sorry to leave you to finish on your own."

"It's all right. I've got this." Kate placed another

glass globe with a battery-operated candle in the center of the tree. "Thank you for the help."

"No problem."

And then MaryJane was off to help Clint. Kate knew she was lucky to work with such generous and kind-hearted people. There was no place like Bayberry—

"Coming through," the delivery man called out.

Kate looked up to find a brown-uniformed man bearing down on her at full speed with his arms full of packages. She backed up without looking and tripped over a box—and stumbled into the Christmas tree.

*Jingle. Jingle.*

The antique ornaments banged together.

*Oh no! This can't be happening.*

She spun around, hoping to catch the tree before it fell over. But there, holding it in place, was Wes. Wes? He had the tree in one hand.

"Wow. Thank you." Kate's gaze skimmed over the tree, checking to see if all of the ornaments had survived. All seemed well. "You saved Christmas."

"I don't know if I'd go that far. But I'm glad I was here to help." He sent her a leisurely smile that made her stomach dip.

Ignoring the sensation, she asked, "Did you just get here?"

"A little bit ago. I was in the file room searching for a report."

"Did you find what you needed?"

"I did. Thanks." His expression turned serious. "You don't seem mad any longer. You know, about the office. Does this mean we're okay?"

She smiled wryly. "We're good."

"I...I should get back to work, unless you need my help?"

She checked her watch and realized that not only had she missed her morning coffee, she had also missed starting on time. It was time to clean up the boxes and get to work. "No. I'm good. I just need to get this cleaned up. But thanks."

Wes walked into her—well, temporarily his—office. Kate turned and started putting lids on boxes. The next thing she knew, he returned and started helping her. Working together, they returned the boxes to the storage room in no time.

"Thanks again," she said.

"There's no need to thank me."

"You've been a big help this morning." She yawned as she placed the last box on the shelf.

She'd taken her laptop to bed last night to work on the online campaign for the candle sale. She'd literally worked until she'd fallen asleep, with the laptop still open. She'd woken up later, closed it and then rolled over and gone back to sleep. Another yawn plagued her. Obviously, she hadn't gotten enough sleep. "And now I really need my coffee."

"You haven't had coffee yet?"

She shook her head. "I didn't have time first thing this morning and then I got busy." Her phone vibrated in her back pocket. She withdrew it and checked the caller ID. It was Aunt Penney. "I've got to take this."

"Sure thing." He moved to leave, but the only way out was past her. She backed up against the metal shelves. He turned to take a sideways step past her. Their eyes caught and it was though they were moving in slow motion. Her heart pitter-pattered much too fast.

He was so tall. So good-looking. And then he was directly in front of her. Were those dimples in his cheeks? She stifled a dreamy sigh. She couldn't take her eyes off him.

And then he passed. The moment was over. It was though they'd been slingshotted back into the normal rhythm of time. And her phone continued to vibrate in her hand.

"You should get that." He nodded toward her phone.

"Oh. Yeah." She lifted the phone to her ear. "H... hello."

"Kate, is everything all right?" Aunt Penney asked. "You sound out of breath."

"Uh, yes." She snapped out of whatever spell had just been cast over her. "I'm fine. What do you need?"

Her aunt had a question about the arrangement for the holiday sale in the warehouse. They were going to enlarge it by a couple of rows. When Kate wrapped up the call, Wes reappeared with a fresh mug of coffee.

He held it out to her. "It's for you. I didn't know how you take it, so here's some creamer packets and sweetener."

She accepted his offerings. "Thank you. That was so thoughtful of you." She moved to a shelf with a little available space. She pocketed the creamer packets but added all three sweeteners.

"It's not a big deal. I'm sure your boyfriend does things like this for you all of the time."

"I don't have a boyfriend." Thoughts of her ex

flashed in her mind and she frowned. "Not any longer, that is."

He shifted his weight from one foot to the other. "Well, anyway, it was no big deal."

"No. It's a huge deal. I just couldn't function any longer without my morning coffee." She lifted the mug to her lips and took a long, slow drink.

"I should be going." Wes turned to walk away.

"I owe you," she called out to his retreating back. "Again."

He paused and turned. "Don't worry about it. I was happy to help."

He turned a corner and disappeared from sight. She stood there, staring at where he'd been as she took another sip. Maybe there was more to Wes than she'd originally thought. And now that he'd not only helped clean up the boxes and brought her coffee, but also saved her family's heirloom ornaments, she might actually be in debt to him.

She didn't like to be indebted to anyone, especially a handsome stranger. She would find a way to pay him back. Maybe something would come to her after she'd had more coffee. Yes, coffee and muffin first, thinking later.

# Chapter Six

THIS ASSIGNMENT WAS GOING TO be more complicated than he'd hoped.

And much more time-consuming.

Wes sighed as he closed his laptop and leaned back in his chair. Pulling the information he needed to do an evaluation of the company was hampered by the candle company's lack of technology. They had no system that collected vital information in a central location.

His head started to ache as he contemplated the monumental task ahead of him. Maybe skipping breakfast hadn't been his brightest idea. Fortunately, it was almost lunchtime.

He glanced through the windows of his office, see-ing employees shrugging on their coats and heading out for lunch. He didn't see Kate among them. He hadn't seen her since she'd cradled that coffee mug in her hands like she was holding liquid gold.

When she'd come upon him in her office yester-day, he'd thought for sure he'd blown any chance of befriending her. The truth was he hadn't had any idea when Penney Taylor had shown him to the office that it belonged to Kate. In fact, it was so neat and organized that he hadn't been sure the office belonged to anyone in particular.

He'd thought of moving somewhere else, but he wasn't sure where. The data he needed access to was sensitive, but when he saw the elder Ms. Taylor, he'd ask for an alternate location.

He usually packed a lunch when he worked at his New York office, but he had yet to get his bearings here in Bayberry, so he'd picked up some snack foods in the break room to tide him over. This way he could eat and work. The sooner he completed this assignment, the sooner he could get back to Manhattan.

He was holding the granola bar and apple when Kate stepped into the doorway. A slow smile tugged at his lips.

"Is that what you're having for lunch?" Kate's nose scrunched up.

"What's wrong with it?"

"I think Bayberry can do better than that." She beckoned for him to come with her.

"Aren't you still upset with me for stealing your office?"

Her lips pursed together and then she shook her head. "I talked to my aunt. You were just doing what she said. I'm sorry I didn't take it well." Kate stepped farther in the room. "I'm really a nice person. Most of the time. I'm just a little worked up about the holiday sale this weekend. Can we start over?"

Wes swallowed hard and got to his feet. "Sure. Hi." He stuck out his hand. "I'm Wes Adams."

She shook his hand. "I'm Kate Taylor. Would you like to go grab some lunch?"

He looked at the heap of work stacked on his desk. This place had more hard copy reports than digital files. Being here was like stepping back into the Stone Age. Well, maybe the Floppy Disk Age.

"The work will be here when we get back," Kate said. "I promise."

She was right. What would it hurt to have a hot lunch? After all, this was Kate Taylor—the girl he'd had a crush on in junior high. It would be nice to get to know the grown-up Kate.

"Okay." He smiled. "Let's do lunch." He got up and put on his coat. "Where do you suggest?"

"Oh, that's easy. Mel's Grille. They can make just about any sandwich you can think of. Come on." She turned, but then paused and looked back at him. "You do eat sandwiches, don't you?"

He couldn't help but laugh. "Yes, I eat sandwiches."

"Good. Come on before the lunch crowd takes all the good seats. And after lunch, I'll give you a quick tour of the town."

He didn't know which to be more surprised about: that there were good seats in a diner, or that Bayberry had a lunch crowd. Or that Kate had volunteered to spend more time with him? The way Kate rushed toward the exit, apparently that was the case.

He hurried out of the office, hot on her heels. Did her change of mood mean she'd remembered him? Unlikely. She'd have said something.

Besides, it wasn't like he ever did much to stand out in junior high. He hadn't been able to take her to the Candlelight Dance like he'd hoped. His father's new job had come through right before the holiday—before Wes had worked up the courage to ask her. He wondered if the town still held the Candlelight Dance. That had been a lot of years ago. And things do change. Like Kate. She'd grown into a strong, confident woman.

A light snow fell as they walked down the street. In the not-so-far distance stood a tall picturesque mountain with its peak all white. Everyone they passed said hello. He looked for any familiar faces, but it'd been so many years since he lived here that he couldn't put a name to any of them.

"Do you know all of these people?" Living in a big city since he'd gone to college had made him forget what life was like in a small town.

She nodded. "With less than a thousand people in Bayberry, everyone knows everyone else."

So the town hadn't grown much since he'd lived here. Interesting.

"Do you ever get bored living in a small town?"

"Not at all. I couldn't imagine living anywhere else."

"But aren't you curious about what else is out there? Different adventures? Different jobs? Different opportunities?"

She shook her head. "I don't have to go away to know my neighbors are some of the best people in the world. My life is here in Bayberry working at the family business. I'm the last of the Taylors, so some day it'll hopefully be mine to run."

He wanted to ask what she'd do if her aunt had to

sell it off, but he didn't want to ruin this reunion of sorts. And it was none of his concern.

"Where are you from?" Her voice drew him from his thoughts.

His first thought was to say Bayberry, but that wasn't exactly true. He'd lived in many states, many towns growing up. Bayberry just happened to be his favorite.

Rather than explain his complicated past, he said, "I live in New York City."

"Well, I hope you enjoy your visit to our little town."

Mel's Grille sat on Main Street, and though the white brick exterior with black shutters didn't stand out, the aroma wafting from the front door as it opened and shut drew him in. He inhaled deeply. He remembered this place having the best burgers and shoestring fries.

"What smells so good?" It wasn't burgers, but he was intrigued.

"Since today is Tuesday, the specials are corned beef on rye and beef stew." She smiled at him. "Go for the stew. It's delicious and comes with a hunk of home-baked bread."

She didn't have to tell him twice. The burger would have to wait for another visit. His stomach rumbled in anticipation. "Count me in."

They hadn't made it to the diner before the lunch crowd descended upon the place. He pulled the door open for Kate and then followed her inside. It wasn't a huge place, but all of the booths and tables were already occupied. People were talking and enjoying their lunches.

A waitress passed with a tray full of food. Everything looked delicious—and huge. He breathed in the aromas and his mouth watered. He didn't know of any place near his Manhattan office that served portions even half this size.

The waitress, in a fifties-style white uniform with red trim, had blond hair pulled up in a perky ponytail. The lines around her eyes said that she was tired, but when she saw Kate, her glossy pink lips lifted into a smile.

"You're running late today."

"I brought a visitor. This is Wes. Wes, this is one of my best friends, Carrie."

The young woman regarded him through stylish red-and-black eyeglasses. "Welcome. The only seating is at the counter. I'll be over as soon as I deliver this food."

Kate led the way to the white Formica counter. How was it possible that everything about the diner was the same as he remembered? Two red stools anchored to the floor had just become available. It was like walking back in time. On the walls were black and white tiles. Even the framed black-and-white photos of racing cars on the wall were the same. He smiled and shook his head.

After they took a seat at the counter, Kate pulled a menu from a holder and held it out to him. When he reached out to take it, their fingers brushed. Their eyes met and held for a second or two longer than necessary.

Kate averted her eyes. "I can vouch for everything on the menu. Except for the sweet potato fries."

"What's wrong with them?"

Her pert nose wrinkled. "Nothing, if you like sweet potatoes."

He smiled at her reaction. "I take it you don't."

She shook her head. "But if you do, I have it on good authority that they're delicious."

"I'll keep that in mind for future reference. I'm already sold on the stew."

Carrie nodded and wrote on her note pad. "Good choice. I promise you won't regret it."

"I'll have the same," Kate said. "Plus coffee."

"Coffee for me too," Wes said.

Kate acted as though they hadn't shared a moment. They had, hadn't they? Or had he just imagined it? Not that he was in town for anything but work. So he let go of the thought—no matter how enticing he found it.

Once Carrie went to put in their order, Kate leaned back on the stool. "I'm guessing you're anxious to get back to the city, since it's the holiday season."

He shrugged. "I guess."

"Do you have a girlfriend or wife waiting for you?"

"I don't have either."

"What about your family?"

"My mother's in Florida and my father passed on."

"How long are you in town?"

"As long as it takes."

"As long as it takes to do what, exactly?"

He had a feeling all of their conversations were going to circle back around to his work at the candle company. He couldn't blame her for being curious. But he was working for her aunt. Until Ms. Taylor gave him explicit instructions to share his project, he couldn't go into details. Confidentiality was a corner-stone of his occupation.

The waitress came rushing back to the counter and slid the now-empty tray beneath it. She placed cups and saucers in front of them. As she filled them with coffee, she said, "Your orders will be up in just a minute."

"Thanks, Carrie. By the way, I have some more ideas for the dance. I'll text you."

"Sounds good."

Once the waitress moved on, Kate turned inquisitive eyes on him. "So, what can you tell me about your work?"

He avoided her gaze. "Nothing."

"Not even a hint of what you're looking for? I might be of more assistance to you if I know what you're after."

He smiled and shook his head. "Are you always this persistent?"

She nodded. "If it's important enough."

"You obviously care a lot about your aunt and the company."

"I do. That's why I want to do whatever I can to help. So talk to me."

"I'm sorry. I can't. My work is confidential. Anyway, I'm still in the information-gathering phase, I'll let you know if there's anything you can help with."

Just then Carrie arrived, saving him from an awkward conversation. She placed a steaming bowl of stew in front of him and one in front of Kate. And then she supplied them each with a few thick slices of bread and a dollop of butter.

The steam was still rolling off the bowls, but that

didn't stop Wes from taking a spoonful. It smelled so good. He just couldn't wait. He blew on the chunky stew a few times and then took a bite. How was it possible it tasted even better than it smelled?

"Mm..."

Kate smiled at him. "So you like it?"

He swallowed. "I do. This is amazing. Do you think they'd give me the recipe if I ask, so I can make it when I return to New York?"

Her smile broadened. "A lot of people have tried, but they don't hand out their recipes. It's a family secret."

Disappointed, he said, "Looks like I might have to make regular visits to Bayberry."

"It's that good, huh?"

He nodded as he took another mouthful. For a few minutes, they ate in silence. He knew he was really hungry, but this was the best beef stew he'd ever had.

"I might have seconds," he said, nearing the bottom of the bowl.

"And you haven't even tried the home-baked bread yet."

He reached for a slice and buttered it. "Don't tell me they churn their own butter, too."

"No, they don't. But don't give them any ideas. After all, Hunter's Dairy is just down the road, so it's a possibility."

He tried but couldn't recall any dairy. His family had always gotten milk at the grocery store, like most people.

He bit into the bread and stifled a moan. He chewed the soft bread and swallowed. "This dairy, they sell fresh milk right there at the farm?"

She smiled and nodded. "They have a small store. They pasteurize and bottle it right there. If you're interested, I can take you. I'm sure they'll give you a tour."

He couldn't believe it. Coming to Bayberry was truly like stepping back in time. He wondered what other things would surprise him—

"Help!" A woman's voice yelled from the doorway. Every head in the diner turned to find out what was wrong. "There's been an accident at the candle warehouse."

## Chapter Seven

*A* COLLECTIVE GASP FILLED THE ROOM.

Everyone jumped to their feet. There was a stampede for the door.

Kate dropped her spoon in her half-full bowl. She stood, grabbed her coat and followed the crowd. Wes did the same. He paused long enough to drop some cash on the counter. Hopefully it'd be enough for the food and a tip. They rushed outside.

The street was filled with people, all wearing the same worried expression. He too was concerned about the people at the warehouse. He hadn't toured that part of the facility, but he guessed a lot of people worked there.

At that moment, the firehouse whistle blew. People crowded both the sidewalks and the street. All were headed for the same destination. Wes slipped on a patch of ice. The breath hitched in his throat. His arms flailed about until he regained his balance. He really regretted wearing his dress shoes, but it hadn't snowed yet in Manhattan, so he hadn't been thinking about the snow when he'd packed.

Kate paused. "Are you all right?"

He nodded and noticed her laced boots. "Go ahead. I'll catch up with you."

He didn't have to tell her twice. She took off, and he just hoped that in her haste she didn't slip on the ice too.

He moved aside for the fire truck. Its red lights flashed as the siren wailed. It didn't have far to go. The warehouse was next to the offices for the Bayberry Candle Company.

Wes inhaled, not catching any hint of smoke. *Please don't let it be that.* He was pretty sure a fire at the candle company would be more than a single fire truck could manage.

So what had triggered the cry for help? Whatever it was, the whole town had responded. At the warehouse, people streamed through the doorway, and came to a halt when they spotted a mountain of toppled cardboard boxes next to a tall shelving unit that had been upended by the forklift.

Kate's aunt struggled to move the debris. "Help clear the boxes." Her face was red from exertion. "Fred is under all of that."

Wes eyed the forklift. It couldn't be moved without risking the rest of the boxes falling. And he had no idea where Fred was trapped.

For that matter, he didn't see Kate. Though he didn't doubt she was nearby. He hoped she was careful. Some of the boxes had split open and there was broken glass on the floor.

The fire chief rushed in and started instructing

people on what needed to be done. To Wes's surprise, no one turned away. They worked as a team. A line was formed and items that could be moved without causing any harm to the handlers were moved to the other side of the building. The damaged items were piled outside on the sidewalk and the parking lot.

When enough boxes were moved, Fred's right leg could be seen, pinned by the compromised shelving unit. The fire department took over, running lines to secure the unit. Penney and other called out to Fred, who responded that he was okay but stuck under the debris.

It was then that Wes spotted Kate. She was standing next to her aunt. Her arm was wrapped around Penney's shoulders as they watched the rescue.

Wes helped to move the heavy boxes, one at a time. They worked slowly. No one wanted the load to shift and make matters worse. While they worked, Kate and her aunt talked to the man trapped beneath the mess.

Twenty minutes later, they lifted the last box. Fred was flat on his back, conscious but disheveled. Everyone insisted that he not move. Doc Watson made his way through the crowd.

"Okay. Everyone step back." The doctor carried his black medical bag, and with quick steps crossed to the patient. "Let me have a look at him."

The onlookers moved toward the door, except for Kate's aunt. Penney moved closer to Fred. She knelt down next to the injured man. Worry lines bracketed her eyes and mouth.

Wes was able to make his way through the crowd to Kate's side. He saw similar lines of worry etched upon her lovely face. He longed to wipe away her worry, but all he could offer were a few words of encouragement. "He looks pretty good."

"Santa just has to be all right," she said.

"Santa?" His gaze moved from her to the man on the floor of the warehouse.

"Fred is always our Santa for the holidays. He's really good at it. You should hear his "ho-ho-ho." He sounds totally legit."

"I'm sure he'll be back on Santa duty soon."

"I hope you're right. Not because we need a Santa, but because I don't want anything to be wrong with him. He's a really great guy." She didn't take her gaze off Fred.

"It appears you're not the only one who thinks so." Wes nodded toward her aunt, who was fussing over Fred.

"I bet that's the best medicine he could have. With her taking care of him, he'll be better in no time."

"Why? Is there something going on between the two of them?"

Kate shook her head. "It's no secret that Fred has it bad for my aunt, but she never gives him a chance. She brushes off any comments about Fred's feelings for her as small-town gossip."

They stood quietly for a bit while the doctor examined Fred's leg. Wes told himself he should get back to work. There was nothing else he could do here. He glanced over at Kate. The worried look was still evident on her face. There was no way he was leaving her—not until they knew Fred was all right.

Still, he felt useless standing around. "Can I get you anything?"

Kate folded her arms over her chest as she shook her head. She wasn't the only one waiting to hear the outcome. Most of the town was within shouting distance, either inside the warehouse or just outside the door.

The doctor straightened and walked over to address the crowd of concerned onlookers. "Fred would like you all to know that other than a few scratches and bruises, he appears to be all right. His one leg is a bit banged up. I've ordered him to get an x-ray and to stay off his feet for the rest of the week."

Applause rose in the crowd followed by relieved murmurs.

Fred was now sitting up, holding his right side while attempting to get to his feet with Penney's help. Wes rushed forward and lent the man his arm. A fireman offered to take over for Penney, and between the two men, Fred was soon on his feet, keeping his weight on his good leg. Penney rushed outside to bring the company pickup to the door, as she insisted on driving him for his x-ray.

Her face was pale and her lips were pressed in a firm line. Wes couldn't help wondering if Penney's concern was purely a coworker's friendly concern, or if perhaps she felt something for Fred, too.

"Ms. Taylor, if there's anything I can do to help, just let me know," Wes said.

"I told you to call me Penney. We don't stand on formality around here."

"Yes, ma'am." When she arched a brow at him, he said, "I mean, yes, Penney."

"That's better." She smiled at him, but it didn't quite reach her eyes. Then she turned her attention to Kate. "I'm going to take care of Fred. Can you see about cleaning this mess up for the sale?"

Kate nodded. "Don't worry about a thing."

"With you here, overseeing things, I won't. It's not like you don't do most of the work around this place as it is." Penney turned back to Wes. "And you'll be here if she needs any assistance?"

It wasn't part of his job, but that didn't stop him from automatically nodding. "Kate doesn't have to worry. And neither do you."

After Wes helped Fred into the pickup, he closed the door and waved them off. There was definitely more brewing between those two than friendship. It was then that Wes gave himself a mental shake. Since when did he wonder about other people's personal lives?

Back in New York, this sort of thinking wouldn't even cross his mind. It must be Bayberry. There was something about this small community that drew him in. How was it that he'd been in town for less than forty-eight hours and was already feeling as if he belonged here?

He'd already considered sending the information to Watson & Summers and completing the report there, but that wasn't going to work. So much of the candle company's data was stored on paper that it made it impossible to complete the project anywhere but in Bayberry.

He turned to Kate. "I should get back to work." And then he thought of something. "If you would like your office back, I'm more than willing to move elsewhere. Just point me in the right direction."

She shook her head. "There's no need. I'm going

to be here the rest of the day, cleaning up this mess and then making sure every screw and nut is secure. I want this warehouse to be perfectly sound."

"I don't think you have to worry."

She arched a brow. "Why do you say that?"

"On the way to the truck, Fred said it was his fault. He had too many things going on and told the new guy the wrong thing. One thing led to another and the forklift hit the shelving unit that fell on Fred. He kept saying it was no one's fault but his own."

Kate breathed a sigh of relief. "I'm just glad he's all right and no one else was hurt. Now to get this place ready for the holiday sale this weekend."

As much as he wanted to get back to work, he couldn't just walk away and leave Kate with this huge mess. "What can I do to help?"

She looked at him as though seriously considering the question. "You can go finish your report for my aunt. I know she's anxious for your results."

"I meant, what can I do here to help you with this mess."

"I know what you meant, but I have plenty of help." They both glanced at the two dozen employees already setting to work. When Kate looked back at him, she said, "I really do need you to finish your report, so we can get things back to normal in the new year."

He resisted telling her that his preliminary evaluation had already established that the business could never go back to the way it used to be. If the candle company could be saved, drastic measures would need to be taken. But for now, that information was only for his client, Penney.

"If you need me," he said, "you know where to find me."

Wes headed back to the office. He had a lot of work ahead of him. And he intended to work late, as he'd already lost a large chunk of the afternoon due to the accident.

Things were almost back to normal.

Kate had worked past quitting time. The warehouse had been cleaned up. The forklift had been inspected, and the accident was confirmed to have been due to operator error. Kate had hoped it would be a mechanical issue, as she knew Fred would feel absolutely horrible about causing such a mess, especially right before the big warehouse sale. Kate and Penney hadn't cared about the mess—they were just glad Fred hadn't been seriously hurt.

Kate was running out of time to get everything in place. She only had a few days until the warehouse was opened to eager shoppers. And with Doc Watson ordering Fred to rest for the remainder of the week, they were also out a Santa, who was a big draw for the kids. The adults enjoyed taking photos of their children with the man in red—comparing little Johnny and Suzie to how they looked in prior years' photos. In a lot of ways, it was more like a Christmas party than a sale. But without Santa, it wouldn't be much of a celebration.

Unless Kate could find a replacement Santa. But whoever she picked would have to be about Fred's size. There was only one Santa suit in town. She started with the men at the candle company.

*Dave? Too tall.*

*Ronnie? Too short.*

She called her aunt to check on Fred, who, according to her aunt, was being a terrible patient. Aunt Penney said she wouldn't be home for dinner and told Kate about the leftovers in the fridge. Kate told her not to worry. She could fend for herself.

Kate was still mulling over the Santa situation when she stopped by Mel's Grille. When she walked in, everyone called her name. The usual crew included Mr. and Mrs. Green, Aunt Penney's neighbors; Reverend Smith and his wife as well as their little girl; and a few others.

Then Kate's gaze settled on her childhood friend. Carrie stood behind the counter in her waitress uniform. Kate smiled as she made her way to the counter. It had been a long day. She collapsed onto a stool with a weary sigh.

"It can't be that bad. I saw that hottie you were having lunch with." Carrie grinned at her from across the counter.

Kate shook her head. "That's just Wes."

"Is 'Just Wes' single?" Carrie waggled her eyebrows.

"Yes, but it's not like you're thinking. He's in town for work, and I was supposed to be showing him around. But then there was the accident."

"I heard about Fred getting hurt, but I heard it wasn't anything serious." Carrie brought a cup, filled it with coffee and placed it in front of Kate. Then she retrieved creamer from the little fridge behind the counter, grabbed the container of sweetener and set them next to the cup. "I hope the gossip mill didn't get the facts wrong."

"They're right, as always. Fred is just a little banged up, but nothing serious. At least that's what Aunt Penney is telling me."

"Aunt Penney?" A definite note of interest rang out in Carrie's voice as her eyes reflected her curiosity. "How would she know?"

"She's taking care of him."

"Really?" Carrie's voice was drawn out as a smile lit up her face. "I knew I was right about those two."

"Slow down there, Ms. Matchmaker. I didn't say they were dating or anything. My aunt is just helping him out since the doc has him resting for the rest of the week."

Kate refused to start any gossip. If her aunt heard, she'd just dig in her heels even further about not getting involved with Fred.

"Bet it won't be long now until Fred convinces her to go out," Carrie said.

Kate muttered under her breath. "I hope so."

"What did we miss?" Abby sat next to Kate.

Sadie Plummer sat on the other side of Kate. "If there's gossip, I want in. I'm always the last to know." When everyone looked at Sadie, she shoved her black-framed glasses further up on her nose. "Not for the paper."

Sadie had left Bayberry after high school. She'd earned a journalism degree in college, to the approval of her father, the editor of *The Bayberry Gazette*. When she landed a job in Atlanta, no one thought she'd return to Bayberry other than to visit at the holidays.

Then last month, she'd quietly moved home. She took the vacant apartment above the newspaper and started working with her father. No one knew why she'd returned. She never said, and they hadn't wanted to pry. When she was ready, she'd share. Till then, it wasn't anyone's business but hers.

Kate shook her head. "We were just talking about Fred."

"And Penney." Carrie piped in.

"I heard she insisted on taking care of him." Abby reached for a menu as though she hadn't memorized the whole thing over the years. The only thing that changed was the daily specials.

"Does that mean they're finally getting together?" Sadie was the romantic in their group. She could quite often be found with her auburn head bent over a romance novel.

"No." Kate really wanted to change the subject.

Carrie's mouth opened, but before she could argue, a customer raised their cup. "Could we get some more?"

"Sure. I'll be right there." Carrie turned back to Kate. "I'll be right back." Carrie grabbed the half-full coffee pot and headed for the table across the diner.

As Abby and Sadie talked about details for the Candlelight Dance, Kate thought about Wes. Why was her aunt being so quiet about his visit? Was he there purely to advise on how they should direct their business in the coming year? Or was there something more?

Wes obviously wasn't the type to share details of

his work. He seemed more like the buttoned-up, all-business, confidential sort of man. But maybe there was a way to sway Wes—make him loosen up. And perhaps she could influence his report to her aunt to say that the Bayberry Candle Company was going to thrive for a very long time. Forever, if she had anything to say about it.

"What has you so deep in thought? You didn't even drink your coffee," Carrie observed, as she placed the almost-empty pot back on the warmer.

This got the attention of both Sadie and Abby.

"Um, nothing." The seriousness of the candle company's problems wasn't something she shared—not even with her closest friends. They all had relatives or friends who worked at Bayberry. She didn't want to put them in the awkward position of keeping a big secret from those they cared about—kind of like the position she was in right now.

Carrie arched a brow. "Something is going on in that mind of yours. It doesn't have anything to do with the handsome guy who's taken over your office, does it?"

"How did you know he was in my office?" Kate was positive she hadn't mentioned it.

"Everyone knows," Abby said.

"You surely didn't think something like that wouldn't make its way around Bayberry, do you?" Sadie said. "Even I heard that tidbit. Because MaryJane told Sue, who told Mike, who told—"

"Okay. Okay." Kate waved off her friends. "I get the picture. I was just hoping people wouldn't notice, or wouldn't care."

"Oh, they noticed. And they're wondering what he's doing here." Carrie looked at her expectantly.

"Don't look at me," Kate said. "He's working for my aunt."

"Uh-huh." Abby placed the menu on the counter. "And your aunt tells you everything."

"Not all the time."

"So the plot thickens." Carrie looked thoughtful for a moment, while Kate drank her cooling coffee. "I know. She's planning to set you up."

"Shh..." Kate choked on her coffee. She glanced around. When Kate was certain no one was close enough to overhear, she turned back to her friends. "Don't say that out loud. People will think you are serious."

"Maybe I am." Carrie grinned. "He's definitely a looker. You should give him a chance."

Kate sighed. "You are forever the matchmaker, aren't you?"

"What's wrong with dating again?" Carrie asked.

"He's not interested," Kate said firmly.

"But you didn't say you weren't interested." Carrie waggled her brows as she smiled.

Heat rushed up Kate's neck and warmed her face. "I'm not ready to date again. Not Wes. Not anyone."

Carrie leaned over, resting her elbows on the counter. "It's been a long time since you and Andy broke up."

"I concur." Abby said, as though that was supposed to spur Kate into action.

Sadie didn't say anything. She was the most reserved of the bunch.

"You mean since he dumped me to go chasing his

dream in Chicago." Kate refused to dwell on her former fiancé.

"But I can't help wondering if you're still hung up on him," Carrie said.

"I'm not." Kate's tone was firm. "Not at all."

"Really?" Abby arched a brow. "You're still friends with him on social media—"

"That's right." Carrie's eyes twinkled with victory. "He tagged you in a post and you commented."

Kate shifted in her seat. Why were they making such a big deal out of this? "It would have been rude not to respond."

"What do you call what he did to you when he just up and left town?" For the first time since the conversation had shifted to Andy, Sadie spoke up.

Both Carrie and Abby started firing off similar criticisms of Andy.

Kate signaled with her hands to quiet down. "Okay. You've all made your points. Maybe I'll mute him—"

"No," Abby said, "Unfriend him and move on."

"I am moving on." Why didn't anyone believe her?

"For that to be true," Carrie's unblinking gaze met hers, "you'd have to start dating again."

At first, her heart had broken when her engagement to Andy and all their plans had been upended. He'd been offered a job as a DJ for a radio station in a big city. No longer was the local radio station enough for him. He was packed and gone before she even had a chance to wrap her mind around what was happening.

Since then, she'd focused on the family business. She wanted to make her aunt proud of her, but it wasn't working out the way she'd imagined. Instead of flourishing, Bayberry Candles was struggling. And she knew her aunt wouldn't retire until the company was back on solid footing.

When Kate noticed her friends staring at her expectantly, she glared at them. "Stop. I get it. And I will date again."

"Soon?" Carrie asked.

Kate nodded.

"You could start with Wes." Abby sent her a teasing smile.

"You guys are terrible," Kate said.

They all laughed.

Carrie wiped off the counter. "What are you going to do without a Santa for the sale?"

"I don't know." It was just one more problem that needed solving. "I'll give it some more thought. Surely there has to be someone in Bayberry who's the same size as Fred and wouldn't mind filling in."

Her friends started naming candidates. One by one, they were excluded, for various reasons.

"Thanks," Kate said." I have until tomorrow morning to find a replacement."

They all apologized for not being much help, and then Carrie leaned forward. "Anyone want dessert? I created a new recipe—banana and blueberry cupcakes."

Since high school Carrie had had one dream: opening her own bakery. She'd been saving every penny. And from the sound of it, she was getting close. Kate was happy for her. That woman had talent that deserved to be showcased.

Kate stood. "Nothing for me. I think I'm just going to head home. I'll see you all tomorrow."

She paid for her coffee and headed for the door. This Christmas was not going like she'd hoped. But there was still time to turn it around.

# Chapter Eight

*P*UNCTUAL.

That's what his year-end evaluation always said.

Wednesday morning, Wes approached his temporary office in the Bayberry Candle Company at exactly eight o'clock. He didn't intend to change up his routine just because he was on a business trip. An assistant vice president needed to lead by example. He couldn't get distracted and bend the rules.

The offices buzzed with people. Most were enjoying their morning coffee and catching up with each other. He noticed that very few were at their desks.

He smiled and said good morning when he was spoken to, but he kept moving. There was work to be done. No wonder this company was in trouble, if this was the way business was normally conducted.

Wes sat down at his assigned desk and immediately opened his laptop to a partially filled spreadsheet. He normally grabbed a cup of coffee to sip on as he worked, but he decided he would wait until everyone had settled into their day before venturing to the coffeemaker in the breakroom. He didn't want to get distracted with idle conversation.

He needed to get this job done. He thought of Chad at headquarters, impressing Mr. Summers as he worked on Wes's hard-earned accounts. Wes's jaw tightened. He had to stay focused and finish early.

An early completion would impress his boss. But would it be enough to get the promotion? He'd already priced senior living apartments for his mother, and the rent would take every bit of his promotion and then some, but he could make it work. And then he could visit his mother more than a few times a year.

He turned his thoughts to work and sorted through the hardcopy reports. It still surprised him that things hadn't been digitalized. It seemed Bayberry was a few years behind the rest of the world. Wes also noticed that the factory relied heavily on human labor instead of automation. He wondered if it had something to do with the unreliability of the machines they currently used. He made a note of it. He'd do an analysis of how much it would cost to automate the candle-making process instead of relying on humans. And he'd figure out how long it would take to recoup the expense.

He had a sinking feeling that no matter how he worked the numbers, the results were going to reflect a need to sell the business. He wasn't sure if one of the larger candle companies would want the actual facilities, but he knew the candle recipes and scents were worth money. Everyone in the New England area had heard of the Bayberry Candle Company. They even sold their candles in New York City during the holidays. He knew because he'd bought one for his mother last Christmas, as a nice nostalgic present. When his family had moved here, Bayberry residents had welcomed them, just as if they were their own. As a teenager, he'd made friends and been truly happy.

Something told him that Kate had no idea just how much trouble her family's company was in at the moment. But it wasn't his job to enlighten her. He was being paid to be discreet and present an evaluation to Kate's aunt upon his departure.

"Good morning."

He looked up from his laptop to find Kate standing in the doorway with a smile on her face. *Wow.* He remembered why he'd had a crush on her back in school. The corners of his lips lifted. When she smiled, the whole world glowed. That hadn't changed either.

"Good morning to you too. Why are you in such a good mood?"

She shrugged. "It's Wednesday. The week is half over. The sun is shining. I just had my first pumpkin spice latte of the year."

"Your first? What took you so long?"

She shrugged. "I held out as long as I could. Everyone has her breaking point."

"Where did you get your pumpkin spice latte?" he asked. "I might grab one at lunch."

"As luck would have it, I have two." She pulled a red to-go cup from behind her back. "And look at that, it has your name on it."

When she handed it over, he saw that it did indeed have his name scrawled in black marker. He took a sip of the warm, rich brew. It had just the right amount of spice, combined with a healthy dose of cream. It was more delicious than the ones they made at his usual coffee shop on the way to the office. And he hadn't thought anyone could top New York City lattes. He'd been wrong.

"Thank you." He reached for his wallet. "How much do I owe you?"

She shook her head. "Nothing. It's on me. Abby, my friend at the Steaming Brew, finally convinced me that it was time to switch over to the holiday flavors. If they didn't have so many calories, I'd drink them all day, every day."

He arched a brow. "Are you sure I can't pay you back?"

"Positive." Her gaze moved to the desk, which was littered with one binder after another. "Looks like I should get going so you can work."

"Actually, I hate to ask you this after you were so kind as to bring me a latte, but could you help me find something? I spoke with Penney on the phone this morning and she won't be in the office today. And, well, I don't know who else to ask for help."

Her phone dinged. She removed it from her back pocket. "Not a problem." She read her phone and sent an answering text, then raised her gaze to his. "Sorry about that. It's work stuff. Now, what do you need?"

"I need the second quarter income statement. The first and third quarters are here, but the second is missing."

"That's odd." She motioned for him to follow her. He set down his latte and stepped around the desk to catch up with her. As they made their way to the back of the building, she said, "Since it appears you're going to be here awhile, you might as well see where we keep our reports." She stopped in front of six aisles of tall gray shelves in the file room. "All of our reports are here."

He stared in astonishment. "Wow. You don't believe in digital files, do you?"

Kate shrugged. "We're hoping to one day get an IT department and automate things, but for now, we make do. Right now, I've been more focused on the marketing aspects of the business."

He followed her to the fourth row of shelves, where she moved halfway back and then knelt to look at some files near the floor. He stopped next to her. "Don't you have a marketing department?"

She stared up at him defensively. "This is Bayberry, not New York City. Our accounting department has been doing the best they can, but time and resources are limited."

He swallowed hard. "Sorry. It's just that I'm used to, well, larger businesses."

Which made him wonder why Mr. Summers had assigned this particular account to him. But instead of worrying about the pending promotion, Wes was surprised to be considering the benefits of returning to Bayberry. He continued to stare at Kate as she sifted through the binders. Maybe he didn't have to be back in New York quite as early as he'd originally thought. Maybe a few extra days in Bayberry would be prudent.

Kate's heart raced.

Even though they were in a busy office, the file area was more secluded. And this aisle seemed to grow narrower with Wes next to her. She wanted to look at him, but she didn't dare. She was flustered enough.

*Just concentrate on finding the report.*

Kate paused from thumbing through the folders. They were out of order. It was going to take longer than she'd originally thought to find the report. And the growing silence was making her even more nervous.

Wes had said something that increased her curiosity, as well as worried her. "If you're used to working with larger clients, how did you end up in Bayberry?"

He cleared his throat. "Your aunt didn't tell you?"

She recalled the conversation in her aunt's kitchen the evening before Wes had dropped into their lives. Aunt Penney apparently had been intending to tell her all about Wes then. If only Kate hadn't put her off to go work on the plans for the Candlelight Dance, she would've had the time to ask her aunt all sorts of questions about Wes's visit.

"My aunt has been busy, and now with Fred being injured, we haven't had much of a chance to speak."

Wes nodded in understanding. "Can I help you look?"

What could it hurt? Some reports were in the proper place and others were not. "You could start there." She pointed to the shelving unit next to the one she was sorting through, pulling the out-of-order files as she went and placing them on an empty spot on the shelf above. "I'll have to get in here after the holidays and put things back in order. There is a system to the filing, but the high school students we had interning here this summer must not have caught onto it."

He nodded again. But he didn't say anything as he started searching for the missing file. He certainly wasn't a chatty one. If she wanted to learn anything, she was going to have to drag it out of him, so to speak.

"Anyway, you were just about to explain how you ended up in snowy Bayberry."

His gaze met hers and held. "Oh yes, I, uh," he glanced away. "It would appear my mother and your aunt know each other."

"Really?" This was news to her. "Well, Aunt Penney does know everyone." She paused to look at him again. He did look familiar. "Does your mother live here in Bayberry?"

"No. She lives in Florida."

She waited, expecting him to continue, but instead he went back to his search. That was all he was going to say?

"But how do your mother and my aunt know each other?"

"My family used to live here."

Kate frowned. "Wonder why Aunt Penney hasn't mentioned it?"

"It was seventeen years ago."

"Oh. So you lived here too?"

He nodded. "We were here for less than a year before my father got a new job—again."

That explained why she couldn't recall him. "I take it your father had a lot of jobs."

Wes nodded. "He was forever searching for the perfect job, but none of them worked out—at least not for long."

So his stay in Bayberry had been brief. That's why

she didn't know him. It was right around the time when her parents had died and she'd come to live with her aunt, her only living relative. But she didn't want to dwell on that, so she asked, "Did your family move around a lot?"

He nodded. "Every time I thought we'd found a place to call home, we'd have to move."

"I can't imagine how tough that must have been. I moved here when I was a kid." She didn't want to bring up her parents' deaths, as this was Wes's story. "And I thought that was hard, making new friends and getting used to a new school. But to do that numerous times. Wow. I'm sorry."

"I wouldn't recommend it to a young family, but we made it work."

Her heart went out to that little boy who was never able to set down roots. "How about now? Do you like to travel?"

He shook his head. "I travel for business because I have to, not because I want to. But the benefit is meeting really nice people." His gaze met hers, causing heat to swirl in her chest. Was he flirting with her? He glanced back at the shelf. "Eventually, I plan to have a desk job and the travelling will be a thing of the past."

"It sounds like a nice goal." When she thought of that desk being all the way in Manhattan, disappointment assailed her. "I hope it all works out for you."

"Thanks. Me too."

As she continued searching for the missing report, her mind played the what-if game. What if Wes didn't live so far away? What if he lived in a nearby town?

Would this be the beginning of something? Would he ask her out? Would she ask him—

"Found it!" Wes held up a file.

The heat that had started in her chest rushed to her cheeks. He'd found that file just in time, because her thoughts had fallen down a rabbit hole—a dangerous hole. She needed to stay focused on business—and helping the faltering company by making this year's sale the biggest and best.

Kate swallowed hard. "You did?" The file shouldn't have been there, but after seeing the condition of the shelves, she wasn't surprised. "You're sure it's the right report?"

He double-checked. "Yes, thank you. I owe you."

Without giving her a chance to say anything, he turned and headed back to her office. She watched him walk away. He didn't talk a lot. She wondered what made him that way. Did he work too much? Or was he used to being alone in Manhattan?

The thought of being alone in that great big city seemed impossible. But something told her that if you wanted to be alone, you could do it even in the middle of millions of people. It just wasn't right that Wes was all alone while his mother was in Florida, especially during the holiday season.

She was so lucky to be part of a close-knit community. As she continued to place the files on the correct shelves, she realized Wes might be leaving soon, but there was enough time to show him some Bayberry holiday cheer. And she had the perfect idea.

# Chapter Nine

*T*HE MORE TIME WES SPENT in Bayberry, the more he liked it.

And then there was the owner's niece.

He smiled as he recalled his earlier conversation with Kate. She blushed so easily that he couldn't resist a little flirting, though he'd caught himself and stopped. Starting something with Kate wasn't a good idea, as he needed to get back to New York as soon as possible.

Still, he'd enjoyed talking with her. Her questions had prompted him to recall all of the places he'd lived as a kid, and there had been many—too many. But it hadn't been all bad. He'd met some wonderful people and visited many amazing places. However, Bayberry stuck out the most in his memory.

When his family moved to Bayberry, he'd thought the town was going to be corny and boring. As a teenager, he couldn't think of anything worse than moving to a little town in the middle of nowhere with no mall, no skate park and no internet. Fortunately, a lot had changed since those days. Okay, maybe not a lot. There was still no shopping mall anywhere near Bayberry, and there was still no skate park—or he might be tempted to relive his youth and brush up on his skateboard skills.

But these days Bayberry did have the internet, which kept him in constant contact with Watson & Summers. Apparently, competition for the promotion was ratcheting up. Chad had just brought in a huge client. Another candidate, June Mason, retained one hundred percent of her clients. And what was Wes doing? Sitting here in this small town with a small client. It wasn't going to mean anything when it came time for Mr. Summers to choose his next assistant VP.

Sure, Mr. Summers had assigned Wes this account. At first, Wes had thought it was some sort of test. Now, he wondered if Mr. Summers was just getting him out of the way so he could concentrate on the other candidates. Wes's jaw tightened.

He tried to tell himself to relax, that Mr. Summers wouldn't do that—he was a fair man. But this was Bayberry. It was a one-light town, and all of the shopping was done on Main Street. It still had a tree-lighting night—this Friday in Bayberry Square, as a matter of fact.

It wasn't that he didn't want to help Bayberry. He knew that without the candle company the town would lose its main source of income and would most likely die off. The young people would all move away for work. As for the older people, some would stay and some would follow their kids, wanting to be near their grandchildren.

But the more numbers he pulled, the more dismal the outlook appeared. And he knew that Kate wanted to help the company with the upcoming sale, but he didn't think there was anything she could do at this late stage.

*Knock knock.*

Kate poked her head inside the office. "Just checking to see if you have everything you need."

He slid a file folder over the report he'd been referencing, and clicked to a blank screen on his computer. It was standard practice he had developed from years of working on sensitive information. "I think I have it. Thank you." She was about to walk away when he said, "What can you recommend for lunch? You know, besides the diner."

"Well, there are a couple of other places." She signaled for him to come with her. "Come on. I'll show you."

He glanced at the clock. Lunch wasn't for another eighteen minutes. "It's not lunchtime yet."

Kate blatantly rolled her eyes. "You're such a rule follower, aren't you?"

He frowned. "And what's wrong with that? It keeps everything neat and orderly."

"But what about spontaneity and breaking up routines? That's important too."

"Not when it comes to work. Strict rules need to be followed. Otherwise you end up in a mess like..." His voice trailed off.

Kate's eyes widened. "So you think if we'd followed a more disciplined lunch schedule we wouldn't be in trouble?"

His lips pressed into a firm line. Why did she make

it sound so ridiculous when she said it? "That's not exactly what I meant."

"Oh, good." Her eyes glittered with triumph. "I was really worried we were going to have to install a bell to let everyone know it was lunchtime, and ring it again when it was time to go back to work."

Even he wasn't that extreme. "I just think if you leave at the proper time that lines don't get blurred."

"And I would work the proper number of hours?"

"Something like that." And then he realized she was taking his words and turning them around. "Never mind. That isn't what I meant." The heat of embarrassment licked at his face. "Forget it."

"Oh good. So that means we can go to lunch now."

*Oh boy. Back to this again.* "You go ahead. I have some work to finish before I go."

"But this can't wait. And your work can." She headed for his desk and closed his laptop. "Come on, Mr. Scrooge."

"I am not a Scrooge."

"Uh-huh." She reached for his coat and held it out to him. "Come on."

He got to his feet. "Has anyone ever told you that you're bossy?"

She tilted her head to the side and stared off into space. Then she turned her gaze back to him. "No. I don't think they have."

He shrugged on his overcoat. Under his breath he mumbled, "That's hard to believe."

She was already headed out the door. "What did you say?"

"Oh, um, I was having a hard time with my sleeve."

They made their way out of the building, with just

about every other employee. Everyone chatted with everyone else. They weren't exactly a quiet bunch. Most of the conversations were about the beautiful sunny day after a week of snow.

It was so different from the conversations at his New York office. Most of the time, the rides in the congested elevator were quiet, except for the occasional buzz of someone's cell phone. And if the winter weather was mentioned, it was noted with abhorrence. Snow, for the most part, was not welcome in the city. It made a mess of everything, and in a city where traffic was a nightmare on a perfectly good day, a snowy day just meant it would be that much longer until people reached their destinations.

But in Bayberry, no one was in that much of a hurry. They didn't push or grumble. They took their time going out the door and walked at a reasonable pace into town and toward the diner. His stomach rumbled as he recalled that delicious stew.

As though Kate were privy to his thoughts, she said, "We have to hurry. We're going to be late."

"Late? For lunch?" He was quite certain they were early.

She glanced over at him. "Yes, late."

As they approached a pickup truck with the Bayberry Candles logo on the side, he said, "We're driving? I thought you walked everywhere."

"Not today. We're going to need the pickup for the food."

Food? How much food was she planning to order? But who was he to argue? The fact he didn't have to walk through the snow and ice in his dress shoes was fine with him. He climbed into the passenger seat.

He rubbed his hands together and then stuffed them in his pockets. The sun might be out today and shining bright, but it was still quite cold. This snow wasn't going anywhere.

Kate started the truck. "What do you think of the candle company?"

Was she really asking about its financial standing? Or his projection for its future? He uncomfortably shifted in his seat and gazed out the passenger window, avoiding her inquisitive stare.

"I think it's impressive that your family established the company more than a hundred years ago, and because of it, a town came to be." He paused, waiting for her to grill him about his work.

"I think so too. Sometimes I try to imagine what it must have been like for my ancestors. You know, moving here in the middle of nowhere and setting up their business. Back in those days, my great-great-grandfather would have to drive a big truck through the mountainous roads and deliver the candles to all of the general stores. And he didn't just do it once a year, he had to deliver them every month. And soon the business grew to the point where he had to hire drivers and more workers. That's when the town started to blossom. Because workers meant they needed food and, well, more of everything."

As Wes listened to her talk about Bayberry, he could hear the love in her voice for her hometown. He'd never known what it was like to have such an attachment to a place. His childhood had been one address after the next, to the point that he could remember writing the wrong address on a form in school.

Now, as an adult, he understood that his father had been doing all he could to keep a roof over their heads, and as such, they'd had to keep moving wherever his father's work took them. But as a kid, Wes hated moving around almost every year. And he especially hated leaving Bayberry and the girl with the long braid.

He glanced over at Kate. He'd never dreamed they would be reunited. Not that she remembered him. But he remembered her. She was the girl who'd been nice to him—who helped him pick up his school books when he'd tripped over his own feet because he'd been staring at her.

But that was years ago. A lot had changed since then. He had changed. And he was based in New York City. He had been there since he'd graduated from college. It was the longest he'd ever lived in one place. So why didn't it feel like home?

When he thought of Manhattan and his cramped apartment, he didn't get the nostalgic look on his face that Kate got when she spoke of Bayberry. But when he was able to move his mother into the city, it would change things. It would make it more like home—

"Hey," he said, pointing out the window, "you passed the diner."

"I thought you said you wanted to try something different."

"I did." He just wasn't sure what he'd gotten himself into. "Where are we going?"

She pulled to a stop next to Bayberry Square. "Here."

He looked around. "Here, where?"

"Right here." She reached behind the seat and pulled out a Santa hat. "You'll need this."

"Need it for what?" He had no idea what Kate was up to, and he got the feeling she liked to keep him guessing. As long as she kept flashing him the brilliant smile that made her eyes sparkle, he honestly didn't mind.

Kate produced a matching Santa hat and put it on. She exited the truck and moved around to the rear.

He still wasn't sure where they'd be having lunch. He was thinking of a nice cozy restaurant and some hot food to warm him up. With reluctance, he climbed out into the sunshine. He walked to the back of the pickup to find Kate had lowered the tailgate.

"What are you doing?"

She smiled at him and then placed a red plaid blanket over the tailgate. She reached for a thermos and sat down. Right there on the truck, she made herself comfortable.

He rubbed the back of his neck. "I thought we were going to get lunch."

"We are."

"And you decided this sub-freezing day was a good time for a picnic?" He didn't want any part of it. He rubbed his hands together, as each breath he took sent a puffy little cloud into the air.

She laughed. "It's not a picnic."

"Then please tell me what you're doing, because I have to be honest, I'm getting a bit worried about you. Do you know how cold it is out here?"

Before she could say anything, a woman in a puffy red coat and white knit cap came trudging up to the pickup with a large box. "Here you go. This is all we can do this year. I got them on sale."

"That's wonderful." Kate set aside the thermos and jumped to her feet. "Everyone does as much as they can. You know that."

"I know." The woman's face lined with worry. "It's just with Joe out of work this month because he hurt his back, things are tight."

"How's he doing?" Kate took the box, which was full of fruit cup snacks, and placed it in the bed of the truck.

"He's doing a lot better. Doc said he might be allowed to go back to work by the beginning of the year."

"That's great." Kate gave the woman a hug.

When the women pulled apart, the woman's inquisitive gaze moved to Wes. "Is he the new guy I've heard so much about?"

Kate smiled. "Yes, this is Wes. Wes, this is Caroline. She works as a nurse at Doc Watson's office."

Caroline smiled at him warmly. "It's so nice to meet you."

Wes stretched out his hand and shook hers. "It's nice to meet you too."

"You poor man. You're freezing." She gave his attire a quick once-over. Caroline turned back to Kate. "You need to help him find some warmer clothes. He's going to freeze out here."

"I'm good," he said, but they both looked at him as if they didn't believe him.

Caroline turned back to Kate. "I'd better be going. If you need any help between now and the big day, let me know."

"Thanks. I will."

After the woman moved on, Wes said. "Okay. What's going on?"

"We're here to collect food for the big holiday food drive. And this year, I'm in charge of coordinating it."

That wasn't what he'd expected. "I thought you said we were having lunch."

"We are. It'll be here soon. And I promise it'll be worth the wait."

Kate settled back on the tailgate and opened the thermos. "Care for some hot chocolate?" Without waiting for him to respond, she poured a steaming cup and handed it to him. "Take this. I think Caroline is right. You're not dressed for this weather."

He accepted the cup and wrapped his bare hands around it, seeking the warmth. "I have warm clothes, but they're back in New York. It hadn't snowed yet this year, so I didn't think about packing my snow gear."

"I think I have a spare pair of gloves." She reached in one pocket and came up empty. Then she tried the other pocket and pulled out a pair of bright red gloves with Santas on the backs. She tossed them toward him. "They stretch."

He thought about refusing the bright red gloves with Santas on the back, but he was too cold to argue. He stuffed his hands inside them. The fingers didn't quite fit his long digits, but they were good enough. "Thanks."

"You could wait in the truck. Sorry, I didn't think about your clothes. We're going to have to take you shopping if you're going to spend much time in Bayberry."

"Shopping for what?" he asked.

"Some warm clothes and sensible shoes."

"I...I can get by."

Kate arched a brow. "We'll go after work."

He opened his mouth to protest but then closed it. He glanced down at his feet, finding his black shoes were now covered with snow and salt. He didn't think there would be any saving them, no matter how much he polished them.

His suits might be fine for New York, where professional wear was expected. But here in Bayberry, his gray designer suit stood out. And he didn't want to stand out. There was something about the way he'd witnessed everyone pulling together to help one of their own that made him want to be one of them again—even if only briefly.

For just a little while, he wanted to experience what it was like to be a part of a tight-knit community. When he'd lived here as a teenager, his family hadn't stayed long enough for him to get over his shyness and join in. While his job had helped him overcome a lot of his shyness, now he wondered what he'd been missing all this time.

Another woman rushed up with her arms full of boxes of canned vegetables. "Sorry, Kate. I could only carry so much. I'll have more later."

"Thank you so much. You can always bring it to the warehouse this weekend."

"I'll keep that in mind." And then the woman turned to him. Her eyes widened. "You're even more handsome than they said." And with that she rushed off.

Kate turned back to him. "It seems you've made quite an impression on the town."

"And I haven't even done anything but stand out here and freeze."

An older man rushed toward them with two foil-wrapped objects. Wes tried to remember him, but failed. The man handed one foil object to Kate. "Fresh-made. It should warm you up." And then he turned to Wes. "I'm glad she has help. Thank you. Now enjoy."

And then the man rushed off as though he were very busy. Wes was about to ask what he was holding, but then he got a whiff. Were those tomatoes? And oregano?

He opened the foil to find a giant meatball sandwich topped with thick slices of provolone cheese. His mouth watered. This looked absolutely perfect. He took a seat next to Kate and took a bite.

He chewed and swallowed. "This is amazing."

"I thought you might like it."

"Is it from the diner?"

She shook her head. "It's from the deli. They make one specialty sandwich a day. And today's happens to be one of my favorites."

He took another bite of the warm, delicious sandwich. "I'm definitely going to have another before I leave town."

She smiled, and he'd never seen anything more beautiful. Her cheeks and nose were tinged with pink from the cold. But it was her eyes that twinkled with happiness, filling him with a warmth that started in his chest and spread outward. His reasons for leaving Bayberry didn't seem so pressing at the moment. He smiled back at her.

As they finished their lunch, a string of people made their way to the pickup. Each and every man, woman and young person greeted them with a smile. It was as though this town had inhaled the spirit of Christmas. It radiated from each of them in friendliness and warmth. If he hadn't lived here previously, he would have written it off as the holiday spirit, but he knew it was this way year-round.

When the rush of people let up, Wes turned to Kate. "This food drive—is it for people in need?"

She shook her head. "It's for everyone."

"I don't understand."

"Years ago, long before my time, the holiday food drive was started for people in need, but this town is made up of very strong, very proud people. They refused to accept a handout. The town elders were stymied. They knew there had to be a way to help their neighbors, but it wasn't until my great-grandmother suggested that the food drive benefit everyone in Bayberry that it took hold."

"Sounds like your great grandmother was a very smart lady."

"She was. I love listening to my aunt and the townsfolk tell me stories about the 'good ol' days'."

"So this food is divided and handed out?"

"Yes. We make baskets. And on Christmas Eve, a group of us delivers all three hundred and nineteen baskets."

"That's a lot of baskets."

"You're telling me. And I have something extra special planned for them. If you're still around, you can help me."

His initial instinct was to brush off the offer. After all, this was no longer his town and these weren't his neighbors, but the more he thought about it, the more he liked the idea—both spreading goodwill and spending more time with Kate.

"Thanks. I'd like that." He paused. "You're so lucky." He hadn't meant to vocalize his thoughts, but now that they were out there, he couldn't take them back.

"How so?" Her fine brows drew together. "I mean, I know I have a lot of blessings for which I'm grateful. I just wondered if you meant anything specific."

He shrugged. "It's this place and these people. They're like one big family."

"No. They are one big family. But just like in every family, nothing is perfect. For the most part, the town pulls together in good times and bad." She balled up the foil from her lunch and stuffed it in her coat pocket. "I take it life in New York is a lot different?"

"It definitely has some differences. Have you ever lived in a big city?"

She shook her head. "I moved away for college, but it wasn't a large city. And then I returned to Bayberry to help my aunt with the business."

He didn't get to explain about his life in Manhattan, as more people were headed toward them with their arms full of donations. Not that he had much to say. He worked. Occasionally, he went out to dinner with friends or to sporting events. But most of the time, he worked. A lot.

As the crush of people dissipated, an older man in a dark gray wool cap ambled up to them with two nondescript cardboard boxes in his hands. "I've got some canned goods for you."

Wes rushed to grab the boxes from the man.

"Well, thank you." The man smiled. He looked familiar. It took Wes a moment to place him. And then he realized it was his former employer, whom Wes had worked for as a teenager. He didn't say anything, though. Wes was certain he'd lived in this town for such a short time that no one would remember him.

Wes placed the heavy boxes in the bed of the truck with all the other donations Kate had collected. He had to admit this town went all out.

When Wes turned back to Kate, she said, "Mr. Plummer, I'd like you to meet Wes Adams. And Wes, this is David Plummer, our newspaper editor."

The man stuck out his hand and as they shook, he said, "Wes, as in Wesley? Wesley Adams? Is that you?"

A broad smile lit up Wes's face. "Yes, it is. I'm surprised you remember."

"How could I forget you? You were one of my hardest-working paper boys."

"But I wasn't here long."

"While you were here, you made quite an impression. It's good to see you again. Have you moved back to Bayberry? Any chance you want to return to the newspaper so I can retire?" Mr. Plummer joked.

Wes shook his head. "I'm afraid I'm only here until Christmas. I'm consulting at the candle company."

"Consulting, huh?" A gray brow arched and an inquisitive look gleamed in his eyes. "Any chance you want to give this reporter a lead?"

Wes laughed. He might've expected something like that in New York, but he'd never expected to be questioned by the press about his job here in Bayberry. "You aren't serious, are you?"

Mr. Plummer pulled back his shoulders and lifted his brushy brows. "Sure I am. I'm a newspaper man and I smell a story. And you wouldn't mind helping an old friend, would you?"

Kate stepped forward. "Mr. Plummer, I don't think Wes has anything interesting to share with you."

The man's sharp gaze moved between the two of them. "Something's going on here. I know it as sure as I'm standing here." He eyed Kate. Then he turned and needled Wes with his inquisitive stare. "Which one of you is going to tell me what's going on? Or do I have to go digging for the story? Because I'm not too old to do it. And the paper could use an eye-catching headline."

Wes cleared his throat. "I'm sorry, Mr. Plummer, but there is no story."

The man sighed. "I'm not giving up. Probably why I'm still running a newspaper at my age, instead of sitting at home and putting my feet up."

And with that he ambled off. Wes guessed the man wasn't as old as he was letting on, but he did look concerned about something.

Wes waited until his former boss was out of earshot before he said, "Can you believe that?"

Kate nodded. "I can. Nothing gets this town stirred up more than some lively gossip. And I know Mr. Plummer is dying to be the first to the punch." Then she turned her gaze to Wes. "But there isn't a story, right?"

His eyes widened and then he lifted his hands. "I don't have a story. I'm just doing my job."

"A job you refuse to discuss with me."

"It's not that I don't want to discuss it with you, it's that I can't. It's not just you. I can't discuss my job with anyone who isn't my client. The stuff is confidential. It's why businesses are willing to open up their books to me. They can trust me. Without that trust, I wouldn't have any clients. Without clients, I wouldn't have a job."

Kate settled back on the tailgate. "When you explain it that way, it makes some sense." Then she turned her face to him. "But it doesn't mean I have to like it."

"Understood. But does that mean we have to be enemies?"

"Enemies? Hey, I don't invite people I don't like to share my hot chocolate and a meatball sub on my tailgate."

"What about the freezing cold part?" He gave her a teasing smile.

"And here I was going to take you on that tour of the town that I promised you, but it looks like we'll have to do it another time."

Wes nodded. "Maybe when it warms up. Say, maybe July."

Kate laughed. "Or we get you some warmer clothes. In fact, I think it's something we need to do right away. Otherwise, you might be an ice cube by Christmas."

"After work will be soon enough."

They stayed at the town square until one o'clock to collect food items from Bayberry's residents. By the time they headed back to the candle factory, the bed of the pickup was overflowing with large cardboard boxes. And Kate promised there would be plenty more come the weekend sale.

He snuck a glance at her as she drove back to the candle company. She really hadn't changed much from how he remembered her. She was still outgoing and friendly.

And once again, he was starting to feel something more than friendship toward her. He refused to name these emotions because as soon as his work was finished, he was leaving Bayberry. His home was now in the city. And soon he hoped to have that promotion.

## Chapter Ten

*I*T HAD BEEN A REALLY nice lunch.

And the food hadn't been bad, either.

Kate smiled, thinking of Wes wearing her Santa gloves. All in all, he'd been a really good sport about the rather unusual lunch. And he'd been helpful.

Thanks to Wes, Kate had gotten the supplies unloaded into the warehouse in no time. It gave her time to make a follow-up phone call regarding her Christmas surprise for the town. She smiled with satisfaction. No one knew about it. Not even her aunt. And that's the way it was going to stay until the Christmas baskets were handed out.

Once her phone call was placed and the date of delivery was confirmed, she had one more errand to run before she went back to work. She needed to check in on her aunt and Fred. It wasn't like her aunt to be away from the business for such an extended period. Kate worried that Fred's injuries were more serious than they'd originally thought.

She headed to Fred's bungalow, which was situated just off Main Street near the candle company. She didn't even get a chance to knock on the door before it swung open. There stood her aunt, looking casual in blue jeans and a red-and-white Christmas sweater.

"Come in. Hurry. It's so cold out there." Aunt Penney moved to the side and made an exaggerated imitation of shivering.

Kate stepped inside, closing the door behind her. Her gaze moved to the crackling fire in the fireplace. And that's when she noticed Fred on the couch. "Hi. How are you doing?"

"Much better. Your aunt is the best nurse."

Aunt Penney blushed. "Oh hush, Fred. I feel really bad that you got hurt. If I hadn't asked you—"

"It's not your fault," he said firmly. "It was my fault for getting distracted."

As the two argued, Kate could tell there was something brewing between them. When her aunt and Fred looked at each other, there was more going on than the banter of casual friends. Did that mean her aunt finally saw Fred in a new light? Hope bloomed in Kate's heart.

Then Penney turned to her niece with concern. "Kate, what's the matter?"

"Why would you think something is wrong?" Kate asked.

"Because you're supposed to be working. I figured if you're here that something must be wrong."

"Relax. Everything is fine. I just unloaded a bunch of food in the warehouse for the Christmas baskets."

"Oh." A smile replaced the worried look on Aunt Penney's face. "That's good. How did it go?"

"Really well. Wes helped me and it went quickly."

"Wes?" Aunt Penney's brows rose.

"Yes, Wes." Why did talking about Wes make her so uncomfortable? They were friends, nothing more. "What did you think I was going to do? Let him sit alone in the office for lunch while you're out?"

"That's true. The poor guy would be bored." Her aunt studied her for a moment. "Is that the only reason?"

"That I asked him to lunch?"

She knew what her aunt was asking. She wanted to know if Kate was interested in Wes. But she wasn't. She'd already dated someone who couldn't be happy in a small town. And she knew she wouldn't be happy living anywhere else.

Aunt Penney nodded. "After all, he's your age, really cute, and single. I checked with his mother—"

"Aunt Penney, you didn't!" Heat rushed to her cheeks.

"Of course, I did. You can't remain single forever."

Kate raised her eyebrows. "You never married. Maybe I'll be like you."

Aunt Penney's smile morphed into a frown, but she didn't say anything.

"We're friends," Kate insisted. "Nothing more." It was time to turn the tables on her aunt. "But don't you think it's time you told me exactly why Wes is in Bayberry?"

Her aunt moved toward the kitchen, just off the living room. Fred sat on the couch and kept his nose buried in the local newspaper, acting as though he didn't hear a word. *Smart man.* But Kate knew he was listening. He didn't take part in the gossip mill that extended from one end of town to the other, but the man always knew more than he let on.

"Have you had lunch?" Aunt Penney asked.

"Yes, Joe made us subs."

"Oh, that's good. Can I get you a drink?" Aunt Penney opened the fridge as though to check and see what there was to offer.

"No, thank you. Aunt Penney, please talk to me. I really need to know what's going on."

Aunt Penney closed the fridge and turned to her. "Now isn't the time to get into it."

Kate sighed. This wasn't like her aunt. They had few secrets between them. "Aunt Penney, please. If it's about the company, I should know. I'm part of the family."

There was the sound of crinkling paper as Fred folded his newspaper. "Penney, you really should tell her. She has a right to know."

Kate's mouth gaped. He knew? And she didn't? She turned back to her aunt with an accusing look. What was going on? And why was her aunt keeping things from her?

The kitchen island stood between them. It was suddenly as if there were a divide between them. Kate didn't like the feeling. After her parents died, her aunt had become her family. It took Kate time to let the citizens of Bayberry in too, but her aunt was her rock—her anchor.

It was Aunt Penney who'd always been there through the good and bad. Through the tears of joy and the tears of sadness. She'd thought they could talk to each other about anything, but now she was wondering what had happened to that easy rapport.

"Don't look at me like that," Aunt Penney said. "I've just been trying to give you a good Christmas before I had to share the news with you."

"What news?"

Aunt Penney sighed. "That's the thing, I don't really know. Wes is here to evaluate the business and let me know if it can be salvaged—"

"Of course, it can be."

"Kate, I know that's what you want to believe, but you know as well as I do that without money to replace our old machines, we can't keep up with the orders. And the bank turned us down for another loan—"

"We'll try another bank. As many as it takes."

"It's not that easy."

"We'll get through this." Kate would be optimistic for both of them. "I've been working on our social media and the big sale this weekend—"

Aunt Penney's face reflected her sorrow. "I know you have. And I'm so proud of you. But I think it's going to take something bigger to turn things around. I've tried other banks and they all said no."

The backs of Kate's eyes stung. She blinked repeatedly. "Without the candle company, there won't be a town."

Aunt Penney's shoulders sagged. "I know." Her voice was barely above a whisper. "That's why I'm doing everything I can to see that there's a future for the company. I'm hoping Wes comes up with something we haven't thought of to save it."

Fred limped up. "Penney's been trying her best, speaking with the bank and other lenders. If there's a way, I'm sure she'll find it."

Kate's gaze moved to her aunt. "Is that right?"

"Of course it is. How could you doubt it? That company and this town are as important to me as they are to you." Her aunt moved around the counter toward her. "Kate, I'm sorry."

Kate shook her head. "It's not your fault."

She moved into Penney's open arms and they hugged. Her aunt's hugs were always warm, tight and reassuring. That much hadn't changed since she was a kid. But she had changed. She was no longer a child.

Kate pulled back. "Aunt Penney, you don't have to protect me. I'm an adult now. I want to be here for you, to help in any way I can."

"You're right." Her aunt looked flustered. "Sometimes I still think of you as my little girl. And I didn't want to ruin your holiday. I know it's your favorite time of the year."

She had that much right. Christmas was always magical, with the lights and the holiday spirit that came over everyone. "It is, but I can still help you with this problem."

Fred stood in the kitchen and rubbed his white beard. His blue eyes twinkled as he smiled, as though he knew it would all work out in the end. When Kate was little and had visited her aunt, she'd always thought that he was Santa—from his deep laugh to the twinkle in his eyes. But now that she was grown up, she realized the reason she'd believed that was because he'd always dressed up like Santa for the holiday parties. Except for this year—

Oh no. She still didn't have a Santa for the party.

She checked the time. She hated to leave, but she had a meeting this afternoon.

"I've got to get back to the factory," she said. "I'm sorry."

"Don't be," her aunt said. "If anyone understands, it's me."

With another hug, Kate let herself out the door. She'd known the company was having problems, but she didn't know they were running out of options. Now that she did, she was going to make sure they had a Christmas miracle. She didn't know how just yet, but she wasn't giving up.

Shopping with Kate was another eye-opening experience.

When he'd heard he was coming to Bayberry, Wes had never expected to be spending so much one-on-one time with Kate. In fact, he'd figured she'd probably married and moved away. And he certainly hadn't expected her to be giving his wardrobe a makeover.

The Men's Shop on Bayberry Square was small, but it was crammed with shirts, pants and even shoes. None of it was very fancy, but then again, Bayberry didn't do fancy. It did practical and comfortable.

Wes, suddenly feeling overdressed, loosened his tie and unbuttoned the collar of his dress shirt. He'd been dressing like this for so long that it would feel strange to go to work in something so...so casual.

"What about this?" Kate held out a red flannel shirt.

Wes shook his head. Flannel? It wasn't really his style.

He looked around, but there was so much to choose from that he felt a bit overwhelmed.

"There's this." Kate held up a gray long-sleeved tee-shirt.

He shook his head. That was way too casual to wear to work—even in Bayberry.

The tall, lanky man with short dark hair who ran the shop walked up to Wes carrying a navy blue knit sweater. "How about something like this?"

The sweater intrigued Wes. He reached out and ran his fingers over the material. It looked nice, and it was soft too. "I think this might work."

Kate came over. "Oh, that would look good on you. And it would keep you warm. Why don't you try it on and I'll see what else they have?"

Wes had to admit the sweater did appeal to him. He'd forgotten how cold it was in Bayberry when the mountain air rushed up through the valley. It could chill a person to the bone.

After he'd tried on the sweater, the salesman peered at him through his bifocals as he handed Wes five more sweaters to try on. And Kate, after learning his size, handed him a stack of jeans from slim fit to loose fit. Some were a dark wash, some faded, and one pair had a greenish tint.

He looked at Kate. "I don't think I'm going to need all of these clothes. I'm not staying that long."

"I thought you were here until Christmas."

"I am, but—"

"Then you need them." She smiled. "We can't have you getting sick or anything."

When all was said and done, Wes walked out of the Men's Store with four sweaters, four pairs of jeans, warm socks, waterproof boots, lined gloves, a knit cap and a lined winter coat. He was already wearing some of his purchases. There was no point in freezing if he didn't have to. He wiggled his warm toes in his new boots. He was certainly prepared for whatever winter weather was thrown his way.

They headed up Main Street to Mel's Grille to grab some supper. Wes knew he should be back in his room inputting data into spreadsheets, but he told himself that even he couldn't go long without eating, especially on this snowy cold evening.

When they walked in the restaurant, the dinner crowd turned as one and called out Kate's name. She waved. Wes smiled and shook his head. He felt like he'd walked into the middle of a sitcom, where everybody knew her name.

Once they were seated at a table, he said, "I don't know how to thank you. Let me know if there's some way I can pay you back."

"Glad to have helped." She worried her bottom lip as though unsure if she should say something or not.

"Go ahead."

Her gaze met his. "What?"

"You have something on your mind. Go ahead and say it. I think if we're good enough friends for you to help me pick me out a new winter wardrobe, we can talk about whatever you have on your mind."

She leaned back in the chair. "Did you really mean it when you said you wanted to pay me back?"

He suddenly got an uneasy feeling. "If this is about the work I'm doing for your aunt—"

"It's not. I promise."

He breathed a lot easier. "Then tell me what it is. Maybe I can help."

"I need Santa."

He smiled, thinking she was joking. "And you would like me to, um, just phone him?"

Her eyes twinkled. "That would be helpful. Do you have his number on hand?"

Wes smiled and shook his head. "Kate, what are you talking about?"

"Well, Fred was supposed to be our Santa, but now that he's injured, I need a new Santa for tomorrow night at the sale."

Wes held up a hand to stop her. "And you think I would make a good Santa?"

She shrugged. "I don't see why not."

"For one, I've never played Santa. And for two, I don't have a Santa suit." He would do almost anything for her, but dressing up like a big red elf wasn't what he'd had in mind. He shook his head. "You've asked the wrong person."

"Please." Her green eyes begged him. "You're the right size to fit in Fred's suit. Most of the other men in town are too tall or too short."

"But I'm just right?"

She nodded. "It would mean so much to me and to the whole town. After all, what's Christmas without Santa?"

Why did he find it so hard to turn her down? When Kate stared at him, as she was doing now, he fell under her spell. And all he could think to say was, "Okay. I'll do it."

"You will?" Her whole face lit up as she shifted in her seat.

For a moment, he thought she was going to jump over the table and give him a hug. But when she settled back in her chair, he was surprised at how disappointed he felt. The thought of pulling her into his arms teased and tempted his mind. He resisted the urge to go to her and give her that hug.

He knew he should look away, but he was drawn to her. Her smile remained, and it caused a funny warm feeling in his chest, knowing he was responsible for her happiness.

"What's going on here?" Carrie asked, as she came to a stop at their table to take their order.

Kate glanced around to see who was listening. No one was seated close by. She motioned for Carrie to lean closer. "Wes agreed to be our Santa this year."

Carrie turned her attention to him. "That's wonderful. The whole town thanks you."

Growing uncomfortable with the way they were fussing over him, he said, "It's not that big a deal."

Kate's expression grew serious. "It's a huge deal. You can't have Christmas without Santa."

"That's right," Carrie chimed in. "And to thank you, dinner is on me."

"What?" Wes couldn't believe what a big fuss they were making about his wearing a red suit and a cap. "I can pay."

Carrie waved him off. "No argument. Would you like some more of that stew you had the other day? I think there's a little bit back there."

"That sounds perfect." He intended to leave her a really big tip.

# Chapter Eleven

" *H*OW'S IT GOING?"

The following afternoon, Wes sat behind his assigned desk at the candle company. He pressed his cell phone to his ear and swallowed hard. He hadn't expected to hear from Mr. Summers requesting a progress report. That never happened with any of his other assignments. It appeared his boss was taking a personal interest in him. That had to be a good sign, right?

Eager to make a good impression, he started with a rundown of what he'd done so far. "But I still have a lot to look at before I can make a preliminary assessment."

"And you'll have that done before Christmas, right?"

That gave him two weeks to get his work done. He was usually given three to four weeks for an in-depth analysis like this.

He softly cleared his throat. "That might be pushing it. They don't have much of their information automated. I'm having to pull data runs and file folders every time I need information."

"I'm sure you can handle it. I'll be looking forward to your report in time for the holidays. And then we'll discuss your recommendation as far as selling."

What? Wes hadn't said anything about Kate's aunt selling the company. He thought back through his conversation with Mr. Summers. No, he definitely hadn't given his boss that impression.

"Sir, I don't think—"

"Hold on," Mr. Summers covered the phone but his muffled voice could still be heard. "Chad, come in. I'll be right with you." Mr. Summers spoke directly into the phone. "I've got to run. We'll talk more soon." And with that the line went dead.

Wes sat there staring at his phone, wondering what in the world had happened. The next time he spoke to the boss, he'd clarify that he wasn't leaning one way or the other about the company's future. That was a big part of his job—staying impartial until the data told him what would be best for the company and the owners.

Maybe Mr. Summers was just anxious to announce the promotion. The usual rush of excitement Wes felt when he thought about receiving the promotion didn't hit him. He assured himself that he just had a lot of other things on his mind. After all, it wasn't every day he played Santa. In fact, he'd never done it before. He wasn't even sure he could do a good job.

He checked outside his office to see if anyone was around. And then, deciding to be cautious, he closed the door. Walking back to his chair, he tried out his Santa imitation.

"Ho. Ho. Ho." A smile pulled at his lips. He lowered his voice another octave. "Ho. Ho. Ho."

That was better. Maybe he could pull this off. He knew how much Kate was counting on him. And he didn't want to let her—or the town—down.

"Ho. Ho. Ho. And how are you? Have you been naughty or nice?"

*Knock knock.*

Wes turned with a jerk. The door was open and Kate had stuck her head inside. "Sorry. Didn't mean to startle you."

"Um, you didn't." Boy, his new sweater was mighty warm. "Did you need something?"

She gave him a funny look. "I was just checking to make sure you're ready for tonight."

"I think I have everything under control." And then he decided to give her a sample of his Santa impersonation. "Ho. Ho. Ho. And has Kate been naughty or nice this year?"

A big smile lit up her face. "Someone's been practicing."

"And someone isn't answering the question."

"Oh. I've definitely been good."

"And what does Kate want Santa to bring her for Christmas?"

The smile slipped from her face. She stepped inside the office and closed the door. "I'd like Santa to present my aunt with a plan to save this company and keep everyone's jobs."

His good mood slipped. "Kate—"

"Don't worry. My aunt filled me in on things the

other day. I know why you're here. And I just want you to know that I'll do whatever it takes to keep this business open and running." Her voice caught with emotion. "Without the candle company, Bayberry will become a ghost town."

He resisted the urge to go to her—to comfort her. "Kate, I don't know if I can deliver that Christmas present."

"Looks like we're going to need a Christmas miracle." Her words hung in the air for a moment. "I actually stopped by to see if you were available."

"Now?" When she nodded, he couldn't help but wonder what she had in mind. "Another food drive?"

"Not this time. I owe you a tour of the town."

"Now?" Why was he repeating himself?

"Sure. It won't be the same if we go this evening, in the dark. It'll be too hard to make out the businesses and landmarks."

His gaze moved to his desk. "I have a lot of work to do."

"It'll still be there when we get back. This won't take too long. Come on." Kate gestured for him to follow her. "I'll give you the grand tour. I only do it for special people."

She considered him special? There was that fuzzy, warm sensation in his chest again. And the way she was smiling at him was making it really hard to remember his priorities.

With great effort, he dragged his gaze back to his desk. "I don't know. I just talked to my boss and he's really anxious for me to wrap up my work here." And he had a lot of work to do. It didn't help that there was always a distraction. An attractive distraction, but a distraction all the same.

Kate smiled, melting his resolve. "This is Bayberry. It's a small town. I promise it won't take long."

It'd be faster just to agree, because he was quickly learning that Kate could be quite determined. And so that's what he did. With an agreement to meet her in ten minutes out front, he finished inputting a few numbers in his spreadsheet, saved it and closed his laptop.

Dressed in his new boots, jeans, sweater, coat, and gloves, he was ready for this adventure. He stepped outside, expecting to find Kate in the pickup, but there was no truck. Kate was standing in the parking lot speaking with someone.

When she approached him, he asked, "Aren't we driving?"

She shook her head. "It's warm today with the sunshine. Even the snow is melting. I thought we could walk. You can get a better take on the town that way."

And so they set off from the candle company, crossing over Candlelight Way and onto Main Street. It hadn't snowed that day. In fact, the sky was a light blue, with sunshine so bright that you practically needed sunglasses. The sidewalks were clear except for the trickle of melted snow. Still, it was nice to have on winter boots.

As they walked along, Kate asked, "You mentioned before about being here until Christmas. Is that still the plan? Or does your boss want you back in the city sooner?"

"I think he wants me back sooner, but I just don't

know if that's possible. I have a lot to do before I can leave." He didn't mention that the lack of digitized reports was really slowing him down.

"And then you'll be joining your mother for Christmas?"

He shook his head. "My mother is going on a cruise with her friends."

Sympathy shone in her eyes. "Do you have any other family to spend the holidays with?"

He shook his head. "I'll probably work."

Her eyes widened. "On Christmas?"

"It's about the only time I have to catch up on things at the office. With no incoming emails or the phone ringing, I can get a lot done."

"That doesn't sound very fun. In fact, it sounds lonely."

"I'm used to it." Used to it and happy with it were two totally different things. The truth was, he buried himself in his work to keep from thinking about the parts of life he was missing out on. But he couldn't attain the promotion to assistant vice president without making sacrifices.

"This is the community hall. Lots of parties and wedding receptions take place here."

He took in the white building with black shutters and candles glowing in the windows. On the double glass doors hung twin wreaths. "Does everyone in Bayberry decorate for the holiday?"

She looked at him like he surely had to kidding. "Of course. It takes the ordinary and makes it extraordinary. I just love the garlands, the twinkle lights and, well, all of the decorations."

From the looks of the town, most of its residents

felt the same way. He had to admit it livened up the town.

"Most of the businesses are found along Main Street, especially surrounding Bayberry Square." As they moved around the square, she pointed out various establishments, from the library to the bakery. And then she moved to the door of Steaming Brew. "And this is the coffee shop, but you've already figured that out."

"I did. And they have the best pumpkin spice lattes ever."

"Good idea. We'll get a couple for the rest of the walk."

When they entered the coffee shop, Abby's eyes widened. She quickly replaced her surprise with a smile as they stepped up to the counter. "Aren't you two supposed to be working?"

"It's her fault," he said, winking at Kate. "She has me playing hooky."

Kate rolled her eyes and shook her head. "I promised him a tour of the town. For one reason or another, it kept getting put off. So while the sun is out and there are no emergencies, I'm showing him around."

"Sounds good to me," Abby said. "If I had someone to take over for me, I'd join you. I just love walking around and checking out everyone's Christmas decorations. So what can I get you two?"

Simultaneously they said, "Pumpkin spice latte."

Abby laughed. "Told you it was good!" When they nodded enthusiastically, she said, "Just give me a moment."

A few minutes later, with lattes in hand, they continued the tour. Kate pointed out Covered Bridge

Street, which led to a pond where people could ice skate once it froze over. She showed him the burger joint and the movie theater, whose marquee boasted a film that had been released about six months ago. Not exactly on top of things, but he hadn't heard anyone complaining.

As they circled back toward the candle company, he did think of one more thing he wanted to see. "Could we head back by Flatlander Way?"

"Sure. Any particular reason?"

He nodded. "It's where I lived once upon a time."

"I'd love to see it."

They walked and talked, mostly about the history of the town. Kate told him about how her ancestors had founded the town. He couldn't imagine what it was like to have roots that went so deep. It's what he'd wanted since he was a kid—to settle in one place and stay there. It would happen if he could land this promotion.

For a while they walked in comfortable silence. He could easily imagine taking more of these strolls with Kate. That is, if he stuck around Bayberry, which he wasn't planning to do.

And then they reached the corner of Valley Lane and Flatlander Way. There sat the beautiful Victorian with bright berry-red paint and clean white trim. He came to a stop. It was just as he remembered it, with the wraparound porch and the sweeping front steps leading up to the double-door entrance. The only thing it was lacking were holiday decorations like every other house on the street.

But that would be simple enough to solve. A single candle in each window. Two wreaths, one for each door. And on the wooden rails should be garlands with white twinkle lights. Nothing over the top. The house deserved a stunning but classic look—

Kate touched his arm, reminding him that she was still standing next to him. "Is it what you remember?"

He nodded, not believing he'd just decorated the whole house in his mind. "It's exactly as I remembered. My mother used to sit with me on the front porch and we'd clean corn for dinner. After dinner, I'd ride my bike all around here." As he waved his arm around, his gaze strayed across a For Sale sign.

And then a woman exited the house. She locked the front door before heading down the steps in their direction.

"Maybe we should move on." He didn't want to linger and cause an awkward situation.

"It's okay," Kate said. "That's Mary Trimble. She's a real estate agent." And then Kate's eyes lit up as though a thought had just occurred to her. "How would you feel about having a look around inside?"

"Really? I'd like that." He didn't usually let himself get caught up in the past, but this opportunity was too good to pass up.

Kate hurried over to Mary. They talked for a few moments. And then Mary went in the opposite direction and Kate smiled at him as she held up a key.

"Come on," she called out.

He rushed to catch up to her. "Shouldn't she be here with us?" He glanced over his shoulder at the agent's retreating back. "Are we allowed in by ourselves?"

"Relax. I know Mary and she trusts me. And I know the owner, Mrs. Harding. She just moved to a senior community. I know she'd be the first to invite you in. So it's all fine. I just have to drop the key off at Mary's office, because she forgot a lockbox for the front door."

Kate stood aside, letting him lead the way. Yet he didn't move. The years rolled away, and in his mind's eye, the property was the way it'd been when he was a teenager. His gaze dropped to the sidewalk. He remembered racing down it on his bicycle. He could still recall the bump-bump-bump as the tires bounced over the gaps between the red bricks.

He could feel Kate's gaze on him. It spurred him into motion. At the base of the steps, he reached out for the railing. He'd hoped that this house would be his family's forever home. He wasn't the only one. He recalled his mother being the happiest he'd ever seen her when they moved here. She'd joined the knitting group and the women's group at the local church. He'd picked up that after-school job delivering papers. Dad had seemed content in his new position, though he'd often been too busy to spend much time with his son. Everyone had been happy.

Kate unlocked the front door and pushed it open. She stepped aside, allowing him to enter first. The house had been emptied, but that was okay. He remembered how it used to look. The wood floors had been well preserved. The banister on the steps still looked perfect for sliding down. He smiled, recalling his mother reprimanding him for not coming down the stairs properly. Not that she was really mad at him.

They toured the downstairs, from the spacious living room where his father used to fall asleep in the recliner with the newspaper open and the news playing on the television, to the kitchen with its many white cabinets, but there was no lingering scent of cinnamon from his mother's famous apple cobbler. His mouth watered at the memory. It'd been so many years since he'd tasted it.

Then he showed Kate where his bedroom had been upstairs. It was so much bigger than his bedroom in New York. This house was more than triple the size of his entire apartment. Not that he was comparing the two places. One was his home and one was a part of his past—nothing more.

As they made their way back outside, Kate said, "You know, it's for sale. You could always buy it."

He shook his head, refusing to acknowledge just how tempting the idea sounded. "My work is in the city. I'd never have time to visit it."

"It's just something to consider. Properties around here sell quickly."

A dog started barking. Wes saw a golden cocker spaniel running through the snow toward them. Wes turned to make a hasty retreat, but Kate had come to a stop in front of him.

The dog was still barking up a storm.

"Hey, Princess." Kate crouched down to greet the dog. "How are you, girl?"

The dog let off one bark, as though understanding Kate's question and answering her. Kate fussed over Princess, who ate up the attention.

And then Princess turned to Wes. He stood per-fectly still as she sniffed his boots and then his pants.

"You can pet her," Kate said. "She's friendly."

He crouched down. He held out his hand for

the dog to sniff. When Princess licked his hand, he smiled.

"You two look good together," Kate said. "Maybe you should consider getting a dog."

"I always wanted one as a kid, but my father said I couldn't have one because we were always moving around."

"Maybe now that you're settled."

He shook his head. "They don't allow pets in my building. And I'm not home enough."

"Kate, is that you?" A woman's voice called out to them.

Princess took off toward the house next door, kicking up snow. The dog's tail swished back and forth.

Kate straightened. "Hello, Mrs. Johnson."

"I hope Princess wasn't bothering you."

"Not at all," Wes said. "She's quite friendly."

Mrs. Johnson smiled. "She was probably excited to get away from the little ones."

"Puppies?" Kate's face lit up.

Mrs. Johnson nodded. "Would you like to see them?"

"We'd love to," Kate said without the slightest hesitation. And then, as though she remembered him, she turned to Wes. "You don't mind, do you?"

Princess barked as though telling them to get a move on.

Wes shook his head. That's all it took for Kate to set off, following Princess's tracks through the snow. He'd already missed part of the afternoon at the office. What was a little more? And he wouldn't mind seeing the puppies.

Once they stepped on the porch, Kate paused.

"Mrs. Johnson, I'd like you to meet Wes Adams. He's here consulting at the candle company. And Wes, this is Mrs. Johnson. She was my math teacher many years ago."

He shook the older woman's hand. "It's nice to meet you."

"It's nice to put a face to the name." She smiled at him, making him feel welcome. "Let's get inside. It's still mighty cold out here."

Inside they slipped off their boots and coats. Princess had already disappeared, undoubtedly to check on her puppies. Mrs. Johnson led them to her spacious laundry room, where five little puppies were running around. A smile pulled at his lips.

When his family moved to Bayberry, he'd hoped that at last he could have what he wanted most—a dog. He recalled telling his mother it was all he wanted for Christmas that year.

Instead, he'd ended up in a small apartment in Atlanta for Christmas that year, far from Bayberry. And there was a no-pets-allowed policy. He never did get a dog.

Kate sat on the floor and let the puppies climb all over her. Her face glowed with happiness. If anyone needed a puppy, it was her. He pulled out his phone and took a picture so he could remember this moment.

"Aww...look." Mrs. Johnson pointed down at his feet.

He glanced down and saw that a puppy had climbed on his foot. Wes had been so caught up in watching Kate that he hadn't noticed.

"He likes you," Kate said.

"He's the runt of the litter." Mrs. Johnson tossed Kate a toy ball for the puppies. Then she turned back to Wes. "We call him Rascal. He's ornery. And he has his own mind. He doesn't take to many people. You must be special."

Wes moved slowly so as not to startle Rascal. The puppy remained on his foot, and let Wes pet him. And then Wes picked him up, expecting the puppy to fuss to get down. Instead, Rascal was docile and settled against his chest. At that moment, Wes was tempted to take the little puppy home.

"He doesn't have a family yet," Mrs. Johnson said. "Would you like to adopt him?"

Wes gazed into the puppy's eyes. Rascal really was cute. Wes's answer stuck in the back of his throat. His mind and his heart were at odds.

"You can have some time to think about it," Mrs. Johnson said.

"Thanks. But I can't have a pet where I live." He ran his finger over the puppy's head and he wished he lived somewhere else—someplace that allowed pets.

Wes didn't know how much time had passed before they said goodbye to the puppies and headed back to the candle company. As they walked, he couldn't shake how nice this afternoon had been and how he would have passed it up if it hadn't been for Kate's insistence. He used to make time for fun and relaxing. Now, his life was all about meetings and deadlines. When had his work become the focus of his life?

He paused outside the candle company and turned to Kate. "Thank you for the tour. I really enjoyed it."

"And weren't the puppies the cutest?" When he

nodded, she said, "You really should adopt Rascal. You two looked perfect together"

"But my apartment doesn't allow pets."

"That's easy. Move."

His eyes connected with hers. The words he was about to say were forgotten. His heart *thump-thumped* in his chest. It was so loud that it echoed in his ears. He wondered if she could hear it. If she did, she didn't let on.

He was certain he could get lost in her big green eyes—just like he was doing right now. But that was not a good thing. He was here to work, not get distracted by a girl, erm, a woman from his past.

He should look away, but she was staring back at him. Wait. She was staring back at him? Was that interest reflected in her eyes?

His heart raced. He was drawn in by everything about her. If he'd thought she was beautiful when they were kids, Kate was an absolute knockout now.

"I had fun too." She looked away, ending the moment. "It was nice to see the town through someone else's eyes. If you liked Bayberry enough, maybe you could stick around longer. Maybe until the New Year."

She didn't give him a chance to answer. She just put that thought out there and strolled into the building. He wasn't sure what to make of her invitation. But it wasn't just the town that he liked.

Was Kate saying she felt something growing between them too? Did she want to spend the holidays with him? His heart picked up its pace once more.

In that moment, he knew what he wanted to do—take Kate up on her offer. He wanted to spend Christmas in Bayberry.

# Chapter Twelve

WHERE HAD THE WEEK GONE? The days were flying by and there was still so much to do.

Kate sat behind the table in the file room that she'd commandeered for a temporary office while hers was being occupied by Wes. She didn't like being pushed out of her office. She knew where everything was and had her comfortable chair adjusted perfectly to fit her back. But it would be worth it if Wes were able to help the candle company out of this tough position.

Her fingers continued to move over the keyboard. She was responding to a bunch of comments on her most recent social media post. Her aunt had taught her that success was achieved one customer at a time. And so Kate made the effort to take a personal approach to her promotion for the upcoming holiday sale.

The only problem with taking a personal approach was that it took time—time she didn't have. Because all this added promotion was taking time away from her regular work—

*Knock knock.*

Kate's fingers hovered over the keyboard as she glanced up, finding her aunt standing in the doorway. "Aunt Penney, what are you doing here? Is something wrong?"

"Relax. Nothing's wrong. I forgot some papers in my office that I wanted to look over later tonight." Her aunt frowned. She lifted her arm and made a show of checking the time on her antique gold watch. "Because there isn't time to look over them now." Her gaze met Kate's once more. "You haven't forgotten about the tree lighting tonight, have you?"

Kate looked at the stack of file folders with reports paper-clipped to each one, waiting for her to review and sign off on them. For the first time since she'd moved to Bayberry, she replied, "I'm not going to the tree lighting tonight."

"What?" Aunt Penney stepped up to the table. A frown pulled at her lips. "But you have to. It's tradition."

"I know. And I don't want to miss it, but I have a lot of work to do."

"I think you've done enough for one day. In fact, I'm certain of it. I saw you head to the office this morning at six. You work so hard."

Kate smiled. "Thank you." Her aunt's praise meant the world to her. "But with the sale coming up, I just can't afford to waste time." She didn't know who was still lingering around the offices so she had to be careful what she said. "It's important. You know how important this sale is."

Her aunt nodded. "I do." It was as if she'd aged ten years in the blink of an eye. "And that's why it's important that you remember that there's so much more to life than business. Trust this old lady who thought she had time to keep putting off living her life. And now it has passed me by. Please don't end up like me."

Kate shook her head. "First, you're not old. Not even close. You have more energy than most women half your age."

"You're just saying that."

"I'm not. It's the truth. Second, I'd be honored to be like you. You're the strongest, most loving person I know."

Her aunt's eyes grew moist. "I...I don't know what to say."

Kate wasn't finished yet. "And third, you still have plenty of time to live your dreams, as soon as you let me take over the candle company." Hope filled her chest. Would this be the heart-to-heart she had to have with her aunt in order for Penney to hand over the reins to the company?

Her aunt sighed. "I can't do that. Not yet—"

"If there's something else I can do—"

"It's not you." Her aunt's face filled with love. "You are amazing and a very hard worker. But I need Wes to complete his report before I can do anything."

Kate nodded. She didn't like it, but she understood. "Just know that I'm here and ready to take over, if you need me too."

Aunt Penney moved around the table and then leaned down to give her a brief hug. "I love you."

"I love you too."

"Now, do me a favor."

"Anything."

"Go to the tree lighting tonight. It's an order. After all, I'm still your boss. At least for a little longer." Aunt Penney gave her a stern look, like she'd done when Kate was a kid and wanted to stay out past curfew on a school night.

Years of experience told Kate that there was no point in fighting her. "Yes, ma'am."

"Then get going. You don't want to be late. Everyone will be there." And with that, her aunt hurried out the door.

Kate was tempted to finishing responding to comments on her latest post about Bayberry Candles. Her fingers moved to the keyboard. But she knew once she started working, time would get away from her.

With a groan, she closed the window and then shut down her computer. Aunt Penney was right. It would wait until tomorrow.

She recalled her aunt's words: *Everyone will be there.* Did that include Wes? She moved faster. Suddenly, going to the tree lighting sounded a lot more tempting.

She reached for her bag. She'd made some preparations the night before, just in case she had time to go. And those preparations included going with Wes.

Kate wondered if he was still working. After all, he didn't have someone in his life to tell him when to call it a day. She was willing to bet he was still in his, erm, her office. But not for much longer.

Someone had to tell Wes that the building was closing. She rushed to finish gathering her things. She was a woman on a mission.

"It's tree lighting night."

He'd know that warm, feminine voice anywhere.

Wes glanced up from his laptop, which was still sitting on Kate's desk among piles of papers and stacks of reports.

He saw her in the doorway. "I hope you have a good time."

"What?" She stepped into the office. "You're not coming?"

He shook his head. "I really need to keep working. This section is taking longer than I thought it would, and I've been out of the office a lot this week."

She checked the time. "But it's after six, and the tree lighting in the square is at seven. We have to get going if we want a good spot."

She sounded as though she was really anxious for him to join her. His gaze moved to the work on his desk. Would anyone really notice if he took the evening off? The thought nagged at him. An evening with Kate was so tempting.

He leaned back in his chair. "You're really excited about this."

"Aren't you?" Her face lit up. "It's Christmastime. A time to celebrate all the good things in life."

"Can you really be that happy when you know what I'm doing? And how it might turn out?"

She shrugged. "Someone just reminded me that there's more to life than work. It doesn't have to be either/or. Work will be waiting for us in the morning."

The longer he was in this small town, the more

he understood why he remembered Bayberry more fondly than the other places he'd lived as a kid. They tried so hard to balance their work and play here. It was too bad his family hadn't stuck around. He wondered whether he'd have been able to escort Kate to the Candlelight Dance if they had.

He remembered as a teenager how he'd had every intention of asking her to the dance. He was only in junior high at the time, so asking a girl to the dance was a big thing. A huge thing. Every time he'd thought of asking her, his hands had grown clammy and his stomach had churned. And so he'd put it off again and again.

Finally, he'd waited so long that it was the week before the dance and his father announced that they were moving—again. Wes had put up a fuss, telling his parents he didn't want to move. But they'd told him he didn't have a choice.

He'd shouted that life wasn't fair and his mother had concurred. After his father had left the room, she'd confided in Wes that she wished they could stay in Bayberry too. The people were so nice and she'd made a great friend in Kate's aunt. He'd tried to persuade his mother to stay here with him while his father worked elsewhere, but she told him that families stick together through the good and the bad.

"Wes, did you hear me?"

He blinked and focused on Kate. He didn't have any idea what she'd said. She frowned at him.

"Come on," she said. "Let's get out of here. Besides, I want to pick your brain."

"Kate, I can't."

"Aunt Penney will be very upset if you're not there.

She has a thing about people working overtime on special occasions, and the tree lighting is a very special occasion."

"But—"

"No buts. Come on. The office is officially closed. Besides, if you don't come with me, your Christmas wish won't come true."

Immediately his thoughts turned to the promotion. It was what he needed to put everything right in his life. Once he had that promotion, he'd be happy. Maybe he could move to a place that accepted pets. His thoughts turned to Rascal. But by then the puppy would be adopted—

"Wes, we don't want to be late."

The eagerness on Kate's face was his final undoing. She was right. The work would be waiting for him. He rolled his shoulders, trying to ease the stiffness from leaning over the desk for hours. He had been in early that day and he'd insisted on eating lunch at his desk.

And now that he had warmer clothes, walking to Bayberry Square wouldn't be miserable. In fact, with his new warm boots, coat, cap and gloves, he had barely noticed the weather when he walked to work that morning.

"Okay. Let's go." He closed his laptop and started to clean up his desk.

"Oh, leave it be."

"I can't. It's a mess." He always cleaned up his work area at the end of each day.

"But it's your mess. Your work mess. Leave it and it'll be all ready for you in the morning."

"How do you figure?"

"Well, you would spend time cleaning it up tonight. And then when you come in Monday morning, you'll have to put everything back where it is now to work with it. Isn't that right?"

He'd never thought of it that way, but she was right. He did arrange his work stacks in the morning. Even though it felt wrong to leave a mess, he got to his feet, grabbed his laptop and slipped it in his messenger bag. His gaze was still on the mess on his desk. He didn't know if he could just leave it be. It went against his sense of status quo.

"Come on." Kate shoved his coat at him. "It'll be fine. I promise. There won't be anyone here to notice, either. Everyone has already left for the tree lighting. And if we don't hurry, we really will be late."

He swallowed hard. "I don't know."

She grabbed his arm and pulled him toward the door. Then she got behind him and gave him a push out the door. "Who knew someone so young could be so set in his ways?"

"This from the woman who has all of these holiday traditions."

"Hey, traditions are good." Kate pulled the door shut behind her. When he stopped and turned back, she braced her arms across the doorway. "There's no way you're getting back in there tonight."

He slipped on his coat and slung his messenger bag across his chest, with an amused look at Kate. "You're serious, aren't you?"

She nodded. "Very."

He shook his head and smiled. "I suppose I can leave it for one night."

"That's the spirit." She looped her arm in his as they headed for the employee exit.

He wasn't sure what to make of Kate's spontaneous action. Oh, who was he kidding? He liked having her on his arm. A smile played at his lips.

He reminded himself not to get too drawn in. After all, he'd be leaving before Christmas. He reassured himself that this wasn't a date. Not at all. It was just two friends—because by now they could call each other friends—anyway, they were just two friends going to spend some time with practically the entire town.

And he did his best to ignore the warm, fuzzy sensation that started in his chest every time she squeezed his arm. Because they were friends. Nothing more.

# Chapter Thirteen

*E*VENING HAD FALLEN OVER BAYBERRY. Streetlamps lit the way.

All the while, fluffy snowflakes flittered and fluttered as they drifted to the ground.

Wes knew he'd made the right decision. Accompanying Kate to the tree lighting felt right—just like her hand tucked in the crook of his arm felt right.

"How is your evaluation coming?" Kate's voice drew him from his thoughts.

He shook his head. "I really can't talk about it."

She frowned. "But it's all right. Remember, Aunt Penney told me all about it."

"It's not that. I haven't completed my study, and to give an opinion at this point would be unwise. There may be something I have yet to uncover that would offset everything I've established so far."

"So you won't even give me a hint which way you're leaning?"

"Leaning?"

"You know, between keeping the candle factory open or recommending selling?"

He gave a firm shake of his head.

"Actually, that's okay with me."

He glanced over at her. "Why is that?"

"Because tomorrow's sale is going to be huge." Her face lit up with a smile. "I've been working so hard on this. I've drummed up a lot of support on social media. You have to admit that it's going to be great." When he couldn't agree with her, the smile slipped from her face. "So what's the problem?"

He really didn't want to rain on her parade. "I didn't say there was one."

"You didn't say anything at all. That's how I know there is a problem." She grabbed his arm and stopped walking. She moved in front of him to look him in the eyes. "Please, you have to tell me."

He sighed. "The sale coupon you printed up and handed out to everyone—"

"It was to get them to the sale. We always do a coupon, and this year I upped the discount to draw in more people. And it's working. Everyone is talking about this sale being the biggest ever."

He gripped the strap on his bag tighter as he averted his gaze. "That's the thing. The markdown is really large."

"Forty percent. It's not that large. I've seen other sales just as large or larger."

"But those other retailers have a means to recoup the loss."

"Such as?"

"Marking up the stock before the holiday season.

Or they limit the discount to just one regularly priced item."

The look of frustration filled her face. "But I made it 40% off the entire order."

He nodded. The sale would draw in people, but it wasn't going to produce the profits needed to turn around the company. He wanted to tell her otherwise. He wanted to tell her that she had a really strong marketing plan, but as accurate as her numbers were on all of the accounting documents he'd reviewed, her accounting skills were not as strong. Sympathy welled up in him.

This wasn't his problem, he reminded himself. He wasn't hired to save the company. It was his job to develop an opinion based on facts. But his growing feeling for Kate was making it difficult to maintain an impartial attitude.

"What else isn't working?" Kate turned and started walking again, but slower this time.

"Do you mean as far as marketing?"

She nodded, but didn't speak.

He really didn't want to ruin the evening that she'd been so excited about. "We can talk about it another time."

"No. I need to know now. If there's something I can do to help the company, I'd like to know as soon as possible. I want to change things. Improve things. I want to know that I did everything I could to help my aunt."

"How about tonight?"

"What about it?"

"How much did the company contribute?"

She shrugged. "Not much. The battery-operated candles and the hot cocoa. And we paid for the tree."

"Why should your company fund it?"

"Because we've always funded it. It's tradition." She kicked a pebble in the plowed road and sent it skidding off into a snowbank. "Besides, it wasn't that much."

"But every little bit counts."

"Things are worse than I'd imagined if you're worrying about cocoa and candles."

He didn't say anything. He knew this was a tender spot for Kate and he wished she'd never brought up the subject. She'd actually gotten him excited about the tree lighting.

As they approached the crowded square, Kate was quiet. From what he could tell, that was a rare occurrence for her. She was no doubt considering what he'd told her. And he felt guilty for stealing away her Christmas spirit. He wanted to rewind time and make her smile again.

"Hey, look at that tree." He pointed to the stately pine, which had to be at least fifty feet tall. "It's huge."

Kate nodded. "It's bigger than last years. They hauled it in from the Spencer Tree Farm."

"They must have used a tractor trailer to haul a tree that size. Could you imagine decorating a tree that tall?"

"I...I have. In the past. Last year, I was in charge, but I wasn't on the tree-decorating committee this year."

It was hard to imagine that there was something about this town that Kate wasn't involved in. "I bet the tree was a knockout last year."

She still looked glum. "Are you trying to cheer me up?"

"I don't know. Is it working?"

And then there was a glimmer of a smile on her face. "No. But I appreciate your effort."

"You have to know that I don't want anything bad to happen to the company, don't you?"

She studied him for a moment. "You really mean that, don't you?"

He nodded. "I do."

Kate inhaled deeply and then blew out her breath. "Enough about business. It's time to enjoy the holiday. And I have something for you."

"For me? I don't have anything for you. Was I supposed to have a gift?"

She smiled up at him. "It's not a gift. Not exactly."

He breathed a sigh of relief. "What is it?"

She reached into her oversized purse and withdrew an ornament. She handed it to him. It was a little red sled made of painted popsicle sticks. It was decorated with holly and red-and-white striped satin ribbon. It was cute.

"Did you make this?" he asked.

"I did. Do you like it?"

"I do. You're talented." Kate definitely had an artistic flair.

He wondered if that was something she could use to give new life to Bayberry—or was a second life even possible for the failing company? The thought dampened his mood. The more time he spent in the town of Bayberry, the harder it was to be objective.

Luckily, numbers by their very nature were oblivious to sentimentality and wishful thoughts. Sure, they could be skewed this way or that, but it took a concerted effort, which he would not engage in.

He looked from the ornament in his hand to Kate, who was greeting one of the people in attendance. What would she do if his report came back with a recommendation to sell the company? Would she forgive him for doing his job? Or would she expect him to tweak the numbers in her favor?

His gut churned with unease. He assured himself that everything would work out. Wouldn't it?

If he'd learned anything about Kate, it was that she was honest and caring. She might love the candle company and this small town with all her heart, but she wanted to find an honest way to keep it all functioning. But was that possible?

Kate turned back to him. "Sorry about that. Is something wrong?"

He swallowed hard. "Wrong?"

"Yes. You're frowning."

He forced a smile to his face. "No, I'm not."

She shot him a look that said she didn't believe him, but she let the subject drop. Her eyes flicked to the ornament in his hand, before meeting his gaze again. "Glad you like it. It wasn't hard to make. I could show you how." And then she withdrew a second ornament from her purse. It was another sled, painted white. "They have our names on the back."

He turned it over and in black paint was his name and the year.

"I don't understand," he said. "What's it for?"

"It's part of Bayberry's tradition. Everyone brings an ornament to hang on the tree and their Christmas wish will come true."

"What do you mean? Like a new car? Or a new job?"

She shrugged. "You won't know until Christmas. But something good awaits each person who places an ornament on the tree."

He eyed her with skepticism. "And you really believe this?"

She nodded.

"What Christmas wishes have you received?"

"Um, well, last year Aunt Penney slipped on some ice and broke her wrist. My Christmas wish was that she wouldn't need surgery. And she didn't."

"But that wish wasn't for you, it was for your aunt."

"Ah, but see, if Aunt Penney had needed surgery, it would have affected both our lives. So technically it was for me, too."

"And this year, what are you going to wish for?"

She frowned at him. "I can't tell you, or it won't come true."

"So if I wish for a sleek sports car, I'll receive one for Christmas?" He didn't really want one, but he certainly wouldn't turn down a free sports car. He was, after all, a guy.

"You could try, but I must warn you that Santa gives you what you need most—not what you think you need. And you have to be a good boy or you get zip, zilch, nada."

"Yikes. I guess this means I'll have to be nice to you until Christmas."

She sputtered. He could tell she was thinking up a good zinger to get him back.

"Don't say it," he warned, trying not to laugh. "Remember, you have to be good, too."

Her lips pressed together in a pout. "You don't play nice."

"I'm just having some fun."

"And it's about time. You obviously spend too much time in the office. Trust me, there's more to life than work. When you get old, the things that will matter most are the good memories you made along the way. Penney was right. No one's going to kick back and think how wonderful it was to spend countless hours poring over reports."

"But sometimes you have to do that if you want to get ahead."

She regarded him. "Is that what you want? To get ahead?"

He hadn't admitted to anyone outside Watson & Summers that he was actively pursuing a promotion, but it felt like he could tell Kate anything. "Yes. There's a promotion coming up at the office, and I'm doing everything I can to get it."

"Do you like where you work?"

Her question caught him off guard. No one had ever asked him that before. "It's one of the top firms in the country. Its name is known from coast to coast."

"But that doesn't answer my question. Do you like working there? You know, the people you work with? The job you do from day to day?"

He'd honestly never stopped to consider the question. He thought of the people at Watson & Summers who said good morning to him each day, smiled at him in the halls and wished him good night. "It's a good place to work. I don't have to move from town to town."

"Like your father did?"

Wes had forgotten that he'd shared that part of his life with her. He nodded. "It's good to stay in one spot."

"And that's what you want? To stay put at your company for the rest of your career?"

Why did it seem like saying yes was the wrong answer? For so long, that's all he could think about—climbing the corporate ladder. But since he'd arrived in Bayberry, he'd seen a part of life that he was missing out on.

He cleared his throat. "That's always been my plan."

"I wish you luck," Kate said. "Let's get our ornaments on the tree."

He let her lead the way. She placed her ornament at eye level and he hung his next to hers. They looked good together—as though they were meant to be a pair.

And then it was his turn to make a wish. His eyes moved over the crowd of smiling Bayberry residents. It was as if he'd stepped inside a greeting card with all its warm and joyous sentiments. His attention moved to Kate as she greeted a young girl and her parents.

It was then that he made his wish. *Please let Bayberry remain the close-knit, welcoming town I've always remembered.*

And then, just because Kate hadn't said he couldn't, he made a second wish. *I wish my mother were here to share this holiday.*

Kate turned to him. "Did you make your wish?"

"I did."

"Good. Come on." She motioned for him to follow her. "We'd better grab a candle before they're all gone."

They stood in line, each taking a candle. Then they moved to a spot next to her aunt, who informed them that Fred was resting his eyes in front of the television, and she'd slipped away for a few minutes.

Wes didn't ask, but he wondered if things had changed between Penney and Fred. She certainly seemed devoted to his care. And Wes didn't think that would be the case if they were really just coworkers. But it was none of his concern. He had bigger things on his mind—like finishing this assignment and getting back to the city.

But as much as he needed to get back to New York, there was another part of him that wasn't anxious to leave. He could easily imagine remaining here in Bayberry until the New Year. After all, he did have weeks of unused vacation time.

The mayor, Mrs. Woodard, climbed up on a small podium. "Welcome to this year's tree lighting ceremony."

She went on to thank each and every member of the decorating committee. Mrs. Woodard did not hurry at all. Her speech was slow and enunciated. Her snow-white hair was trimmed short, with every strand in place, as though it wouldn't dream of misbehaving. She wore large pearl earrings.

Wes tuned her out as she droned on about all of these people he didn't know. For lack of anything else to focus on, he studied the mayor. She wore just a hint of makeup and red lipstick. Her attire was prim and proper. She wore a black dress coat that stopped short of her knees. A large Christmas tree-shaped brooch sparkled in the spotlight. And instead of snow boots, Mrs. Woodward wore sturdy dress shoes. She was definitely a bit on the formal side for Bayberry.

She looked a bit familiar, but he couldn't quite place her in his memories. Maybe it was the way her eyes lit up when she spoke of the holidays. It reminded him of his mother. Just like Kate, this was his mother's favorite time of the year. If only his Christmas wish to have her here could somehow come true. She'd love it.

But she had plans for the holiday this year. She was looking forward to a Christmas cruise with her friends. She'd be fine. Besides, he had work to do and a promotion was within reach.

Next year would be different. Next year, he'd be a corporate AVP and his mother would live in the same city. Hope pumped in his veins. Next year, he'd be able to take his mother to the tree lighting at Rockefeller Center. The thought made a smile play at the corners of his lips. Next year, he wouldn't spend Christmas alone.

"Sorry she keeps going on and on," Kate whispered in his ear.

He leaned over to her and whispered back, "I'm used to it. My boss is the same way."

And then he realized he wasn't spending this Christmas alone. He continued looking at Kate, wondering what he'd done to deserve a second chance, of sorts, with her. And then a thought came to him.

He leaned close again. "Do they still have the Candlelight Dance on Christmas Eve?"

"They do. I'm surprised you remember that."

"I never got to go, but I just might this year." His nerve wavered. He shouldn't ask her. After all, it wasn't as though he was going to be around after the holidays. Why start something that he wouldn't be able to finish?

"You should," she said, interrupting his thoughts. When he looked at her in confusion, she added, "You should go to the dance."

Was she asking him to the dance?

He gave himself a mental shake. Of course she wasn't. He was just letting his imagination get the best of him.

He shook his head. "I don't know."

"Why not?"

"I've got two left feet."

"That's the best excuse you can come up with?" When he shrugged, she said, "You do know you don't have to have a date."

"Really?"

She nodded. "I'm going solo. Lots of people do it."

She was going solo? How odd. "I would think you'd have your choice of dates."

It was her turn to shrug. "I'm not interested."

He sensed there was more to it than she was letting on. "Want to talk about it?"

Kate fidgeted with her purse strap. "There's not much to say. I dated this guy for almost a year. I thought we were happy here in Bayberry. But when Andy got a job offer in Chicago, he accepted it without even talking to me. He expected me to give up my life here and follow him."

So she was suffering from a broken heart. He

couldn't believe a guy would choose a job over Kate. Andy sounded a lot like his father—chasing his dream and forgetting that moving involved more than just himself.

Wes sympathized. "You had roots in Bayberry and he wanted you to just drop everything—job, commitments and friends?"

"Yes. Exactly."

"I'm sorry you were put in that difficult position, choosing between the life you love and the person you love. Talk about an impossible decision."

She shrugged. "Deep down, I must have known it wasn't going to last. We were better as friends than we were as a couple."

Her admission that she wasn't pining for her ex lightened Wes's mood. "It's good to learn that earlier rather than later."

"Agreed." She glanced his way. "Have you had a similar experience?"

He shook his head. "I've been too focused on my career to devote the time to a relationship. Maybe someday, when my life slows down."

"Your career sounds like it's on the fast track. Do you really think it'll slow down? To me, it seems like life just gets faster and more chaotic. If you want something bad enough, you have to make the time for it."

She had a good point, but the thought of backing off the career he'd been working toward all his life didn't sit well with him. He shifted his weight from foot to foot. Maybe he could change the subject.

"I hear they have the biggest Christmas tree in New York," she said.

"You must mean the one at Rockefeller Center."

Her eyes sparkled with excitement. "How impressive is it in person?"

"I don't know. I've never seen it." He knew how bad that sounded. He always spent his holidays working—until now. "If you're ever in New York at Christmastime, I'll take you."

"It's a date." Her cheeks, already pink from the cold, turned a deeper rosy hue.

He liked the thought of dating Kate. He liked it a lot. "Yes, it is."

Kate looked away. "You're probably in a hurry to get home. What would you be doing if you were in New York right now?"

He shrugged. "Nothing special."

"I bet you'd put up a Christmas tree."

"I don't have a Christmas tree." In fact, he didn't own any decorations.

"Really?" Her fine brows lifted in surprise. "No Christmas tree at all?"

He shook his head. He hadn't given it much thought. Or rather, he tried not to think about it. "After I got my own place, it just didn't seem worth the effort to decorate just for myself."

Kate frowned. "That...that's so sad."

He stared down at the snow. Is that how she saw him? As a sad man? It wasn't true. He was fine. He had a small but nice apartment and a good job. And maybe he'd consider moving and getting a puppy like Rascal.

"I'm fine." Did his statement sound as hollow to her as it did to himself?

Her gaze searched his. It felt as though she could

see through him. He couldn't tell what she was thinking. He didn't want her feeling sorry for him. He was happy with his life. Wasn't he? Or had he been wearing blinders all these years, blocking out everything he was missing out on?

"Is everyone ready for the countdown?" the mayor asked the crowd.

"Yeah!" Everyone in the crowd cheered.

Needing to look at anything or anyone who wasn't Kate, Wes glanced around. He noticed that the crowd had multiplied since they'd arrived. He'd be willing to bet that everyone in town had shown up.

"Ten, nine, eight..." Everyone continued to count down, including Wes. Excitement pulsated in the air. "...Two...one!"

With a flip of the switch, the mayor turned on the tree lights. They were shaped like white candles. It was quite stunning. And way at the top was a large angel holding a candle in each hand. It was really quite remarkable. And according to the mayor, the decorations were beaded ornaments made by the children of Bayberry.

Everyone clapped. And then the mayor started to sing "O Christmas Tree." Wes wasn't a singer—not that he'd actually tried since he was a kid. When Kate started singing and glanced expectantly at him, he shook his head. Her brows gathered into a frown until he mouthed the lyrics. He was rewarded with a smile from Kate that sent his heart racing. What would it hurt if he really sang? And so he uttered the words softly.

His phone vibrated in his pocket. Who would be

calling him at this hour? His mother? Maybe something was wrong.

He slipped the phone from his pocket. Mr. Summers? What did he want?

As everyone continued to sing "O Christmas Tree," Wes moved away from the group. He pressed a button and held the phone to his ear. "Hello."

"Wes, how are things going?"

"Good, sir." He went on to give him a summary of the reports that he'd been able to complete so far.

"What—" Applause from the crowd drowned out Mr. Summers' voice.

Wes pressed a palm to his other ear. "I'm sorry, sir. What were you saying?"

"The five-year projection." Agitation vibrated in the older man's voice. "I want to know if it's complete."

Wes inwardly groaned. "I haven't been able to get that far, as I've had to pull each number by hand."

"This isn't good." There was a pause. "Is that singing in the background?"

"Um..." He kept walking until he was next to the deserted street. "Yes, sir."

"You mean you're out partying instead of working?" There was a distinct note of disapproval in his voice.

Wes knew this wasn't going to help him when it came to the promotion. In fact, it would probably hurt him. He should have gone with his instincts and remained at the office.

"No, it's not like that," he began.

"What's going on?"

"It's a tree lighting, sir." As he said the words, he could feel the promotion slipping from his grasp.

"Tree lighting?"

"Yes, sir. It's when they light up a Christmas tree in the center of town—"

"I know what a tree lighting is. What I don't understand is what my employee is doing there when he doesn't have his work done."

Wes shifted his weight from one foot to the other. "Well sir, the owner's niece invited me and she wouldn't take no for an answer. I will be working overtime to make up for this."

"Hmph. See that you do." And then the line went dead.

Wes stared down at his phone, alarmed. He'd never been pressured to wrap up a job this quickly. What was going on?

Kate hurried over to him. "Is everything okay?"

He shook his head. "It was my boss checking in."

"Oh. Did you tell him how hard you've been working?"

"I tried."

"But?"

"But it doesn't matter." Wes shook his head again, trying to clear the confusion. Perhaps he'd read more into the other man's tone than he should have. Maybe Mr. Summers was tired. Or maybe he was jealous that he didn't have anyone to drag him to a tree lighting. "What did I miss?"

"Nothing. Everyone is singing carols, and then we'll make our way over to Mel's for food."

"If you don't mind, I think I'll head back to the B&B." His good mood had escaped him.

"Are you feeling all right?"

He nodded. He just had some thinking to do,

not to mention all of the work awaiting him. He had enough information stored on his laptop that he could go back to his room and start an initial consolidation of the numbers. The rest would have to wait until he had access to the company office and all the hard copy reports contained within its walls.

"Okay, good night then," she said. Did he imagine that she looked disappointed?

"Good night," he replied.

As Kate headed back to the caroling, he watched her go. More than anything, he wished he could spend the rest of the evening with her.

With a deep, resigned sigh, Wes turned away.

He made his way over to the diner, where he ordered a burger and fries to go. He might have to work, but that didn't mean he had to starve. And he recalled from his youth that Mel's had the crispiest shoelace fries.

# Chapter Fourteen

ODAY WAS THE ANNUAL BAYBERRY Candle sale.

It was going to be perfect. Okay, maybe not perfect, but close to it.

On Saturday afternoon, Kate's stomach quivered with nerves. It was almost time for the sale. Make it or break it time. Well, maybe not that drastic, depending on what Wes's report said.

Speaking of Wes, she needed to help him with the final touches on his costume. As she picked up the Santa hat from her desk, she noticed a slight tremor in her hands. She told herself it was because she was wound up about the sale. It had nothing to do with smoothing the red velvet suit jacket over Wes's broad shoulders, or the way he'd looked at her as though he'd wanted to say something, but then changed his mind.

She was overthinking things. That was all. She drew in a deep breath and then blew it out. This evening was about helping the business. Nothing else.

Still, when she approached Wes and he sent her a

slow, lazy smile, her heart fluttered in her chest. She assured herself that he smiled like that with every-one. Didn't he? Part of her hoped not. She wanted to believe there was something growing between them, even if she had no idea where it would lead.

"We just need to add this." Kate held up the hat.

"I can't believe I let you talk me into this."

"But you're so cute." Wait. Did she just say that? She inwardly cringed as heat swirled in her chest. "As Santa. You're cute as Santa."

Amusement twinkled in his eyes. "You can't take it back. You think I'm cute."

She inwardly groaned. "As Santa."

"Uh-huh." He was grinning at her, making her stomach dip.

She adjusted the Santa cap on Wes. Being so close to him made her heart race. *Stay focused.* A little to the left and a little to the front. And then it was situated perfectly atop Wes's white-haired wig. It was almost show time.

For a while there, she'd worried that Wes would back out of playing Santa. If he had, she had con-sidered donning the suit and practicing her ho-ho-ho, but she knew she would never be able to pull it off. The suit wouldn't even come close to fitting her, no matter how many pins Aunt Penney put in it. And then there was the fact that Kate could never lower her voice deep enough to make her Santa imitation sound authentic. But thanks to Wes, she didn't have to worry.

She stepped back to inspect her work. "What do you think, Aunt Penney?"

"I think he looks great, except for one thing." Penney moved to the desk and pulled out a pillow. "I think he's thinner than Fred. He's gonna need some extra stuffing."

Wes frowned. "I think I look round enough."

Kate walked around him. "Penney is right. Your bowl of jelly isn't full enough."

"What?" he asked.

"You know, 'Twas The Night Before Christmas, and all through the house...oh, never mind. Just take our word for it. You need some more stuffing."

Aunt Penney helped Kate open Wes's wide black belt and stuff a pillow inside his suit. Once it was properly positioned, they stepped back.

"I think he's perfect now," Aunt Penney said. "What do you think?"

"I think I was better without the extra pillow." Wes frowned.

Kate smothered a laugh. "You look adorable. And that beard looks good on you."

He ran a hand over it. "You really think so?"

She nodded. "I do."

"Ho. Ho. Ho." He patted his very round stomach. "What do you think? I've been practicing."

Both women laughed. Kate was glad to see that Wes had at last found his Christmas spirit. And then his blue gaze landed on her, causing her stomach to flutter again. She felt a magnetic pull toward him. Her gaze dipped to his lips. She wondered what it'd be like to be kissed by Santa—

"You're going to be perfect," Aunt Penney said, as though oblivious to the vibes floating through the room. "This is going to be such a special evening."

*It already is.* Kate's gaze met Wes's. He winked at

her. Kate jerked her attention to the green elf hat that went with the rest of her costume. "Aunt Penney, I hope you're right."

Aunt Penney gave Kate's arm a pat. "It will be. You'll see."

But would they make enough money to replace the necessary equipment? That remained to be seen. But if social media buzz was anything to go by, it was going to be their biggest turnout.

"I'll meet you kids out there," Aunt Penney said. "I should go greet people."

"Go ahead," Kate said, knowing her aunt loved the meet and greet. "We'll be fine."

And with that, Aunt Penney made her way to the warehouse, leaving Kate alone with Wes. She fidgeted with the elf hat, avoiding his gaze. "You seem to be in much better spirits today."

"I do?"

"Yes, you do." She needed to keep their conversation focused on anything but how he made her feel. She couldn't explain it to herself, so how could she explain it to him? "After that phone call last night with your boss, you seemed to have lost your holiday spirit."

"I was just tired. It's been a long week."

Kate arched a disbelieving brow at him. She had a feeling it was something more, but she didn't have anything concrete to go on.

"Does your boss always call you after hours and expect you to still be working?" That didn't seem right to her.

Wes shrugged. "Honestly, he's never called me after hours before this particular account."

"Wow." She could tell that it worried him, but she had a different take on it. "Must mean you're doing a good job—no, a great job."

His eyes met hers. "You think so?"

She nodded. "Would someone at the top of management take time out for someone who wasn't performing well?"

He paused to consider her words. And then a smile lit up his face. "Have I ever told you that I love the way you think?"

"No. But I'll be reminding you of that tonight when the little ones are pulling on your beard or spilling their drinks on you."

The smiled slipped from his face. "They wouldn't."

Kate's smile brightened. He was so much fun to tease. "Let's get you out there."

And without waiting for him to agree, she led the way. This evening was going to be great. It was just what the company needed to get itself back on track—no matter what Wes said. Everyone would remember what they loved about the Bayberry Candle Company, from great-smelling candles to glassware, and everything in between. The orders would keep coming in long after the holiday was over.

The place was crowded.

As in, it was hard to move for all the adults and children crowded into the cordoned-off section of the warehouse. The din of voices and the Christmas carols on the speaker system carried throughout the warehouse, reverberating off the walls. The sale was definitely more like a great big holiday party.

Wes hadn't been here since Fred's accident. He'd been holed up in Kate's office, sorting through report after report. He'd never appreciated digitization so much until he came to Bayberry. Some things were best done the old-fashioned way, like hot cocoa and pastries, but not numbered reports. But he pushed aside his frustrations for the evening. Tonight was about cookies, offered to him by many of the children; Christmas wishes, among which there were some heart-jerkers; and holiday greetings, extended by everyone.

As Wes sat atop Santa's big red chair on a platform, he could see around the warehouse. Kate and Penney had outdone themselves. Twinkle lights were woven above the crowd. Just a few of the light strands blinked. Not enough to be annoying, but enough that it gave the area an extra bit of bling.

There were giant plastic candles throughout the designated sale area, along with red and white poinsettias, as well as large boxes wrapped in colorful metallic paper, from silver and blue to pink and yellow. There were illuminated snowmen and reindeer decorations.

He saw a long banquet table laden with Christmas cookies, punch and coffee. And beside him were boxes of Christmas gifts for the little ones, of which he'd handed out approximately half so far.

But now it was time for his break. Wes was looking forward to it. Who knew listening to Christmas wishes and smiling for the camera could be such exhausting work?

He made his way over to Kate, who was speaking with an older couple. She was putting them at ease and making them laugh. She really loved the residents of Bayberry, and they obviously felt the same way about her. And he could see why. Kate was warm and bubbly. She truly cared about people—even an outsider like him.

She had drawn him into the community despite his complaints, and reminded him that there really was more to life than trying to impress Mr. Summers. If only his boss could see him now, he'd be appalled. Wes started to laugh at the thought of the man's horrified look.

"And what has you so amused?" Kate made her excuses to the older couple and approached him.

"I was just thinking about the people at my office seeing me all dressed up."

Kate gave him a quick once-over. "I think they'd be impressed. You make a pretty good Santa."

He frowned at her. "Pretty good?"

She sent him a teasing smile and nodded.

He dug down deep and then he said, "Ho, ho, ho. And have you been naughty or nice?"

Kate turned to him with a smile that made his insides feel as if a swarm of butterflies had just been released in his chest. "Very nice."

"Hm..." He eyed her through the gold-rimmed glasses that were part of his costume. "I guess Santa will have to get you a special present this year."

"Well, there is one thing..."

He was intrigued, as he'd been considering getting her a gift to thank her for all she'd done to make his stay in Bayberry not just nice, but really nice. "And what would this one thing be?"

She leaned close to his ear, so close that he caught a whiff of her lavender perfume. He inhaled deeply, enjoying the subtle floral scent. He was certain that for the rest of his life when he smelled lavender, he would always think of Kate.

And then softly she whispered, "I'd like Santa to save Bayberry."

His heart stilled in his chest. He should have expected that response, but he'd been hoping for something easier. Right now, he had no hope of giving her her heart's wish. Because so far, the numbers weren't panning out in Kate's favor. How did he prepare her for something like that?

She pulled back, still smiling. "What do you think, Santa? Can you make my wish come true?"

Before he had a chance to answer, he heard a woman's voice call out, "Santa! Santa Claus!" It was hard to make out where it was coming from over the din of voices. He turned around. And then he blinked, to make sure he wasn't seeing things. But she was really there. His mother was headed straight for him.

"Mom! What are you doing here?"

Her smile faltered. "Is that any way to greet your mother?"

He stepped forward and swept her up into a big hug. He'd forgotten about his belly of pillows, making the hug awkward and a bit funny. He'd been thinking of her since he'd arrived in town and now, she'd just magically appeared. Maybe there was something to that Christmas tree wish thing.

Not that he really believed in that sort of thing. But

no matter what had drawn his mother to Bayberry, he was happy. It might not have been the Christmas he'd imagined, with his mother situated close by in New York, but something told him this was going to be better.

He pulled back and smiled at his mother. She'd never looked happier. They'd been apart way too long, what with his crazy work schedule and her unwillingness to fly.

"But what about your cruise?" Wes asked. "Why aren't you on it?"

She smiled and patted his arm. "I had a much better offer. I can go on a cruise any time, but to spend the holidays with dear friends and my son—well, that's something very special."

His brain was rushing to catch up with everything. "How did you get here?"

"I took the train. It was a lovely ride this time of year. Everyone was in such a great mood. I met a young couple from Miami on their way to Connecticut. They're expecting their first baby." Her eyes twinkled. He knew she hoped that one day he'd make her a grandmother. "Anyway, I can tell you more about my adventures later. You have a job to do, Mr. Claus."

He checked the time. His break was over. It was time to get back to Christmas wishes and cookie crumb hugs. And he had to admit he'd never enjoyed a job this much.

He turned to the podium but then paused and turned back. "Mom, you'll still be here when I'm done, won't you?"

"Of course, son."

"Wow!" A little boy of about four or five with reddish hair and freckles stared at Wes's mother. "You're Santa's mommy?"

A big smile lit up his mother's face. "Well, yes, I guess I am."

"I didn't know Santa had a mommy." The little boy's eyes filled with wonderment.

"Aren't I lucky? Ho ho ho," Wes chuckled, with a grin at his mother.

And then the boy's mother smiled and took his hand, leading him off to the sale items. Wes couldn't stop smiling. It isn't every day you can create such a look of awe on a child's face. It was magical.

It'd been a long time since Wes enjoyed the holidays. But this year was turning out quite different. This year he was losing his focus on work and getting caught up in the joy of the season. And it was all thanks to Kate.

He'd been right about her all those years ago. She was something special. And she hadn't really changed, not in the important ways. She was still kind, thoughtful and generous. And he was lucky that she considered him a friend...but was it wrong that he wanted more?

He didn't know the man who'd let her get away, but the guy must be kicking himself. There was no one in the world quite like Kate. And he was fortunate enough to get to spend this Christmas with her. He was definitely going to have to work up the nerve to ask her to the Candlelight Dance.

He'd missed out on the chance to escort her in the past. He couldn't let history repeat itself. Most people didn't get second chances. He'd been given one, and he wouldn't squander it.

The amazing evening was over.

How had the time gone by so fast?

Maybe because it had been a wildly successful and fun event.

Kate had smiled so much throughout the evening that her cheeks were a bit sore. Yet she continued to smile. She blamed most of it on Santa. He was forever glancing her way. Though he didn't say anything, just the mere fact of their glances catching and holding a moment longer than necessary sent her heart racing.

She knew not to let herself get caught up in Wes, though. He was only here for work, and once the holidays were over, he'd be gone—back to the big city and his promotion. She'd been down a similar road and it hadn't ended well. It saddened her to think that Wes would soon be so far away. She was getting used to having him around.

"What's the matter?"

She turned to find Aunt Penney standing next to her. "What did you say?"

Aunt Penney studied her with that insightful gaze of hers. "It's okay."

"What is?"

"To like him."

"What? Who?" Heat rushed up her neck, settling in her cheeks. "You mean Wes?"

Aunt Penney's brow rose as she nodded. "I've watched you two, and he's good for you."

"He...he is?" She wasn't sure she was comfortable with the direction of this conversation.

Aunt Penney continued to nod. "I watched you after Andy left. You closed off that part of your life. You didn't make any big proclamations or anything, but anytime someone asked you out, you were always busy with this or that. But with Wes, you've let down your guard."

"It's not like that. We're not dating. He's just here, doing work for you. I...I was just trying to make him feel welcome."

In the beginning that might have been true, but lately things were changing. When she thought of doing something, she immediately thought of inviting Wes. But that was just what people did for visitors, right?

She was able to distinguish between romantic feelings and friendly vibes. And this thing with Wes was nothing but a good friendship, nothing more. Because she'd already had her heart broken. She didn't want to go through that again. And there was no way she'd be happy in the big city. After all, New York City was even bigger than Chicago.

"How would you know how things could turn out if you won't even give Wes a chance?" her aunt asked. "After all, it's the season of miracles."

Not giving Kate a chance to respond, Aunt Penney strolled away. Kate stood there holding a stack of orders, pondering her aunt's words. She hadn't planned to be alone forever, but that didn't mean she should jump for a man who obviously had priorities that took him away from Bayberry—

"Kate? Yo! Kate?" Wes waved at her, trying to gain her attention.

She blinked. When her gaze landed on him in his

Santa costume, a flush once again engulfed her face. She hoped he hadn't overheard them. "Sorry. I...I was just, well—" There was no way she was admitting she'd been thinking about him. "I guess I'm just tired."

"You had a huge turnout. I think everyone in town, and then some, showed up. Is it always like this?"

She shook her head. "This was our biggest Christmas sale ever."

"Very impressive. Looks like your online campaign and coupon did the magic trick."

"Thanks. I think they certainly helped."

He glanced down at what she was holding. "Are those tonight's receipts?"

She glanced down. "Oh. No. These are the special orders."

"Special orders? That sounds impressive. Do they have to be done in time for Christmas?"

"Most of them. And some of them are quite large, such as shipments for churches and community events."

"Do you think you'll be able to get them out in time?"

She nodded. "Everyone here knows how important these orders are, and they'll make sure everything gets turned around in time." Then she paused and worried her bottom lip.

"Kate, what is it?"

"I don't know if the conveyor belt will hold up. If we can't get these orders out, we'll never be able to raise the money for the necessary repairs." Tears of frustration stung her eyes. Why was everything so hard lately?

"Kate, everything is going to be okay." Wes stopped and pressed his lips together, as though he realized he couldn't promise such things.

"How can you say that? You know the bind we're in."

When he spoke, it was in a soothing tone. "And I know the employees have kept the machines running one way or another until now. I believe they can keep things going until the New Year."

She felt bad for taking her frustrations out on him. "Sorry." She took a deep breath, trying to calm her rising emotions. "I think working all these late nights is catching up to me."

However, she noticed that he'd said they'd keep things going until the New Year, but nothing about after it. The three cups of coffee she'd had that evening churned in her stomach.

She couldn't give up on the company. She couldn't let her aunt and the town down. Maybe the sale alone wasn't enough to revitalize the place, but she'd find another way.

But for now, she needed to change the subject to something less worrisome.

"You were amazing as Santa. If Fred isn't available next year, I'll know who to call."

A smile eased the frown lines on Wes's face. "When you first asked me to be Santa, I didn't want to do it. No way. No how."

"And now?"

"And now, I can't remember when I had such a good time. Those kids are amazing. They're so full of hope and love for others. If I had the power to bring their Christmas wishes to life, I would do it."

"So what you're saying is that you want to be a real-life Santa?"

He made a funny face. "We all know there's no real-life Santa."

"Do we?"

He smiled and shook his head. "You're probably going to tell me you know him."

She was saved from answering when Aunt Penney and Wes's mother, Martha, joined them. Both women were smiling. It appeared everyone had had a great night.

"That was a wonderful event." Aunt Penney turned to Kate. "Thank you for taking over for me. I'm starting to think you don't need me hanging around this place."

"It was a record-breaking evening," Kate said. "And I will always need you."

"Everyone I saw had their baskets and carts overflowing as they headed to the checkout," Martha said.

"I was just looking around. Most of the shelves have been emptied," Wes added.

"And that's after we restocked throughout the evening. The new hurricane lamps were a huge hit." Kate glanced around, appreciating the empty shelves.

"The bayberry-scented candles are all gone," Aunt Penney said. "That's no surprise. They sell out every Christmas. But we can talk about the sale later. I'm sure everyone is tired and anxious to get off their feet."

Wes turned to his mother. "Where are you staying? There's no room at the B&B, but I'll give you my room."

His mother frowned. "But where would you stay?"

He shrugged. "I can sleep on the couch in the office."

"Nonsense," Aunt Penney said. She turned to Martha. "No one is sleeping on a couch or giving up a room. I have a lovely guest room and it's just waiting for you. Would you like it?"

"I'd love it." Martha beamed. "Thank you."

"It'll give us plenty of time to catch up," Aunt Penney said.

Martha nodded. "We have a lot of that to do."

Kate noticed that her aunt seemed so much happier than she had for a while. It was only then that Kate realized just how much the business had been weighing on her aunt. Now that Penney had shared the true state of affairs with her niece, Kate was determined to turn the company around.

# Chapter Fifteen

KATE WAS UP BRIGHT AND early the next morning. Her first thought was of Wes in that Santa suit. He'd looked adorable. Who'd have thought he'd take to the role so well? And the kids had loved him.

Even she'd been tempted to sit on Santa's lap and tell him her Christmas wish. But what was her wish? To save the company? Yes, but there was something else she wanted—something she hadn't allowed herself to think about since her split with Andy—a family of her own.

Wes's image came to mind. And then she dismissed it as quickly as it had come to her. He'd told her what he wanted more than anything: a promotion at his job in the city. He wanted to remain in New York and stay with the company. And so she couldn't let herself fall for his dreamy blue eyes or flirtatious smile. She knew it wasn't going to be easy, as there was something about Wes that was just so easy to like.

But once bitten, twice shy, as they say. No way

was she going to get left behind again. She'd learned her lesson. She would wait until a good guy came along who loved Bayberry as much as she did.

Even though it was Sunday, she made her way to the office, anxious to discover the results of last night's sale. She did a preliminary tally of the warehouse and internet receipts. They were impressive, but not as impressive as they'd have been if she'd been more conservative with the discount or limited the number of items sold at a reduced price. She regretted letting her desperation for a large shopper turnout drive her to give deep discounts. It wouldn't happen again. She made a mental note for next year.

Still, the money they'd made gave her hope. This was hands-down the biggest sale in Bayberry's history. Somehow, some way, they could save the candle company.

But she knew if she were going to make that happen, she needed some help. She picked up the phone and dialed Wes's number. When he didn't answer right away, she worried that she'd called him too early. She checked the clock. It was just barely seven. Some people liked to sleep in on the weekends. She disconnected the call.

Kate tried to make herself comfortable in her office, but it was virtually impossible, as Wes had stuff piled everywhere. But she was hesitant to move the stacks of papers, folders and binders, as she was afraid he'd lose his place. There was no way she wanted to make this job harder on him.

And so she pulled the files from her desk drawer and moved to the conference room, where she had the big long oak table all to herself. She'd just refilled her coffee and sat down when her phone rang. It was Wes. She was expecting him to be half asleep and grumpy that she'd woken him up.

She braced herself. "Hey, Wes."

"Sorry. I was in the shower when you called."

"It's fine. I just wanted you to know that the party last night renewed my drive to save the company."

"I was thinking about it while I was out jogging."

"Jogging? In this weather?" She glanced out the window at the falling snow.

"It was a really nice run. Usually I'm on a treadmill in the city, but it was nice to get out and enjoy the fresh, crisp air. Do you run?"

"I, um, used to. I haven't in quite awhile."

"You should join me tomorrow before work."

"That would be nice." The words passed her lips before she calculated just how early in the morning she'd have to get up to run, shower and make it to work on time. "Can I think about it?"

"Sure. It's an open invitation." He cleared his throat. "You called. Did you need something?"

"Oh, yes." She'd gotten so distracted that she'd totally forgotten her reason for calling him in the first place. "I've done a lot of thinking since the sale—"

"It was just last night."

"I know, but I was excited and couldn't sleep. We did really well, and I want to keep up the momentum. I had some thoughts I wanted to run past you."

When he was quiet, she added, "If you help me, I promise to make this up to you."

"Kate, you don't have to bribe me. I'll do what I can to help you."

"But now you have a surprise to look forward to."

"I'm meeting my mother for brunch. Can we get together after that?"

"Yes. That would be perfect. I have some more things I want to look at before you get here."

"You're already at the office?" He sounded shocked.

"Yes. Remember, I couldn't sleep. My mind was racing, so I decided to put the time to good use. I have a company to save." Anticipating his response, she rushed on. "Don't say it. When it comes to the future of this company, I intend to prove your projections wrong."

"I just don't want you to get your hopes up."

"Too late." Kate doodled a heart next to her list of possible cost-cutting measures. And then, realizing what she'd drawn, she scratched it out. "My mother always said, you have to have faith that things will work out. My aunt says that good thoughts aren't enough. You have to back them up with actions. I'm doing both."

After they hung up, Kate realized that none of her ideas so far were big enough to significantly impact Bayberry's bottom line. Another cup of coffee and a clean sheet of paper, and she sat there determined to plan a way out of this predicament.

Brunch was over.

Their coffee cups were almost empty.

Wes leaned back in his chair at Mel's Grille. It was his favorite food stop in town. Not that the Italian restaurant and the burger joint weren't good. They were.

He just preferred Mel's. He wondered if he could find something like it in New York, near his office.

Wes finished his coffee and then set aside the empty cup. "Mom, it's so good to see you. I have to admit you really surprised me. Why didn't you tell me you were coming to Bayberry?"

She smiled at him. "Because I didn't want to mess up your plans."

"My plans?"

She nodded. "It seems like every time we try to meet up, you have other obligations, and we miss each other."

Guilt hit him like an avalanche of snow. "I'm sorry. I know I've been working hard. But I promise it won't always be that way."

His mother's smile faded and worry reflected in her eyes. "Your father used to always say the same thing—after this job, he'd settle down—or after this promotion, he'd be able to stay put. I know he believed those words when he said them, but circumstances always changed and we were forever moving around, never settling down and putting down roots. And I know how hard it was on you. But I just hope you're not staying with your current company because you don't want to be like your father."

"That's not it." He said the words too quickly, too vehemently. His mother arched a brow. He sighed. "Okay. Maybe that's part of it."

"Are you really happy at your job?" Her gaze searched his.

"I am. I might even get a promotion."

"Another one?" When he nodded, his mother smiled brightly. "I'm so proud of you."

"Thanks." His mother's happiness meant the world to him. He'd always strived to make her proud of him. And he had something to tell her that he hoped would make her extremely happy. "Mom, it means so much that we're together for Christmas."

His mother reached out, placing her hand over his. "I feel the same way. It's why I cancelled my travel plans. I couldn't think of any other place I wanted to be."

"If I get this promotion, we'll be able to see each other as much as we want."

His mother's brows drew together. "I don't understand."

"This promotion means you'll be able to move to New York. We'll find you the perfect apartment—"

"Wesley." The way she said his name let him know she wasn't pleased. "What makes you think I want to live in New York City?"

He opened his mouth and then closed it without saying a word.

"Oh Wes, I wish you'd said something sooner. I would have told you that I want something quieter, a slower pace of life."

He searched her face. "Are you saying you don't want to be near me?"

"Not at all. But I'd rather it be someplace like Bayberry."

He rubbed his jaw as he considered what she'd just told him. And then his eyes met hers. "Are you sure? I mean, we can find something outside of Manhattan."

His mother shook her head. "I've decided where

I'm moving. It's going to be my last move. I want to put down roots. It's time."

"Where?" He wasn't sure he wanted the answer.

"Right here in Bayberry. I should have done it years ago."

His mother was moving here? When his report would most likely recommend closing the town's primary employer? His jaw tightened. This assignment was getting more complicated with each passing day.

"Wes, what's wrong? I thought you'd like the idea. I'll be closer to you."

Obviously, his thoughts were transparent on his face. He swallowed hard and did his best to relax his facial features. "Nothing's wrong. I'm happy to have you close by. We'll be able to spend holidays together."

His mother smiled. "I can't wait. This is going to be such a special Christmas."

Unless the Bayberry Candle Company was forced to close its doors. He shoved aside the troublesome thought.

Not sure what to say, he checked his watch. "It's getting late. I've got to get to the office."

The frown returned to his mother's features. "It's the weekend."

He reached out, giving her hand a squeeze. "Don't worry. Kate asked me if I could stop by and help her with something."

His mother's eyes widened. "Well, in that case, don't let me hold you up." She shooed him away. "Go. Enjoy your afternoon."

He headed out the door to find the sun shining brightly, but with the freezing temperature, the snow wasn't going anywhere. He pulled a pair of sunglasses from his jacket pocket to help with the glare.

How had he been so wrong about his mother? He'd thought for sure that she'd be up for a new adventure. And what could be more exciting than living in the Big Apple?

Maybe she just needed some time to think about it. That was it. When she realized how great it'd be if they lived in the same city, she'd change her mind.

The walk to the candle company wouldn't take him long at all. That was one thing he loved about Bayberry: everything was within walking distance. But there were so many other things to love about it too. Just then Mr. Plummer, the newspaper editor, approached him.

The men greeted each other as they kept walking in opposite directions. A moment later, Mr. Plummer called out to him.

Wes turned back. "Yes?"

The man studied him. "I was wondering if you had any leads, or perhaps a quote for the paper."

Wes knew what the man was fishing for, but he decided to play dumb. "I don't know what you mean."

"Sure you do. You've been in Bayberry for quite awhile now. Surely you must know if the candle company—the heartbeat of this community—has a future."

Wes liked the guy—he really did. And he also knew the editor was just doing his job. "Mr. Plummer, you have to realize that I can't comment on my job."

"But surely you can confirm that you're here to determine the future of the candle company."

"I can't confirm anything. Now I'm late. I must go."

And with that, Wes walked away with determined steps.

As he passed other Bayberry residents, he smiled and waved. They returned the gesture, but he could also see worry in their eyes. It was apparent that news of his assignment had gotten out. Everyone was concerned, and he couldn't blame them. Nor could he give them the reassuring words they were desperately hoping to hear.

That bothered him. Sure, he'd been in similar situations before, but not with people who'd welcomed him to their town—people he was getting to know on a personal level. This was hard—very hard.

Usually he came to a city, did his work, kept to himself, submitted his report and left town. He wasn't around to see the devastation that the report could wreak on lives. But here in Bayberry, he didn't have to submit his report to know what would happen should the findings be negative. And Kate's aunt had already told him that she didn't have the personal resources to bail out the company—not that he would ever recommend such a thing.

He was still thinking this all over when he arrived at the office. As he strolled through the holiday-decorated building, he found Kate in the conference room. She had a mug of coffee on the table, as well as her laptop, a tablet, and a bunch of crumpled papers. She seemed to be deep in thought, to the point that she didn't notice him standing in the doorway.

"Knock knock."

Her head jerked up. "Sorry. I was just thinking."

"It must be pretty serious."

"It is. I've been giving a lot of thought to the company. And the sales yesterday were good, but they could have been better if I hadn't offered such a large discount." She stood, grabbed her cup and headed for the half-empty coffee pot. "Can I get you some?"

He shook his head. "I just had some."

She refilled her mug and moved back to the table, where he joined her. "Kate, I know you really want to save the company, but you have to realize that one night of great sales isn't going to be enough—"

"I know. And now that I know about the company's trouble and your evaluation, I want to do every single thing I can to save Bayberry. I can't let our employees down." She turned to him. Her eyes stared straight into his. "But I need to know where to start."

Wes sighed as he raked his fingers through his hair. He was not used to getting drawn into saving a company he was evaluating. He should just back away. It'd be the smart thing to do. But would it be the right thing?

He was beginning to see that it was impossible to separate Kate from the business she loved so dearly. It left him in the position of telling her that he couldn't help, and walking out on both her and the company. Or he could roll up his sleeves and help her.

His gaze searched hers, making his heart pound harder. What was it about this woman that got to him? There was just something about the way Kate smiled, the way she wore her heart on her sleeve and how she cared so much for the people around her that drew him to her.

"Please." Her eyes pleaded implored him. It was his final undoing.

"Okay. But I'm not sure if there's anything that will work."

"I have to try. So many people are counting on this company—including me."

"Kate." He waited until he had her full attention. "I want you to understand that the company is in serious trouble. There might not be anything you can do to save it."

"If the company goes under, so will the town. I couldn't live with myself knowing I hadn't done everything in my power to save it."

He made the mistake of gazing into her big green eyes. It melted away his resistance.

With a resigned sigh, he said, "Let's see what we can come up with."

They started with the results from last night's sale. And he had to admit it had been a success. Kate proposed another sale, but Wes slowed her down. Too many sales, too close together, would produce diminishing returns.

"What else do you have?" he asked.

"Well, the supply contracts are up for renewal." She slid a stack of papers in front of him. "I've gone over all of them, and each supplier has requested an increase. Some are asking for as much as ten percent more."

Wes glanced down at the contracts. "Where are your quotes from competing vendors?"

"I don't have any. My family has been doing business with these companies for years. My aunt has known most of them since she was just a girl. It wouldn't be right to go behind their backs."

"Kate, this is business."

"I know that, but there's also such a thing as loyalty."

He paused. "I'm going to tell you something, and I know you're not going to like it."

She frowned at him. "Then why say it?"

"Because I think you need to hear it, and then you can do with it what you will. Sentimentality has no place in business." When she went to protest, he held up his hand, stopping her. "Let me finish. You are amazing, and you have a generous heart. You want to see the good in everyone, even me." He smiled reassuringly. "But when it comes to business, you have to close off your heart and think more like a shrewd businesswoman."

"I...I don't know. It doesn't sound like me."

"It's not easy. I get that. But if you want to protect Bayberry, some tough decisions must be made." He looked her directly in the eyes. "Are you up for the challenge?"

"I'm just not sure about upsetting our regular suppliers."

"Trust me. They're all familiar with this process."

"But—"

"It'll be fine. Trust me."

He shouldn't be doing any of this. Saving a company wasn't part of his job duties. He was supposed to give an impartial report. If his boss had a clue what he was about to do, Wes could kiss his promotion goodbye.

He didn't stop. He didn't hesitate. Instead, his fingers moved over the keyboard of Kate's laptop. There was something about Bayberry and its residents that had him anxious to do whatever he could to help the town survive.

He looked at Kate. Most of all, he didn't want to let her down.

# *Chapter Sixteen*

*T*HIS WENT AGAINST EVERYTHING SHE'D been taught growing up.

It had been impressed upon her from an early age that loyalty meant everything.

Kate was torn between faithfulness to the suppliers she'd been doing business with for years, and doing what was needed to save Bayberry. Sometimes adulting was so tough. Still, what would it hurt to prove that the companies she did business with wouldn't take advantage of her?

And so they started searching the internet, looking for other suppliers from whom Kate could request quotes. And that's exactly what she did. Each email she wrote was a challenge for her. Even though she'd told Aunt Penney that sometimes change was for the best, the truth was, she liked tradition, too. She liked loyalty. She liked believing in the good in everyone.

And things had been done this way year after year—long before Kate was a Bayberry employee. It was hard to believe her aunt would have kept renewing contracts with these firms if she didn't have a really good reason.

"What's wrong?" Wes's voice drew her from her thoughts.

Kate's fingers hovered over the keyboard. "What did you say?"

"You're frowning. I was wondering what's wrong."

"It's nothing."

His gaze prodded. "Kate, talk to me."

She searched for the right words. "It's just that you probably think I'm naive for believing these companies are being up-front and honest."

"Whoa. Wait. You misunderstood me. I think they're honest. The part I have an issue with is how much they're charging you. There's nothing dishonest or illegal about it. They're allowed to submit whatever quote they feel is reasonable. And the candle company has a fiscal responsibility to make sure it obtains the best offer out there."

"I can do that." Wes's words made sense to her.

"You know, I think it's great you believe in those qualities," Wes said. "I do too."

She stared into his eyes, his dreamy blue eyes, and for a moment she forgot what she'd been about to say. Her pulse raced. No one had ever made her feel that way with just a look—certainly not Andy.

Remembering her ex—the man who'd skipped town for his job and left her behind—reminded her of why she couldn't let herself get caught in this rush of attraction for Wes. She wouldn't let herself get hurt like that again.

But Wes wasn't Andy. The two men were very different. While Andy was all about hanging out with his friends on the weekends and watching sports on television, Wes was taking his mother to brunch and then helping Kate. While Andy liked to talk about himself and his career, Wes would rather listen to Kate. And whereas Andy only heard bits and pieces of what she said, Wes heard every word.

She was fighting these feelings for Wes, but it was so hard. He was such a great guy, almost perfect for her, except for one thing. His future was in New York. And her future was here in Bayberry.

"Kate? What is it?" His voice drew her from her thoughts.

"Um..." She looked back at her computer monitor. "So you think we need to do this with every contract?"

"I do. And I think it should be done every time contracts are renewed."

She nodded and jotted a note to update the office procedures. She wondered what else needed to be brought up to speed. She had a feeling there would be quite a bit, as Aunt Penney was one for routines.

"How much do you know about each of your suppliers?" he asked.

She paused to think about it. "I know a couple of them, as they're local, but as for the others, I know the sales reps by name. We exchange Christmas cards, but that's about all."

"So you don't know if they hold the same principles as you?"

"I suppose not." That soothed her guilt about potentially canceling business with firms that her family had been dealing with for years.

"It may not be fun, but it's your responsibility to protect the company—to protect the town's company."

"The town's company." She smiled. "It's true. Without this town, there wouldn't be a company. They really are intertwined."

"Seems they go hand-in-hand."

Kate smiled. "They do. Let's hope it stays that way."

Once Kate had an email written up for each type of vendor, she was able to replicate it for all of the potential vendors. And in the end, she felt good about taking steps to safeguard the company.

"Now we just have to wait to hear back from them," Kate said.

Wes sat next to her. "And let's hope that since you mentioned the urgency of the matter, they'll get back to you quickly."

Done with work for the day, Kate and Wes cleaned up the conference room. Together they had everything back to rights in no time.

*Deck the Halls...*A cell phone tinkled.

Wes raised his brows. "It's not me."

"It's me. I switched my ringtone to something festive." Kate checked her caller ID. "It's Aunt Penney." After a brief conversation, she disconnected the call. "She invited us to have dinner at her house."

"What about Fred?"

"He's invited too. Those two have been practically inseparable since the accident. Aunt Penney would say it's because she doesn't want to leave him alone in case he needs anything."

"And you would say?"

"Between you and me, I'd say my aunt has never seemed happier. If only I could prove to her that the company is safe with me, she might retire and relax."

Wes moved to stand in front of her. "Your aunt knows what she's doing."

Kate knew he was trying to make her feel better, but it wasn't working. Deep inside, where no one could see, her doubts and worries weighed on her. "I don't know if she'll ever trust me to run Bayberry Candles."

"From what I can tell, she trusts you implicitly."

Kate's gaze searched his. "You really believe that?"

"I do." Sincerity shone in his eyes—as well as something else. But in a blink, it was gone. "When that accident happened with Fred, you were the person she turned to. Relax," he urged. "You're doing all the right things to help the company."

She smiled at him. "Then let's get out of here. I have to pay you back for all your help."

He arched a brow. "What exactly do you have in mind?"

"Oh, you'll see."

"Should I be worried?"

She grinned. "Not at all. Just trust me."

"That's what worries me."

Kate laughed as she turned off the lights and headed for the door. What was it about this man that made her worries seem less significant? When she was with him, it felt as if everything was going to work out for the best. She hoped that meant that Bayberry Candles would survive.

The pickup truck bounced down the snow-covered road.

At least Wes hoped this was a road. All he could see in front of him was a break in the trees and snow. Lots of snow. It was everywhere, and they were headed into the wilderness. What exactly did Kate have in mind?

The truck slowed down, and the next thing he knew, the tires were spinning and snow was flying. They were stuck. He glanced all around, but there wasn't any sign of civilization. The thought of hiking back down the mountain to Bayberry did not appeal to him in the least.

"Don't worry," Kate said, as though she'd read his thoughts. "I've got this."

She downshifted and they started to move again. Kate looked totally in control and in her element. She was definitely not a city girl. The thought dampened his mood.

He was growing accustomed to having Kate around. She reminded him that there was more to life than just work. She got him to laugh—to enjoy himself as he hadn't done since he was a kid. And she reminded him how special Christmas could be, if you let it into your life.

"Thank you," he said.

She never took her attention off the path in front of them. "For what? Taking you into the snowy forest?"

"No, for helping me to remember how Christmas used to be. When I was little, my mother would create the best Christmases. We didn't always have a lot, but she made them fun."

"I've just met your mother, but she seems like a really special lady."

"She is. Very special. When I'd ask her how Santa would find us, since we never spent Christmas in the same town, she told me that Christmas was always in my heart, and as long as I had the spirit, Santa would find me."

"Aww...that's so sweet."

"Yeah, my mother is great, but the problem is, somewhere along the way I lost the spirit."

"Are you getting it back?" She slowed to a stop and turned to him.

"I am—with some help from you." He looked around. "Obviously, no one lives out here in the middle of nowhere. So what are we doing here?"

"Haven't you ever cut down a Christmas tree?"

He sat there for a moment, hoping this was some sort of joke. Did she have any idea how much snow was out there? But she got out of the truck. When he looked around, he found Kate standing at the rear of the pickup.

He got out and joined her. "I must admit, I've never done this. When I was a kid, if my family had the money, which wasn't every year, we would get a tree from a lot in town."

"Then let's get busy." She lowered the tailgate and withdrew a chainsaw.

He looked at her with admiration and a little bit of apprehension. That was a mighty large chainsaw. Still, she turned and trudged off. She was going Christmas-tree hunting with or without him. And he wasn't about to let her go alone.

He yanked up the zipper on his coat, grabbed the knit cap from his pocket and pulled it down over his head. With a resigned sigh, he trudged after her.

The cold air nipped at his face. A gust of wind sent

the snow from a tree limb showering down upon him. He shrugged deeper in his coat. Still, he could feel the cold clear down to his bones. He swiped at his sleeves, brushing off the snow. What part of this was fun?

Kate laughed. "And here I was beginning to think you weren't going to join me."

"And miss all this fun?" He let the sarcasm drip from his voice. "Never."

She laughed again. "You'd think you weren't used to snow, but I know for a fact there's snow in New York City."

"Except they plow the roads and shovel the walks." He stared down at the snow covering his boots. "It's nothing like this."

"This is mountain living." She inhaled a deep breath and blew out a cloud of warm breath. "You don't have this crisp air in the city."

Another gust of icy wind made him clench his teeth. "But we stay dry and have a coffee shop on almost every corner."

"You just had a pot of coffee." She started walking toward the line of trees. "Come on. It's warm, with the sun out."

Warm? They definitely had different definitions of the word. Very different indeed.

His boots creaked as they moved over the deep snow. The cold seeped in every opening in his clothing. He frowned as he hunched down in his new coat, minimizing exposed skin. He wondered how she would describe the weather in Florida—warm, sunny Florida. Right about now, a warm Christmas was sounding pretty good.

They moved past a line of really tall pine trees lining the path. A hundred yards farther on, they came to a grouping of smaller trees. He was relieved to realize they didn't have to hike to the top of the mountain.

He stopped next to a tree that was almost as tall as he was. "How about this one?"

Kate paused and scrutinized it. "Too short."

"Wait. Are you calling me short?"

Amusement twinkled in her eyes. "For a man, you're tall. But for a tree, that one is short."

They both started walking again. He noticed how quiet Kate had become. She must really take this Christmas-tree hunting seriously.

"I still think you're calling me short," he called out, hoping to tease her into a good mood.

She shook her head and kept moving, stopping at a tree, inspecting it from every angle and then moving on to another one.

"Mind telling me what you're looking for?" he asked.

"I'm thinking seven or so feet would be good for me. For Aunt Penney, she won't go for anything less than nine feet."

"Nine feet? Seriously?"

Kate nodded. "Is that a problem?"

"I guess not. If you don't mind hauling an entire forest to town in the back of your pickup."

"Nothing that hasn't been done before."

"I was afraid you were going to say something like that." He stopped and leaned on his shovel. "Is hiking around in the snow and freezing temps really what you consider fun?"

Kate stopped in front of yet another pine tree. The sun beamed down on her, highlighting the pink of her cheeks. "What's not to love?"

"A lot. I think I lost the feeling in my feet."

She pursed her lips and scrunched up her brows. "We haven't been out here that long."

"Seems like forever."

She shook her head. "I never would have guessed you'd be so wimpy."

"Wimpy?" He pulled his shoulders back. "I'll show you who's wimpy." He moved to stand beside her. "Looks about the right height. This wimpy guy is going to cut down a tree for you."

She placed a hand on his shoulder. "Wait."

"Why?"

"I need to check the trunk and make sure it's straight."

"Really?"

"Uh-huh. You don't want it falling over, do you?" She walked the whole way around the tree. She knelt down and stared up at it. "This is it."

"Okay. I'll cut this one down while you find the second tree." He set to work sawing the trunk.

Together they worked for the next couple of hours until the trees were cut, loaded and delivered to town. He didn't want to admit it, but he'd had a really good time. His complaining had succeeded in making Kate laugh. And that was a sound he loved.

He knew the future of the company weighed heavily on her mind, but he didn't want it to zap her holiday spirit. When Kate talked about Christmas and all of the holiday festivities, her face lit up. And her excitement was contagious.

He wanted to drag out this report until after Christmas. After all, what good would it do to provide the results before the holiday?

## Chapter Seventeen

*H*ER INSIDES SHIVERED WITH NERVES.

Why did this feel so much like a date?

Kate assured herself that it wasn't one. She'd invited Wes over to help decorate her tree. What else could she do, let him sit alone at the B&B? He'd inevitably start working, and he'd done enough of that this weekend.

So inviting him over was a perfectly reasonable thing to do. They were friends, nothing more. He was a man without a home for Christmas, and she was sharing hers with him. It was what she'd do for any stranger in town for the holidays. But she sighed. It was no use. She couldn't sell that story, not even to herself.

Wes was different. She liked him more than was wise. She knew all too well that in the end, she would get left behind when work drew him back to the city. And yet, she told herself to live in the moment, because she'd never known anyone like him before.

On their way into her garage apartment, she'd

stopped to plug in the strings of colored lights outlining her aunt's house and the garage. A large inflatable reindeer as well as a seven-foot snowman filled the front yard. If she'd ever had any doubts where she'd gained her love of the holidays, it was abundantly clear now. It must be something in the genes.

Once inside, she moved from room to room, plugging in the white candles in the windows. With the apartment all lit up, Kate returned to the living room, where Wes had divested himself of his boots and coat. "After dinner we can set up my aunt's tree." Kate opened a box of Christmas ornaments and withdrew a string of colored twinkle lights. She glanced up when he didn't say anything. "That is, if you're still up for it."

"I'm always up for decorating." He perched on the side of the couch. "You're making me a convert."

"I am, huh?" When he nodded, she couldn't help but smile. "You might not say that after we get done decorating trees this evening."

"How hard can it be?" He reached for the strand of lights. He plugged them in and all the little bulbs lit up. "See, even the lights work."

Together they set the tree in a stand and began stringing it with lights. Wes stood on one side and handed the strand to her on the other side. Every time his fingers brushed over hers as they wrapped the lights around the tree, a rush of excitement raced through her.

If she could let go of reality for just a little while, it'd be so easy to imagine that Wes was here in Bayberry for good. Her gaze caught his. Her heart leapt into her throat.

They stared into each other's eyes for what seemed like forever. The truth was that she wanted him here—she wanted to share this very special time with him. A smile lit up his face. He was always handsome, but when he smiled, he was drop-dead gorgeous.

His smile broadened. *Oh no.* Did he know what she was thinking? Heat rushed up her neck and set her cheeks ablaze.

Kate turned away, focusing on situating the little ceramic cow and sheep around the manger. She moved them this way and that, giving herself a moment to regain her composure.

Even so, she couldn't stop thinking how lucky she was to be able to share this time with Wes. She might not get to have him forever, but sharing right now wasn't so bad. She watched as he untangled a strand of lights. It wasn't so bad at all.

This was cozy. Very cozy.

It'd be so easy to think of this as a date.

Wes looked from the string of lights he was wrapping around the tree to his beautiful hostess. Surrounded by all these holiday decorations, she was in her element. She practically glowed as she hustled around the room, making everything merry and bright. Even he was getting in the holiday spirit.

With all of the lights strung, Wes knelt down and plugged them in. The Christmas tree lit up in a colorful glow. "See? We're almost done."

"Not quite." Kate moved to the kitchen. "We haven't done the most important part."

"And what would that be?" Wes moved to the kitchen island and sat down.

She removed the popcorn maker from beneath the cabinet and placed it on the counter. She didn't say a word as she grabbed a container of kernels and a large bowl.

"You want a time out for a snack?" he asked.

"Not quite." She filled the popcorn maker. "This is for the tree."

He'd thought stringing popcorn was something they did in the movies, not in real life.

She smiled as the popcorn maker hummed in the background as it warmed up. She'd already gathered the supplies they'd need and placed them on the island.

In no time, they were seated on the couch with a fresh bowl of popcorn between them. He wasn't sure about this. He'd never made a popcorn string before. And he was not familiar with a needle and thread. He certainly felt like a fish out of water.

"I don't know about this," he said, not wanting to make a fool of himself in front of her. Because it mattered what she thought of him. He hadn't wanted to admit it before, but it was the truth.

"Oh, come on. You can do this." She moved the bowl onto her lap and shimmied closer to him on the couch. "Can you thread a needle?"

"Uh..." He stared at the needle and thread.

And then he watched her dampen the thread between her glossy lips. With ease, she put the thread through the eye of the needle. "See. Easy."

He skipped putting the thread in his mouth and went straight to aiming the thin thread through the impossibly small eye of the needle. His first try missed. The second try missed again. And the third try missed too.

"Here." Kate held out her hands to take the thread and needle. "Let me."

She didn't have to ask him twice. He handed over the items. And again, she moistened the thread and easily threaded the needle.

"You make that look so easy," he said.

"Practice. Lots of practice."

"Do you always do this?" Wes asked.

"Always. It was something my mother used to do when I was a kid. She even got my father to join us. What I loved most about it was that we were all together." She slid a piece of popcorn down the thread. "How about you?"

He stabbed a popcorn kernel with the needle. It fell apart. He sighed as he glanced over at Kate. She made it look so easy. He reached for another kernel to try again. "How about me what?"

"What are some of your favorite Christmas memories?"

He stabbed at another kernel. It stayed on the thread, but barely. With care, he pulled it down the thread. "I don't know."

"Surely you have to have one. Come on. Share."

He didn't normally talk about his family holidays. Christmas had been different each year—different state, different city, different home. It was difficult to have traditions when you were always moving around. It was so different than Kate's upbringing.

"What is it with you and Christmas?" Wes asked.

"What isn't there to love about Christmas? There's

something magical in the air. Add a few snowflakes and it's perfect."

"Perfect, huh?" He knew that if her beloved company went under, Christmas might never have that magical element for her again, and that saddened him. He'd never known anyone to be this excited over a holiday. He didn't want to be responsible for stealing away that twinkle of merriment in her beautiful eyes.

"Hey, you're changing the subject. What's your favorite Christmas memory?"

He didn't have to think really hard to find the answer. "My favorite Christmas memory was when I was four or so. We'd gone to visit my grandmother in Michigan. There was a bad snowstorm that took out the power, and my father built a fire in the fireplace. I was so worried that Santa wouldn't be able to reach us, because he couldn't come down the chimney with a fire burning. So my grandmother took me out to the garage with her. We carried a tall wooden ladder to the back of the house and leaned it against the back door. She told me, that way Santa could get down from his sleigh on the roof. We even left the back door unlocked. It was the last year I believed in Santa and she made it great. And in the morning, there were footprints on the roof."

"Aww...that's a great memory." Kate smiled.

"It was." He hadn't thought about that Christmas in a long time.

Back in those days, his parents had been happy. His father had been working a steady job in Ohio, and Wes had believed in happily-ever-afters. It wasn't too long afterward, though, that Wes had learned what it was like to say goodbye to the only home he'd ever known. And from then on, he'd spent Christmas in a different city every year.

At last, he was settled. So why was he wishing for things he didn't have? He should be thankful for the opportunities presented to him and not thinking about how things could be so much different. He didn't know if it was the cozy atmosphere of Bayberry or being around Kate, but the life he'd carved out for himself in New York no longer seemed like enough. And he didn't know what to do about it.

He finished the string of popcorn and then joined her at the tree. "It's really coming together."

"Isn't it? But we haven't even started on the ornaments. I have so many I inherited from my parents, and then a bunch I added to the collection. So each Christmas I'm able to do a different theme."

There was something driving him to know her even better. "Kate, what happened to your parents?"

She paused and gazed at him. The pain of loss reflected in her eyes. She didn't say anything. She didn't have to. He immediately regretted his words.

"I'm sorry," he said. "I shouldn't have asked."

"No. It's okay." Her voice was soft. "It's not like I didn't dig into your past." She turned back to add the string of popcorn he'd just finished to the tree. "I was fifteen, and it was autumn. My parents were on their way home from an evening in Boston. There had been rain and a heavy fog. A...a truck coming in the opposite direction crossed the center line and my parents were hit head-on."

Sympathy welled up in Wes. He remembered how hard it'd been when he lost his father, and he'd been an adult at the time. He couldn't fathom the over-whelming pain of being a child and suddenly losing not one, but both parents.

"Kate, I'm so sorry. I can't even imagine."

"At least I had my aunt. She was there for me. She bundled me up and moved me to Bayberry."

It was in this moment that he realized she'd moved to Bayberry the same year he had. As he replayed his memories of seeing her—of her not speaking to him—it gave him a different view. She had been grieving. And the kids who had crowded around her were giving her a shoulder to lean on, to help her through this difficult period in her life. Guilt assailed him as he realized he should have tried harder back then to be her friend—to learn what she'd been going through.

He cleared his throat. "So you came to Bayberry the same year I did."

"Really?" She looked at him as though trying to picture him as a kid.

He nodded. "I remember you. Ninth grade, right?"

She stared at him. Her fine brows drew together as she pursed her lips. "You look familiar, but I can't place you. I'm sorry. I wish I could."

"It's no big deal." So then why did it feel important to him? "We were just kids."

She gave him a funny look. "I can't believe I would forget you."

"I didn't forget you." Now why had he gone and said that?

Color filled her cheeks. "I don't even want to know what you thought of me back then. I was shy and scared of life without my parents."

"I thought you were wonderful." He smiled shyly. "In fact, to be totally honest, I had a crush on you."

Her mouth gaped. "You did?"

The room grew uncomfortably warm. Why did he keep admitting these things to her? She didn't even remember him, and yet he remembered everything about her, including the small, unsteady smile she'd given him when they bumped into each other, quite literally, after math class. Her pen had fallen to the floor and he'd picked it up for her. It had happened right before his father uprooted them once again and moved them to Atlanta.

His gaze met and held hers. His heart was pounding. "I did."

"I feel really bad I can't remember you. There was just so much going on back then."

"I understand." He really did, now that he knew her past. "It's no big deal."

The next thing he knew, she was reaching out to him. He froze, not sure what to do. He didn't want to do anything to scare her off. It took all his self-restraint not to pull her into his arms.

But then she was there, next to him. Her arms reaching out and wrapping around him. That contact knocked down his wall of restraint. He couldn't resist her any more than he could resist drawing in his next breath.

He opened his arms to her, drawing her close. She fit into them as if she was always meant to be there. His heart pounded against his ribs. He inhaled the delicate lavender scent of her perfume. He'd never smelled anything quite so enticing. He could stay like this forever—

She pulled back. The hug was much too brief, but it was a hug all the same.

He swallowed hard, hoping his voice sounded normal. "What was that for?"

"Just because." And then she turned back to unpacking her Christmas ornaments as though nothing had happened.

He wasn't able to act as though nothing had happened, though. He stood there trying to make sense of it as his heart slowed its pace. Should he say something? Should he do something? Or should he act like it was no big deal?

"Could you take these?" She held out three jingle bell ornaments with snowmen attached.

She acted as though it hadn't meant anything to her. His heart rate slowed. Had he read the signals all wrong? Obviously that was the case, but he wasn't about to let his disappointment show.

Totally deflated, he forced himself to act normal. "Where do they go?"

"You can put them near the top of the tree, since they're small."

He did as she asked, looping the hooks over the prickly limbs. "Done. Do you have more?"

"Hang on." She opened another box. "I have some really old decorations around here somewhere." She opened box after box.

"Can I help you?" He wasn't quite sure what to do.

The more boxes she opened, the more of a mess she made. He started to wonder if perhaps he should close up the boxes behind her. He looked around for the packing tape and scissors.

"Here they are." She straightened, holding a star

covered in silver glitter. "When I was a kid, I loved this ornament. I have no idea where it came from, but I loved the way the Christmas lights made it twinkle."

He glanced at the ornament. It was nice, though not anything special, but he knew it was the memories tied up with the ornament that made it special for her.

And then she frowned.

"What's wrong?" he asked.

"It's just that I usually do a theme with each tree."

"And?"

"And the ornaments that are already on the tree won't go with these."

"Well, if that's all, it's easily remedied." He moved to the tree and carefully removed the ornaments. They hadn't put many on, so it wasn't hard to take them off. The hard part was remembering which box they went in, but with Kate's help, he got them all put away.

And then Kate started to unwrap each old ornament. They all looked delicate, and he knew how much they meant to Kate, so he was hesitant to touch them. Each one was adorned in memories.

"It's okay." She stood and held out a blown glass ornament. "You can take it."

"But if I drop it—" He didn't want to be responsible for stealing away a piece of her past.

"You won't."

"But if I do—"

"Then we'll clean it up and move on."

His gaze met hers. "You'll never speak to me again."

She burst out laughing. "Don't be ridiculous. You'll have to do a lot worse than that."

Like recommending the candle company be closed? He slammed the door on that thought. He refused to let the possible scenario ruin the wonderful here and now.

"Okay." He took the ornament from her. "Just remember you said that." He hung it on the tree, taking time to make sure it was secure.

"See? You're doing fine."

One by one, she unwrapped the ornaments and guided him as he hung them on the tree. There was something special about these ornaments. They had a lot of character. Some of them were even hand-painted. And there were so many that the tree was becoming quite crowded.

"Kate, I don't know if we need any more." When she didn't respond, he turned to her. "Kate?"

She had unwrapped another ornament and paused to stare at it. It was a little angel with a gold pipe cleaner halo. Wes had forgotten all about it until that moment.

Kate's gaze met his, and her eyes shimmered with unshed tears. "It was you."

He wasn't sure what to say or do. He stood there transfixed.

Kate blinked repeatedly. "I remember now. You gave me this in school. You sat across from me in art class. I was having a really bad day. I was missing my mother, who used to do all sorts of Christmas things with me. And since it was the first holiday season without my parents, I was having a hard time."

"I didn't know. I'm sorry." He'd just been a totally oblivious teenager at the time.

"Don't be sorry. You gave me something precious. You gave me this ornament and you didn't expect a thing in return. It was so kind, and it made me smile. But then, before I could thank you, you disappeared. And then a couple of days later, you left school."

"My father got transferred again." Wes looked down at the painted wooden angel in her hand. "I can't believe you kept it all this time."

"Why wouldn't I? It was the perfect gift at the perfect moment. It was like a reminder that my mother was always looking down on me—that she wasn't completely gone. She's still in my heart."

He glanced at the angel. "You got all of that from an ornament?"

She nodded. "I never got a chance to thank you."

He stepped closer to her and gazed deeply into her eyes. His heart started to thump-thump, harder and faster. "You just did."

His gaze dipped to her lips. He shouldn't even be considering kissing her. She lived here and he lived far away in the city. But right now, they were only inches apart. And it would just be one quick kiss. Okay, maybe not that quick.

Still, he was supposed to be impartial. He had a job to do and an evaluation to prepare. His hands moved to her waist. Heat emanated through her clothes.

As she continued to stare into his eyes, he was starting to forget why kissing her was a bad idea. Right about now, it was sounding like a great idea— the best idea he'd had in a long time.

In that moment, all the reasons not to kiss her escaped him. All he could think about was pulling her close and finding out if her lips were as sweet as the powdered sugar donuts that appeared in the office break room each morning.

His head started to lower just as she tilted her head upward—

*Buzz. Buzz.*

The sound of his phone ringing made them both jump back. The spell had been broken. The moment escaped them. And he felt as though he'd missed something very, very special.

*Buzz. Buzz.*

"You'd better get that," Kate said.

She moved away. His gaze followed her as she placed the ornament he'd made for her many years ago front and center on the tree. It was for the best that they hadn't kissed. But it sure didn't feel like it. Still, he wasn't going to be in Bayberry much longer. Though a lot had changed since he'd arrived in this small town, the one thing that had remained constant was his career—a career that he hoped was on an upward trajectory.

And the last thing he wanted to do was hurt Kate. She'd already had her heart broken once. He wouldn't do that to her. So it was best to remain friends and nothing more.

*Buzz. Buzz.*

He lifted the phone to his ear. "Hello, Mom."

"Honey, it's time for dinner. Can you kids come over now?"

"Sure. We'll be there."

He disconnected the call. "It's time for dinner."

Now that the moment had passed, he welcomed the invitation. With other people around, especially his mother and Kate's aunt, he wouldn't be tempted to try and kiss Kate again. His gaze meandered to her, but then he glanced away.

Because that had been just a fleeting moment, not to be repeated. They'd simply gotten caught up in the past. Nothing more. He needed to concentrate more on his work and less on celebrating the holidays with Kate. And then everything would go back to the way it used to be. Wouldn't it?

Dinner dishes had been cleared.

Coffee had been poured.

Everyone was sitting around Aunt Penney's dining room table.

Kate added some sweetener to her coffee, giving it a stir. She enjoyed the way conversation flowed easily without her having to say a word. Wes's mother and her aunt got along so well. Kate could easily imagine them being the best of friends if they lived in the same town.

And Fred had been able to make it to dinner, since he was getting around much better. Aunt Penney had said she didn't want to leave him alone at home all evening. She'd insisted he wasn't up for cooking for himself, but from what Kate had witnessed, Fred had made a miraculous recovery. Was there more to his injuries than she could see? Or was her aunt just using the accident as an excuse to invite Fred over?

"How are you doing, Fred?" Wes asked.

"Good." Fred jerked back, looked guiltily at Aunt Penney, and then leaned under the table to rub his leg. "Erm, I mean as well as can be expected."

Kate caught her aunt frowning at him. What was going on? Her aunt was up to something, but she didn't know what. Or was her aunt just hoping to spend more time with Fred?

The thought of her aunt falling in love filled Kate with hope. Her aunt had sacrificed everything to keep the family company going, as well as to raise her niece. Over the years, her aunt had assured Kate that raising her had been enough, but Kate worried that her aunt had missed something by not having a love of her own.

It was another reason Kate wouldn't consider leaving Bayberry. Her aunt had given up everything for her, and she would give up everything for Aunt Penney. It's what family did: They stuck together.

"Isn't that right?" Aunt Penney looked expectantly at her.

Kate had no idea what they'd been discussing. The only thing she could do was agree and then maybe everyone would stop staring at her. She was never comfortable being the center of attention.

"Um, sure."

Aunt Penney gave her a bright smile before turning her attention to Wes. "So, it's up to you. Would you be willing to help Kate with the decorations for the Candlelight Dance, since Fred is too injured to do it this year?" Penney turned to Fred. "Isn't that right?"

Fred's white brows lifted. "Oh. Yeah." He rubbed the left side of his ribs. "Definitely too sore to help."

Wait. Wasn't it Fred's right side that had been injured? Kate definitely smelled a bit of scheming going on here. Her questioning gaze moved to Aunt Penney, who conveniently glanced away.

"Oh, Wesley wouldn't mind helping out," Martha supplied.

"That's right," Wes said. "Don't worry. Just point me in the direction of the decorations."

Aunt Penney took a sip of her coffee. "Wes, it's a great thing you're in town this year."

"Glad to help." His gaze met Kate's.

His heated gaze sent her heart racing. She recalled the almost-kiss they'd shared. If only his mother had called a minute or two later.

Suddenly it was very warm in her aunt's dining room. Not wanting anyone to pick up on the vibe between them, she looked away, reached for her water glass and took a long drink.

"And how's your job going?" Aunt Penney asked.

Wes hesitated. "You know I'd prefer not to discuss my results until I'm finished."

Aunt Penney nodded. "Sorry. I meant your position in New York—"

"Oh yes," his mother said. "Tell us about your job. He has big news." Martha beamed as she looked at her son. "Tell them."

"Well, uh…" Wes looked a little flustered. "I'm, uh, up for a promotion. But nothing has been decided yet. There are some other people in the running too."

"He's going to be a vice president," his mother said.

"Assistant vice president," Wes corrected. Everyone congratulated him on being up for such a prestigious position and wished him well, but he avoided meeting anyone's gaze. "I don't know if I'll get the promotion."

"You will," his mother said confidently, and with such obvious pride in her son's abilities. "There's no one more dedicated to his work." She turned to Aunt Penney. "He never takes time off. He works weekends and holidays."

No one responded. Not even Wes.

The truth was, Kate felt sorry for him. The weekends were bad enough, but holidays too? Who worked every single holiday unless they absolutely had to? Holidays in Bayberry were always a big deal, from New Year's fireworks to Spring Fling, to the Labor Day picnic and everything in between.

"Mom, we'll see," Wes said. "Nothing is for sure."

Seeing that Wes was uncomfortable in the spotlight, Kate spoke up. "He's been working hard while he's been here. I've been trying to talk him into staying until the New Year. After all, he's working on a big project."

Wes glanced at her. "And you've been a lot of help. You know, with tracking down information." Heat rushed to her face.

She knew now wasn't the best time to broach the subject, but she didn't think there would be a good time. She turned to her aunt. "I know you haven't wanted to discuss this, but we need to. What are you going to do if Wes's report isn't what we were hoping for?"

Aunt Penney shifted in her chair. "I've given the business a lot of thought. Of course I want to be able to hand the business over to you, but I won't hand you a troubled company."

Kate glanced at Wes, but instead of a smug, I-told-you-so expression, his eyes conveyed compassion. She turned her attention back to her aunt. "But I don't mind. I want to do everything I can to continue the family business."

"I know you do, and that means so much to me. But before I'll let the company go under and the people of Bayberry lose their jobs, I'll sell the business." Aunt Penney met her gaze. "Will you be all right with that?"

Sell the company? Sell her heritage? Panic set in. Kate clasped her hands to keep from fidgeting with her napkin. As a child, she'd dreamed of one day following in her aunt's footsteps.

Kate glanced around. Everyone was waiting for her response. She had to be a responsible adult now and let go of those childhood dreams. Or so she tried to tell herself, because there was still a part of her that was in denial that it could ever come to this.

She clenched her laced fingers tightly and swallowed. "You know how much I love the company. I can't imagine working anywhere else." Her heart squeezed as she considered the worst-case scenario. She took a deep breath and let it out. "But like you, I have to think beyond myself and what I want. If the worst happens, I'd rather the business be sold and remain in operation than for it to die a slow and painful death."

Aunt Penney gave her a reassuring smile. "Don't worry. It's all going to work out."

Kate wished she could be that certain. The thought of losing everything she knew in life—once again—was staggering. Kate imagined Carrie, Abby,

Sadie and every resident of Bayberry moving away. The thought sent an arrow of sorrow into her heart.

She refused to let that happen. If she had to work around the clock, she was going to do everything she could to keep the town of Bayberry the way she'd always known it—with the candle company running and its residents employed.

# Chapter Eighteen

ONDAY ROLLED AROUND MUCH TOO quickly. And there wasn't enough coffee to keep Kate from yawning.

After Wes had left the prior evening, she hadn't been able to sleep. She'd stayed up brainstorming and baking. When she was worried, she liked to keep her hands busy. And she thought a tray of Christmas cookies would help smooth the Monday morning transition for everyone at the office.

With a wrapped tray of cookies in one arm, she rushed down Main Street. Her usual smile was lacking that day. There was so much to worry about that not even the Christmas decorations and a fresh layer of snow could lighten her mood.

*Jingle. Jingle. Jingle.*

There stood that Santa again, with his brass bell and red kettle. She still didn't know his identity, but she was too distracted to figure it out right now. It was best to keep going. The Steaming Brew was just ahead.

"Kate, slow down."

The mention of her name made her stop in her tracks. "How do you know my name?"

"I know many things, Kate. And I know you'll find the answers you need. Just don't give up."

"Wait. What?" Did this guy always talk in riddles?

"Keep searching. You'll get there."

"Get where?'

Two little girls all bundled up in pink hats and gloves came running up the walk, yelling, "Santa!"

Their mother was just steps behind. "Girls, slow down."

The girls moved between Kate and Santa, putting an end to their conversation—if you could call it a conversation.

"I'm sorry about the girls," the mother said.

"Not a problem." Kate smiled. "Merry Christmas."

She puzzled over who was inside the Santa suit as she made her way to the coffee shop but was soon distracted as she said good morning to passersby with their Santa hats or red coats with holiday pins or just an extra bright smile. Christmas brought out the best in most everyone.

When Kate went to open the door of the Steaming Brew, she found patrons lined up to the entrance. Not even the cold, snowy weather could keep people at home when the number of shopping days before Christmas was dwindling.

With every seat taken, Kate remained at the counter after placing her order. For the moment, there was a lull in new customers.

When Abby handed over her coffee, Kate asked,

"Do you know who's down the street pretending to be Santa? He's saying some strange things."

"Someone's playing Santa at this hour of the morning?" Abby looked baffled. And then Kate repeated what Santa had said. Abby called someone to take over the register.

When Abby started for the door, Kate followed. "Where are you going?"

"I want to see this fortune-telling Santa."

When they stepped onto the sidewalk, they looked in every direction, but there was no sign of Santa anywhere. How could that be? Kate had just been talking to him a couple of minutes ago.

Abby turned to her. "Are you getting enough sleep?"

"I didn't imagine him." When Abby just nodded as she headed back inside, Kate said, "I didn't. He was as real as you and me."

Abby picked up the red to-go cup with Kate's name on it and handed it to her. "You sure you don't want to add one or two shots of espresso?"

"I'm positive," Kate said firmly. She wasn't imagining him.

The rest of the way to the office, she replayed the scene with Santa. What was he trying to tell her? Was he referring to the business? Or her thing with Wes? Then, deciding that some stranger was just pranking her, she shoved aside the thoughts.

Inside the candle company, she brushed the snow off her coat and hung it up. She carried the tray of cookies into the kitchen, where she bumped into Wes. "Hi. You're in early."

He filled a coffee mug. "I didn't get any work done this weekend, so I thought I'd get an early start."

"Sorry. It was my fault."

"Don't be. I had a really good time." He smiled, setting her stomach aflutter.

She placed the tray of cookies on the counter and removed the plastic wrap. "Want one?"

He arched a brow as he took a snowman cookie. "Did you make these?"

She nodded. "I had some time on my hands last night."

He studied the very full tray. "Looks like you had a lot of time."

"I had a lot on my mind." And today she would get some answers. "Speaking of which, I need to get to work. I'll see you later."

She hurried out of the kitchen, but got sidetracked by a couple of employees. There was a problem with an order.

It was nearing lunchtime by the time Kate made it to the conference room where she had established a makeshift office. She sat down and opened up her laptop. Immediately, her email window popped up on the screen. She had mail. Lots of mail.

She opened the first email. It was in response to the quotes she'd requested. The tone of the note was friendly. The vendor was happy to have a chance to bid on the candle company's account. She was impressed at how quickly they'd gotten back to her. Apparently, Wes wasn't the only one to get a jump on the week.

"Is everything all right?"

Kate glanced up to find Wes propped against the door jamb. "Yes, fine."

"It's just that you rushed out of the kitchen so fast I was worried something might be wrong. But then you got pulled away before I could find out."

She shook her head. "I wanted to see if we'd gotten any responses to our quote requests, and the first one just came in. I was just about to compare it to the existing contract."

Wes's brows rose. "That was fast. Would you like some help?"

She didn't need any help, but she didn't want to pass up the offer to spend more time with him. "Sure. Come on in."

He took a seat while she pulled up the corresponding contract. Together they evaluated the terms and numbers, and found that the new vendor would be able to provide substantial cost reductions.

Wes seemed pleased. And Kate was too, initially, but then she started to think about the implications of dropping a vendor. She knew what it felt like to end up in a crunch, especially over the holidays.

"What's the matter?" Wes's voice drew her from her thoughts.

"I was just thinking that my suppliers might be financially hurting as much as we are."

Wes smiled at her. "Did anyone tell you you have the biggest heart?"

"You think so?"

"I know so."

And then he set to work on the laptop. His fingers raced over the keyboard. She wondered what he was up to, but she remained quiet as she waited for him to finish.

"See this?" He pushed the laptop around so she could see the monitor. "Your existing supplier is projected to have record profits this year. You don't have to worry about going with someone else."

"How did you find that?"

He showed her. "But you can only get this information for companies that are publicly traded."

As they continued to discuss the new quote, another quote came in. It was also cheaper than what their current supplier could offer. Kate knew they were headed in the right direction, but she was wondered if the savings would be enough.

"I should get back to my work," Wes stood up.

"Wait. Can you give me any other ideas about how to cut expenses?"

Wes didn't say anything at first. Frown lines furrowed his brow.

"I'm sorry if I'm overstepping. You've already helped me so much."

"It's not that," he said. "I'm just not sure you'll like what I'm going to suggest."

She pressed her lips firmly together. Saving the company—saving the town—wasn't going to be easy. She'd known that from the onset, but it was easier thinking of it in broad terms than examining it in detail. But she had to do this—it was so much bigger than herself.

She leveled her shoulders and lifted her chin ever so slightly until her eyes met his. "Tell me what it is and I'll work on it."

"Let me ask you a question first." He shifted his

weight from one foot to the other. "Is the candle company the sole sponsor for the Candlelight Dance?"

"Yes. We always are. It's a longstanding tradition." Where was he going with this? And then the worst thought came to her. "Surely you're not suggesting we cancel the dance?"

Yes, she'd said she would do whatever it took to keep the company and town afloat, but at the same time, she hadn't thought it would mean abolishing an institution that had been around longer than she had—longer than her aunt had been.

The Candlelight Dance had been started by her great-great-grandfather when there was nothing else to do in the dark of winter, because there were no other towns close by. He had factory workers to entertain for the holidays. If they left, there was a good possibility they wouldn't come back to the remote town of Bayberry, which spent much of the winter under snow.

And so with nothing more than a barn, some candles and her great-great-grandfather's fiddle, the Candlelight Dance had begun. Over the years, the event had grown and the traditions had expanded. But at the heart of it, the purpose of the dance was still the same—bringing neighbors together to celebrate the holiday.

"I'm not suggesting you cancel it." His gaze searched hers. "But I am suggesting you modify it."

She was at last able to take an easy breath. "Modify it how?"

"Your company can no longer afford to pay for everything. Cuts must be made and they must be substantial."

Kate's shoulders sagged. "It won't be much of a dance—"

"Wait. I don't think you understand. I'm not asking you to eliminate anything. From what I could glean from the financials, there's quite a lot involved." When Kate nodded, he said, "All I'm asking is that instead of the company taking on all the responsibility, it's divvied out to the whole town."

"You want me to ask everyone for help?"

"Sure. They can all chip in."

She shook her head. "I don't think so."

"Why not?"

"Because...because it's never been done that way. It's all about tradition. And...and I just can't let everyone down." Perhaps she was more like her aunt, who insisted on routines, than Kate had ever thought.

"You won't let anyone down. That's the beauty of it. Instead of taking on everything yourself, you'll be asking the town to take part in the preparation. Then the dance will truly become a community event."

"I don't know." Would people be willing to step up and help out? It had never been done before.

"Will you at least consider it?"

She nodded slowly. What would it hurt to propose the idea? After all, she had said she would do anything to save Bayberry. This appeared to be anything. "I'll need to figure out the details."

"While you do, I have some more reports to go over. I'll catch up with you later."

Just before he walked out of sight, she remembered to say, "Thank you, Wes."

He glanced back. "Sorry if it wasn't what you wanted to hear."

"But it's what I needed to hear. If I'm—if we're—going to save this company, I need to realize that things can't go on the way they've been done for years. Change is coming whether I like it or not."

"Change isn't all bad."

And with that he walked away, leaving Kate alone with her thoughts. The dance hadn't changed at all since she'd moved to Bayberry. She wondered how her aunt would feel about it—how the town would feel about it.

The rest of the day, thoughts of the dance plagued her.

Change was coming.

But would people be willing to accept those changes?

By evening, Kate was ready to take the first step. She headed for Fred's place. A knock on the door, and Wes's mother opened it and greeted her with a warm smile. She stepped inside, finding a smallish Christmas tree in the corner of the living room. It was trimmed with red and white ornaments. The fireplace crackled as flames danced upon the logs.

Her aunt was in the kitchen at the stove. Fred was nowhere to be seen, but she knew he wouldn't have gone far. The aromas of homemade chicken soup and bread wafted through the house, making Kate's mouth water. In the background, "White Christmas" played. Kate smiled. It was most definitely Christmastime. She just hoped her aunt felt like singing after their talk.

"Aunt Penney, can we talk?"

"Sure. But it'll have to be here. I'm making a chocolate cake for dessert. Fred's favorite." Aunt Penney moved to the kitchen island with a big mixing bowl. "What do you have on your mind?"

Kate's gaze moved to Wes's mother, who was standing at the counter, chopping vegetables for what appeared to be a salad. "Maybe now isn't the time."

"It's fine. Martha doesn't mind. Do you?"

"Not at all. But I can step out of the room if it'd be easier."

Then, realizing she was making a big production out of this, Kate said, "No, please stay." She slipped off her coat and turned back to her aunt. "How would you feel if I made some changes to the Candlelight Dance?"

Aunt Penney reached for the flour. "What kind of changes?"

"Well, Wes and I were talking—"

"You and Wes were working on this, as in together?" Aunt Penney raised an eyebrow.

Was that a bad thing? She wasn't quite sure from the tone of her aunt's voice. After all, Aunt Penney was the one who'd hired him to give an unbiased review of the company.

"I've been asking him questions."

Aunt Penney resumed gathering ingredients for the cake. "What sort of questions?"

And then, realizing her aunt might be worried about confidentiality, Kate said, "Don't worry. He hasn't said a word about the report he's working on for you. These were other questions about how I could change things to help the company."

At some point, Martha had gravitated over to the island. And now they were all huddled together. It felt strangely normal, even though Martha was new to her.

"I hope my son was helpful." Martha wiped her hands on a towel.

"He's been very helpful. More than I ever could have imagined." And then Kate told them about the supplier contracts and the new quotes.

"That's wonderful," Martha said. "It'll save the company so much money."

Aunt Penney didn't say a word.

Kate eyed her aunt, watching for her reaction. "Aunt Penney, are you okay with changing suppliers after using the same ones for so many years?"

Her aunt sighed. "The truth is, I should have been more diligent. If I had, the company might not be in the state it is now. You're doing the right thing. You're doing what I should have done. And I thank you. Tomorrow morning, come to my office and we can go over those quotes."

When her aunt sent her a reassuring smile, Kate knew her aunt meant it. And the worry she'd been feeling about all of these big changes rolled away. She pulled out her phone and made a note on her calendar. "Now I won't forget."

"But I don't understand," Aunt Penney continued. "What does this have to do with the dance?"

"Wes thinks that instead of the company solely sponsoring the dance, we should ask the town to participate. He says it will make the dance a truly community event. And it will take some of the financial pressure off of us."

Aunt Penney didn't say anything at first. Kate's palms grew moist. Martha remained quiet, as though sensing the seriousness of the subject. Traditions weren't easily broken or modified.

Worried that her aunt was upset, Kate said, "Don't worry. I won't change—"

"No. Stop. This is perhaps what we need. And Wes is right about making it more of a community event." Aunt Penney's gaze met hers. "You go right ahead and do what you feel is best. I'm right behind you. Is there anything you want me to do?"

Kate shook her head. "I've got this."

Just then Fred entered the kitchen, walking just fine, until he spotted her. Then he took on an exaggerated limp. Kate struggled not to roll her eyes. Who did he and her aunt think they were kidding?

"I thought I heard someone else." He smiled at Kate. "Can you stay and have some dinner with us?"

"I would love to, but I have to go. I need to talk to Carrie, Abby and Sadie about some changes to the Candlelight Dance." Kate got up from the stool and put on her coat.

Fred's bushy brows drew together. "I hope there's still going to be a dance."

"I'm pretty certain there will be one," Kate said. "As long as I get to work on it."

"Then you'd better get moving. I have plans for the dance this year." His gaze moved to Aunt Penney.

Her aunt's face took on a rosy hue. "Oh Fred, you know the doctor said you have to be careful with your ankle."

"By Christmas Eve, it'll be good as new. And I'll be ready to dance with my favorite gal."

The color in her aunt's face increased. Martha smiled as she returned to peeling carrots for the salad. Kate quietly headed for the door. Fred didn't need any help. He was doing fine winning Penney over all on his own.

# Chapter Nineteen

*H*AD HE DONE THE RIGHT thing?

The thought had been plaguing Wes ever since he'd given Kate advice that morning. Sure, it was part of his job to hand out recommendations, but those should be based on cold, hard facts.

This morning, his advice had been based on his gut. None of it had been part of his job. And he knew that with each bit of advice, his hope was growing that somehow the candle company could be saved. And if he was holding out for a miracle, he knew Kate was even more invested in the outcome. He just hoped all these changes would bring the miracle they needed.

*Jingle. Jingle.*

He glanced over at the front door of Mel's Grille, where a young guy was holding the door for an older woman using a walker. The young man paid the woman a compliment that made her smile. It was such a friendly town.

Wes took the last bite of a hot turkey sandwich smothered in gravy, and then a bite of mashed potatoes. There was no way they were anything but home-made. He finished every last bit of the delicious meal.

But as good as the food had been, he couldn't stop thinking about Kate. He sure hoped she wasn't upset with him or the advice—

*Crash!*

The sound came from across the diner. He spotted what looked like a broken coffee cup on the floor. Before he could get to his feet to lend a hand, three people rushed over to help the waitress clean up the mess.

This small town was full of heart. People helping people. And that's why he thought his suggestion about the town chipping in with the dance would work. The only thing he didn't know was if the cost-cutting measures would be enough, or come soon enough, to save the candle company.

Without drastic changes, the company was sure to be sold. But if Kate and her aunt were willing to make the changes, he would take them into account when he completed his evaluation. He never got this involved with his clients or their businesses. But Bayberry was different—the small family-run com-pany was different, and the owners were different. He wanted this story to have a happy ending. But would it?

Carrie stopped by his table. "Can I get you more coffee?"

He nodded. "Thanks, that would be great. Hey, is everything okay?" He gestured to the area where they were still cleaning up the mess.

Carrie leaned down and lowered her voice. "It's a new girl and she's nervous. She'll be fine once she gets the hang of things. The dishes, on the other hand, might not fare so well."

He smiled. "Glad it's nothing serious."

"How about a slice of that blackberry pie? I baked it."

He'd been eyeing the pie displayed on the counter on a pedestal with a glass dome. He hadn't had berry pie since he was a kid. And it looked picture-perfect. If he stayed in Bayberry much longer, with all of its sweet treats, he was going to have to start running twice a day.

Before he could respond to Carrie, the door opened and the bells jingled. They both looked toward the entrance. When Kate entered, Wes sat up a little taller. He waved at her. When he caught her attention, she smiled. Again, that warm fuzzy feeling filled his chest, making his heart beat faster. He motioned to the empty stool next to him.

Carrie glanced back at him, expecting an answer.

"It looks delicious," he said. "Can you give me a minute?"

Carrie smiled knowingly. "I have a feeling it's going to be pie for two."

Wes grinned, but didn't say a word.

"I'll check back." Carrie waved to Kate before walking away.

Kate brushed snow from her coat, pulled off her knit cap, stuffed it in her pocket and then headed for his table. "It's starting to snow out there."

"Did you have dinner yet?" he asked.

She shook her head. "I didn't have time. I was talking to my aunt about the changes to the dance."

His body tensed as he waited to hear how Penney

had taken to the idea. He didn't push, but quietly waited for Kate to direct the conversation.

"When I told her about your idea, I wasn't sure she'd go with it. But she surprised me, and told me that, basically, change is inevitable. And then she said she should have done these things a long time ago. So I have her blessing to start switching things up with the contracts and the dance and whatever else needs changing." Kate smiled, but it didn't quite reach her eyes.

Sympathy welled up in him. He knew she was relieved to have her aunt's blessing, but that didn't mean changing things was going to be easy. Routines were comforting. Change could be unsettling at first. He knew, because his life had been a constant series of changes until he'd settled in Manhattan.

He reached out and squeezed her hand. "It'll be okay. Everything will work out. You'll see." He just hoped it would work out in their favor.

Her eyes met his. "Do you really believe that?"

"I do. But sometimes there are detours, and the result isn't exactly what you imagined."

"That's what worries me."

"All you can do is your best. The rest just has to work itself out."

"I wish you were staying to see it all through to the end." There was a sadness in her eyes that reached out and touched his heart.

He cleared his throat. Still, when he spoke his voice was deep with emotion. "As tempting as that sounds, my life is in New York. But I'll be here until the New Year."

"I guess we'll have to make the most of the time you're here."

"Let's get you some dinner."

"What about you?" she asked.

"I already enjoyed a nice hot turkey sandwich."

"Oh, that sounds good. I haven't had one in a long time."

When Carrie returned to the table, Kate ordered the sandwich. Wes went ahead and ordered a slice of pie.

Kate had asked Carrie to stop back when she had a free moment. Carrie did just that after most of the dinner crowd cleared out. "It's my break," Carrie announced. "What did you want to talk about?"

"You'd better sit down for this one."

Carrie's smile morphed into a frown. "What's wrong?"

"Nothing...exactly." And then Kate went on to explain the changes she planned to make to the Candlelight Dance. "So, what do you think?"

Wes remained quiet the whole time, waiting and wondering how his idea would be greeted.

"I think it'll work," Carrie said. "We need to talk to Abby and Sadie."

Kate called the two and put them on speaker phone. After hearing the proposal, both were hesitant, but agreed it was worth a try. Wes didn't say it, but he was uneasy. He knew he was messing with an age-old tradition and if it went wrong, it'd be his fault.

"We have to jump on this right away. The sooner we talk to all the business owners and the women's guild, the sooner they'll be able to get started." Carrie glanced at the clock. "It's too late tonight. Most of the shops are closed, but I'm off tomorrow afternoon."

"And I have a meeting with Aunt Penney in the morning, so the afternoon works for me too," Kate said.

Carrie nodded. "I can start on the south end of town."

"And I can start at the north end," Kate said. "And eventually we can meet in the park and compare notes."

"Let's text each other and decide on a time to meet."

"Sounds like a plan."

His fingers were a blur as he typed.

The preliminary report wasn't good. Not good at all.

The next day, Wes skipped lunch as he rushed to get his work done quickly. Mr. Summers had request-ed that Wes send it as soon as possible. And that's exactly what Wes intended to do. After a phone call from Jan, Mr. Summers' assistant, he knew that the promotion still hadn't been announced. He needed to do what he could to secure it.

But as he was typing the email to his boss, Wes's thoughts strayed to that Victorian home—the one where he'd experienced his first crush, the house that had felt like home when he walked through the door-way. It was for sale, and he kept imagining what it might be like to own it, to settle here in Bayberry with its friendly residents and its family feel.

He shook off the thoughts. It wouldn't work. His career was in New York. Everything he'd been striv-

ing for since college was in the city. The company he
worked for was the best at what it did, not only in
this country but around the world. So why would he
think of giving that all up to settle down in this small
town? What would he even do here?

No. It wasn't going to happen. He had to stay focused on the promotion. And even though his mother
didn't want to move to the city, it shouldn't change
his plans. Achieving the assistant VP position had
been his goal since he'd graduated from college. And
it was within his grasp.

With the email sent, he closed his laptop and went
to find Kate. Since it had been his idea to switch
things up for the dance, he felt like he should go along
and try to explain things to the town's residents. He
worried that it wouldn't go over well.

At least that's what Wes told himself was the reason for taking part of the afternoon off to walk shop-
to-shop with Kate. She welcomed his company, and
they set out in the lightly falling snow. The flakes
melted as they landed on the sidewalk and road, but
they added to the accumulation of snow in the yards,
giving them a fresh, glittery appearance.

Everyone was bundled up against the distinct chill
in the air, but it didn't stop them from sharing warm
holiday greetings. Wes knew he'd been in the town for
awhile when he was able to put names to many of the
faces.

There was MaryJane from the candle company office. She'd told anyone who would listen that she was
taking the day off to finish her Christmas shopping.
By the number of packages in her hands, she'd succeeded.

Wes said hello to the reverend and his wife. And there was Joe from the deli. Wes was quite pleased with the number of people he recognized.

He met even more of the townspeople as they went along from business to business. Soon he would know them all. They were a quirky bunch, but very friendly and welcoming—just as he'd remembered.

They'd just stepped in Tara's Tasty Treats when the young woman behind the counter greeted them with a smile. "Hello, Kate." The woman turned to Wes. "Hi. You must be Wes."

He wondered how she knew his name, but then he realized that in this small town, gossip flowed faster than the small creek that ran through Bayberry.

"Yes, I am." He held his hand out over the glass countertop. "And you must be Tara. It's nice to meet you."

"And he has manners too." The woman beamed at Kate as she shook his hand. "I like this one."

When Wes glanced over at Kate, her face was bright red and her gaze didn't quite meet his. Was it possible that she felt something growing between them too? Or was it all in his head?

But as he continued to look at Kate, he realized that the feelings he had for her had nothing to do with his head, and everything to do with his heart. And that's when he knew he couldn't let her down. He had to find a way to keep her family's company going—her town thriving—and put that enchanting smile back on her face. Even if his numbers didn't agree with him.

Kate stepped forward. "Tara, we're going to try something different for the Candlelight Dance this year." Rushing on before Tara could ask a long string of questions like the last person had, Kate added, "We're trying to make the dance more of a community affair. And we're asking residents and businesses what they can volunteer or donate."

The woman's brows rose, but to her credit, she didn't ask for an explanation. "That sounds like a lovely idea. What sort of things do you need?"

Kate read off the lengthy list, and Tara volunteered to make favors for the dinner before the dance. They both thanked her and headed out the door. Kate texted Carrie so she could cross favors off her list too.

They continued knocking on house doors and businesses alike. By the time they reached the town square, the temperature had dropped as the sun sank lower in the sky. When they spoke, their breath came out in little white puffs. Fortunately, there were only a handful of items left on the list.

When they met up with Carrie in Bayberry Square, Kate said, "We can provide these last few items." She sent Wes a questioning look. "Don't you think?"

If it meant they could get in out of the cold, he'd agree to anything. He stuffed his hands in his coat pockets. Considering that Bayberry Candles had gone from supplying everything for the dance to fewer than five items, he said, "I think that will work just fine. And everyone seemed excited to chip in."

"They did," Carrie agreed.

"It's wonderful," Kate said. "I don't know why I didn't think of this a long time ago."

Long shadows stretched over the park. And just then the Christmas lights flickered on. People passing through the square on their way home from work or to admire the Christmas tree greeted the three with a warm smile, a wave or a kind word.

Wes used to think he liked the hustle and bustle of the city. Perhaps it was what he needed when he was fresh out of college, but now that he was a bit older, he was seeing the benefits of both worlds. It would be so easy to settle here in Bayberry. The thought teased and tempted him.

But his life was in New York. He had his job. A potential promotion. A chance to move further up the corporate ladder. And...

His thoughts stuttered. Surely, he had to have more than that. Right? He did have his friends—to whom he still needed to send Christmas presents. Perhaps a gift card to a trendy restaurant in the city for Jan. And then there was Joe in the mail room. They chatted about sports every Monday morning like clockwork. All before hours, of course. Well, most of the time. Some conversations leading up to the Super Bowl took a little more time.

The thing that struck him the most was that he had nothing to go home to. Not a person, especially now that his mother had made it clear she didn't want to move there. Not even a pet. His thoughts turned to Rascal. The thought of adopting the little guy wouldn't leave him. But then there were the long hours Wes put in at the office, plus the travelling. Someday he'd like to get a dog. And he couldn't help thinking how Bayberry was the ideal place for a dog—

"Wes, did you hear me?" Kate asked, giving him a strange look.

"What did you say?"

"We were talking about the toboggan race this weekend. You're coming, aren't you?"

"Yeah," Carrie said, "you can't miss it."

"I don't know," he said. "I might be too old for sled riding."

"It's not sled riding," Carrie said. "And you're never too old."

"It's toboggan racing," Kate said. "Totally different."

He shrugged. "If you say so. I'll watch."

"The thing is," Carrie pouted, "I have to back out." Her eyes met Kate's. "I'm so sorry. I have to work. The diner is shorthanded and you know how everyone piles in after the race wanting something hot to drink and eat." Carrie turned a hopeful look in his direction. "You'll help her out, won't you?"

Kate shook her head. "It's okay. I don't have to race. I can just cheer from the sidelines."

Carrie gently elbowed her. "You can't. You promised Sam you'd race. That's the only reason he agreed to do it with his son."

"Stop." Kate's nose and cheeks, already pink from the cold, took on a deeper hue as she shot her friend a dirty look. Then Kate turned to him. "Don't mind her. I'm fine."

Carrie's eyes were twinkling with mischief. "The rules say you can't enter without a partner."

Wes wondered if that was the truth. Or was Carrie trying to set them up? He quickly dismissed the idea. If somebody had matchmaking in mind, surely they'd plan something more romantic than racing down a freezing hill.

But with both of the women looking eagerly at him,

he didn't have the heart to let them down. "Okay. I'll do it."

They both cheered.

Between now and the weekend, he had a lot of work to do. Numbers to pull. Spreadsheets to complete. And figures to crunch.

But at the end of all that, he would have a very pleasant reward awaiting him. And it definitely was not the sled riding, erm, tobogganing he had in mind.

# Chapter Twenty

*I*T WAS RACE TIME.

And Wes didn't have a clue about the difference between a sled and a toboggan.

Just then snow flurries started to fall. They were fat, fluffy flakes that slowly drifted down in the still air. As he stood on the hill staring down at Bayberry, he couldn't help but think that with the snow blanketing the ground and dusting the rooftops, the town looked like one great big Christmas card.

"Another new experience," he said.

"You mean you've never been on a toboggan?" Kate looked at him with astonishment.

He shook his head, feeling as though he were the only one in Bayberry to have never ridden a toboggan. "My father preferred the southern states, so as a kid I didn't have much exposure to snow. And though it does snow in New York, I'm always working."

"Well, you aren't working right now." Kate flashed him a smile. "We'd better hurry and take a test run or two."

"Is that necessary?" He couldn't believe it would be very challenging.

Kate nodded. "We want to win."

"We do?"

"We do," she said firmly.

Wearing borrowed snow pants and boots that climbed halfway up his calves, as well as his new coat, he followed her toward a prime spot on Barkley's Hill. From that vantage point, he was able to stare across the dip to his old house. That house was never far from his thoughts these days.

He couldn't help but wonder about the people who would move in next. Would they be as happy as his family had been there? He didn't recall exactly why they'd had to move, but it was probably for a higher-paying job. He couldn't help but wonder if it had been worth it, as his dad had barely stayed at the new company for a year.

They trudged farther up the hill, dragging the toboggan behind them. He held one side of the rope pull while she gripped the other. Working together, getting it up the hill was so much easier. Teamwork: it was something that his position at Watson & Summers didn't allow him. The more he climbed the corporate ladder, the more alone he felt.

In fact, the closer he got to the assistant vice president position, the more he felt as though he and the other candidates were pitted against each other.

It wasn't until he was away from the office that he'd noticed the way Mr. Summers pushed people, and casually mentioned other employees' achievements to get more productivity from him.

Wes frowned as they reached the top of the hill.

Why had he put himself through all that stress and worry over accounts and quarterly results, when every quarter had to be bigger and better than the last? And then he remembered wanting to move his mother close to him. But now, knowing that wasn't what she wanted, he had to decide what he was willing to put himself through for the promotion.

But that thought would have to wait, because right now there was snow and a sled—a toboggan, that is— and it was time to have some fun—

*Whack! Whack!*

Two snowballs smacked him, one on the shoulder and one in his chest. What in the world? He glanced around. Immediately he spotted Kate off in the distance.

She grinned at him. Her eyes sparkled with merriment. And then, not waiting for his response, she bent to gather more snow. Her arms moved quickly and then she straightened with a devilish smile. She wasn't going to—

Kate winged a snowball in his direction. The lady had a good arm. He ducked. The snowball hit the ground behind him.

When he straightened, she was gathering more snow—more ammunition. Oh no. He wasn't going to stand around and be a target. Two could play this game.

He grinned as he gathered snow, squeezing it into a firm ball. But as he stood back up, a snowball drilled into his shoulder, exploding. Snow showered over his face and left him sputtering.

"The war is on!" He launched a snowball, hitting her in the back.

She gasped. He laughed. Once she shook off the snow, she turned with an extra-large snowball and let it fly.

He ducked. And the battle continued until they were both laughing so hard, neither could catch their breath. He couldn't remember the last time he'd had this much fun. Usually his time was rationed out, making the most of each minute, whether it was time spent at the gym in his office building or working over a late dinner in front of the television. But this was a totally unproductive use of time, and he couldn't think of anything he'd rather be doing, or anyone he'd rather be doing it with.

Snow had slipped beneath his jacket, but he wasn't going to let that stop him. Not a chance.

He needed more of this in his life. Maybe not snow-ball fights, exactly, but just letting loose and having fun. He tried to imagine doing this in New York. But when he left home, he was almost always in a suit. Not exactly conducive to adventures in the snow. Bayberry had forced him into boots, jeans, a sweater and a down jacket, as well as a knit cap and gloves. It was everything he needed to have winter fun.

As another round of snowballs flew through the air and laughter rang out, he realized it wasn't Bayberry that had drawn out his inner kid. It was Kate. She could work as hard as the next person, but she made time to let down her pretty reddish-brown curls and have some fun.

At last, Kate waved her arms and cried uncle. He couldn't blame her; he was getting tired too. But it didn't diminish his good mood. Not in the least.

He made his way over to her. "I could use a hot chocolate. How about you?"

She moaned her approval. "That would be awesome. But it's going to have to wait. We have some sledding to do."

"Okay. But later, we're getting hot chocolate."

She smiled at him. "It's a date."

A date? Had he asked her on a date? He rolled it around in his mind. No. It wasn't a date. When he asked her out, she would know it. But it did give him an idea. A very good idea.

"Come on." Kate grabbed his hand and they headed for the toboggan.

His idea was going to have to wait. He settled in the back, letting Kate sit in front of him. And off they went, flying down the hill. He hadn't done this since he was a kid. If he stayed in Bayberry much longer, he wondered what else Kate would convince him to do. The wind whistled in his ears and Kate shrieked with laughter. He held her tightly against him.

The toboggan slid to a stop at the bottom of the hill. Kate jumped to her feet. She turned to him. "Come on. We have time for one more run. This time I'll sit in the back."

He stood up. "Are you sure?"

"Positive," she bubbled. "We have to see which way is faster: me in front or you in front."

When she looked at him like that, she warmed him from the inside out. He'd never seen her so excited. And though he wasn't looking forward to trudging up the hill again, he didn't want to ruin this moment for her. And truth be told, he was having as much fun as she was. It'd been a long time since he'd allowed himself to enjoy the snow.

"You got it," he said. "I'll race you to the top."

"Race?" Her expression was one of horror. "In the snow?"

"Sure." And up the hill he went, with snow kicking up all around him.

He stumbled once, but recovered quickly. With his long legs, he was able to outpace Kate. It wasn't easy rushing up a hill in so much snow, but his pride refused to let him slow down. When he reached the top, he turned around to find Kate taking her last steps to the top. When she came to a stop next to him, she pressed her hands to her sides as she huffed and puffed.

It took her a moment to catch her breath, and then she gasped, "You cheated."

"Cheated? How do you figure?"

A teasing smile lit up her face, puffing up her pink cheeks. "You must have—or I'm really out of shape."

He wasn't touching that comment. No way. He wasn't that foolish.

When he glanced away, he noticed the toboggan at the bottom of the hill. He'd been so distracted by Kate that he'd totally forgotten about it.

"I'll be right back," he called out as he rushed back down the hill, trying not to stumble in the deep snow.

"Where are you going?" Kate yelled.

He knew she'd figure it out soon enough. When he reached the toboggan, he turned and found Kate laughing. Wow! She stole his breath away. He was never going to forget this day. Or her. Not ever.

Then, realizing he was just standing there staring

at her, he started climbing the hill once more, but this time with the toboggan in tow.

When at last he came to a stop next to her, his heart was pounding, but it wasn't just from the physical exertion. No. It was the way Kate was looking at him—as if he was the only person around—the only man for her.

She tilted her chin up and gazed deep into his eyes. She looked so adorable with her pink cheeks and nose. And the cold air had given her lips a deep rosy hue. No one had ever looked so beautiful.

His gaze lingered on her lips. What would she do if he were to lean forward and steal a kiss? It wasn't as if she was moving away from him. Was it possible she was tempted by the same idea?

He hadn't gotten this far in his career without taking chances. Maybe it was time to take chances with his personal life. And kissing Kate was definitely a chance worth taking. In fact, he couldn't think of anything he wanted to do more.

He started to lean forward. Her eyes drifted shut—

"Hey guys!"

Wes and Kate jumped apart, as though a bolt of lightning had struck in the middle of the snowstorm. Wes ducked his head as he turned away, pretending his heart wasn't hammering against his ribs.

Kate turned to the kid standing behind them. "Hey, Sammy. I see you got your dad here."

"Thanks to you." The young boy's face lit up with a wide smile.

His father, Sam Sr., walked over, greeted Kate and then shook Wes's hand. While Kate went to look at the boy's new toboggan, Wes stayed behind.

The tall man with the friendly smile asked, "Are you enjoying your visit to Bayberry?"

"I am." Wes adjusted his gloves. "I've always enjoyed this town."

"So you've been here before?"

"Yes. When I was a kid, we lived here briefly."

"Not many people move away from Bayberry. The ones who do usually make their way back—like you."

Wes shook his head. "I'm not staying. I'm just here until this project is done."

Sam's eyes lit up with comprehension. "You're the one determining whether or not to shut down the candle company. Looks like you have the fate of the town in your hands. That's definitely not a position I'd ever want to be in."

Wes shifted his weight from one foot to the other. "So the word got out?"

Sam smiled. "The word has been out. You wouldn't believe the efficiency of Bayberry's gossip chain. It would beat the speed of light. They had you figured out from your first day in town."

"And here I thought I was flying under everyone's radar."

Sam let out a deep laugh. "You came to the wrong town for that. So how are things looking?"

Wes shifted his weight again. He wanted to talk about anything but this. "I can't discuss it."

"I understand." The man's expression grew serious. "But you have to recommend the candle company stays in business. This town won't survive without it. I don't work there, but my wife does, and her sister." When Wes didn't say anything, the man continued. "That's right, you can't discuss it."

Wes's gaze sought out Kate, but she wasn't looking in his direction. Her back was to him as she was examining the boy's toboggan.

Wes searched for a topic of discussion that had nothing to do with the candle company or the future of Bayberry. "This is my first time in a toboggan race."

"Mine too. I wasn't even planning on doing it, but your girlfriend—"

"Kate's not my girlfriend."

Though as Wes disputed the man's assumption, he couldn't help but ponder the idea. It'd been a while since he'd had a girlfriend. He missed the companionship, but his job, with its long hours and travel, just wasn't conducive to relationships.

He was surprised Kate wasn't already involved in a relationship. And based on the way she interacted with Sammy, he couldn't help but think she'd make a great mother—encouraging, patient and engaging.

And then he thought about the Candlelight Dance. It was little more than a week away. He'd meant to ask her to the dance all those years ago, but he'd missed the chance. And he had been toying with the idea of asking her out on a real date. This was his opportunity to do it. He could ask her tonight, over a cup of hot chocolate after the race.

Sam eyed him. "She's a great gal. You'd be foolish not to ask her out."

"I think you're right. I'm going to do just that."

The man smiled his approval. "Good luck. She doesn't date much. The last guy she was with up and moved away."

Wes didn't let on that Kate had already confided in him. If she wouldn't follow Wes to New York, how would they ever maintain a relationship? It wasn't like he could just up and quit his job...but of course, she probably felt the same way.

It was just a date—a dance. It wasn't like they would be embarking on a serious relationship. Right?

"I'm sure things will work out for Kate," Wes said. "Any guy would be lucky to have her in his life." And then deciding he didn't want to dissect his relationship with Kate, he said, "I should go. We have just enough time for another practice run before the race."

"I guess we should do that too."

Wes hadn't known Sam before this evening, but the man had certainly given him a lot to think about. If circumstances were different, he imagined they'd be good friends. What would his life look like if he moved to Bayberry? Would Kate want to start something with him?

Moving to Bayberry would mean giving up everything he'd spent his adult life working toward. And if he didn't, could he walk away from Kate? Her smile filled his thoughts at all hours of the day. When he closed his eyes at night, she filled his dreams. And when he woke up in the morning, he was eager to see her again.

But there was something big standing between him and having to make those decisions—the candle company. He knew that if the business went under, Kate would blame him. Sure, she said she wouldn't, but things would be different if it became a reality. He just couldn't let that happen.

He'd been giving the problem a lot of thought. He had an idea of how to save the candle company, but there would be a lot of details to iron out. And he'd need Penney's blessing. Would she approve of his un-orthodox solution?

It was the most amazing evening.

Mel's Grille was hopping with people from the toboggan race. Every table was occupied. Each stool at the counter was taken. And every waitress in her fifties-style uniform with a red apron was rushing from table to table.

And Kate couldn't be happier. She knew she should be at the office with Aunt Penney consider-ing more cost-cutting measures or building up the company's online presence, but there was something about being with Wes during this magical time of the year that was irresistible. Somehow, some way, she'd make time for both work and Wes. Because the more time she spent with him, the more time she wanted to spend with him.

He made her smile. He made her want to believe in happily-ever-afters. He made her want to take a chance with her heart.

He made her believe that anything was possible. He made her want to think she was capable of far more than she'd done so far.

Kate beamed across the table at Wes. "That was awesome."

"Is that what you call that wipeout at the bottom of the hill? Awesome?" His eyes twinkled with merri-ment.

"It was pretty spectacular when you had all that snow on your head." A big grin pulled at her lips.

Wes returned her smile. "No funnier than you wiping the snow from your face."

"I guess you've got me there. But before we wiped out, we did win the snowball trophy." She placed it on the table between them. "Can you believe it?"

"No. I've never seen a trophy with a tennis ball painted to look like a snowball."

Kate's mouth dropped open. "It's not a tennis ball."

"It's not?" He leaned in closer and squinted. "Sure looks like it."

She looked at the trophy. Maybe he had a point, but it was too much fun to banter with him to stop now. "It does not."

He shrugged. "Okay. Maybe it doesn't. But I sure had you wondering for a while."

"Oh, you." She smiled, realizing he'd been teasing her all along.

Carrie delivered their cheeseburgers and fries. With all of that trudging through the snow, they'd really worked up their appetites. They made short work of the meal, and then leaned back in the booth.

"How about dessert?" Kate asked. "After all, we have to celebrate."

"Celebrate, huh?" When she nodded, he asked, "What did you have in mind?"

"Hot chocolate with marshmallows." Her mouth watered just thinking about it. "Theirs is so creamy and rich. It's like chocolate heaven."

"You don't have to twist my arm. I was sold at chocolate and marshmallows."

Her eyes lit up. "A man after my own heart." And then her face reddened. "Well, you know what I mean."

When Carrie returned to their table, they ordered a couple of hot chocolates. Silence fell over them. Kate tried to come up with something to talk about other than the candle company. They'd already talked about it more than enough.

Wes fidgeted with a spoon. "You know, I was thinking about the candle company—"

"No." She held up her hand. "Tonight's too good to ruin with work talk."

"I'm sorry. I was just trying to help."

Carrie arrived with their hot chocolates smothered in little marshmallows. It was just the way Kate loved it. She immediately took a sip of the rich, creamy concoction. She moaned in delight.

"Perfect," she said before returning to their conversation. "It's just that I'd rather think about you in the snowbank. It makes me smile."

He feigned a frown. "I like how my near-death experience amuses you."

"It's the little things in life." A small giggle escaped her lips before she took a drink of her cocoa.

"Then I guess that chocolate mustache of yours is another one of those small amusing things." He sent her a teasing smile.

Heat flooded her cheeks. She quickly reached for a napkin and wiped her mouth.

"Better?" she asked.

"I don't know. You looked kinda cute with the 'stache."

She sighed before stirring the marshmallows into her cocoa. "It won't be long until the dance. Everyone is chipping in. I just hope it turns out okay."

He stirred his own cocoa. "It'll all work out. Just wait and see."

"Tomorrow, everyone is meeting at the community hall and we're going to start looking through last year's decorations. We'll see what needs to be replaced. Abby let me know the quilting group has agreed to do the baking instead of having to buy desserts. And Carrie arranged to have everyone bring a covered dish instead of having the event catered. And the young man I was talking to after the race? He rearranged his calendar and he's able to DJ the dance, so we won't have to pay for a band."

"Do you want to go with me to the dance?" The words came out of his mouth in one big garbled rush.

Had he just asked her to the dance? Her heart leapt into her throat. But his words had been so rushed, she wasn't quite sure. She really hoped she'd heard him correctly.

Kate swallowed hard as her palms grew damp. "Did...did you just ask me to the dance?"

His gaze met hers. "I've been waiting to ask you that question for seventeen years."

Her eyes widened as her brows rose. "You have?"

He nodded. "I'd planned to ask you to the Candlelight Dance all those years ago. I was so nervous because I'd never asked a girl to a dance before, and I was pretty certain you were going to turn me down. It took me a while to work up the courage, and just when I did—just when I'd promised myself I would ask you the next day at school, my father came home from work that night and told us that we were moving—again. We were leaving right away—before the dance."

"And so you never got to go?"

He shook his head. "So I've been waiting a very long time to ask you. And I have to admit that after all these years, I'm still nervous. I know that sounds silly."

"Not at all." Her insides trembled with excitement. "Go ahead." When he gave her a puzzled look, she said, "Ask me."

A look of comprehension dawned. "Oh." He visibly swallowed and then took her hand in his. His touch was warm and sent goosebumps up her arm, setting her heart aflutter. "Kate, I would be honored if you'd agree to be my date to the Candlelight Dance—"

"Yes! I'd love to!"

"You would?" He stared at her for a moment as though digesting her words. "I mean, don't feel like you have to—"

"Did it sound like a pity acceptance?" She threw him a dazzling smile.

He shook his head. "No. It didn't. And lucky for me, I have a suit to wear."

"So you do. But now I need a dress."

"You don't have to dress up on my account. I think you look great in anything. Honestly. You could wear what you've got on now and I would think you were the most beautiful woman in the room."

She glanced down at the navy-blue suspenders from her ski pants over the white long-sleeved shirt. And then she ran a hand over her messy bun with a million flyaways. "I look terrible."

"Not to me."

She met his eyes, her cheeks flaming, nervous and thrilled and scared.

As much as she wanted to convince herself that she wasn't falling for Wes, she knew it was too late. She was falling head over heels for this man who lived far from her tiny town. She didn't have a clue what she was supposed to do about these feelings. Not an inkling. Because she'd never expected this to happen. And a long-distance relationship was the last thing she wanted.

# Chapter Twenty-One

*H*AD THAT REALLY HAPPENED?

Had Wes really asked her to the dance?

It was as though they were meant to be together. Nothing—not distance nor the passage of time—could alter their lives being intertwined. Their fate had been written in the stars.

In the light of a new day, Kate tried to tell herself that she was being ridiculous. After all, it wasn't as if they were in high school anymore. But that didn't stop the sensation of butterflies fluttering through her belly, or the worry of finding just the right dress.

In fact, she'd been so caught off-guard the previous night that she wasn't even sure her feet had touched the ground when she'd walked home. She replayed the scene over and over in her mind. And the part that touched her the most was that after all these years, he'd finally had an opportunity to ask her to the dance.

She couldn't remember ever being this excited about a date. She tried to temper her excitement with the thought of Wes leaving after the holidays and returning to New York, but not even that realization could dampen her anticipation. She was going to the Candlelight Dance with a date—a very handsome, very sweet, very kind date. And she couldn't wait.

But she had to wear something extra special. It couldn't just be something out of her wardrobe. There wasn't anything there that was special enough for a date that had taken seventeen years to transpire.

And then it came to her. She sprang out of bed and grabbed her phone. She called her aunt. The phone rang once, twice, three times, and she was beginning to think her aunt wasn't going to answer. Where could she be? It was Sunday morning.

"Hello?" Aunt Penney's voice sounded a bit groggy.

"Aunt Penney, I can't believe it. I just got asked to the dance."

"You did?" Her aunt's voice grew peppier. "I take it you're excited about this, since you called me at 6:13 on a Sunday morning."

Kate gasped and looked at her bedside clock. It was indeed early—way too early for the weekend. "I'm so sorry. I didn't realize. I'll let you go back to sleep."

"That's okay. When you get to my age, you don't need as much sleep. And I couldn't go back to sleep now. I'd be wondering about this date of yours."

"Wes asked me."

"I figured that. Give me all the details. On second thought, I'll meet you in my kitchen in two minutes. You can fill me in over coffee and the muffins I made last night for Fred."

"Fred, huh?" Kate smiled. With every passing day, those two were getting closer and closer.

"Oh, hush. See you soon." And with that, her aunt hung up.

Kate scrambled out of bed, rushed to her closet, grabbed her warmest robe, and headed for the door. She paused long enough to slip on her boots, and then off she went into the wintry morning. Luckily, she only had to go down the steps and across the driveway.

Once inside her aunt's warm kitchen, she slipped off her boots and headed for the coffeemaker. Kate put in a new filter and then added the grounds. Once she'd poured in the water, she pressed the start button. What her aunt didn't know was that Kate had gotten her one of those coffeemakers that uses pods for Christmas. Instead of a pot of coffee sitting around getting burned, Aunt Penney could have a fresh cup each time. And then there were all of the flavors—so many to choose from.

As the coffeemaker sputtered, her aunt entered the room with a smile on her face. They quietly moved around the kitchen, gathering the sweetener and creamer. Neither of them was a big talker before they'd had their morning boost of caffeine.

At last the coffee trickled into the pot. That heavenly aroma wafted through the room. Anticipation thrummed in Kate's veins, when she at last poured them each a large mug.

With coffee in hand, Aunt Penney said, "Tell me everything, and don't leave anything out."

They settled down at the kitchen table with their coffee and one of Aunt Penney's famous blueberry muffins. Kate started with how she'd been paired up with Wes for the toboggan race. Then she mentioned their dinner afterward. Aunt Penney listened with rapt interest. Finally, Kate shared that Wes had wanted to ask her to the dance all those years ago, but had never gotten the chance.

"That's remarkable," Aunt Penney said. "The fact that he was drawn back to Bayberry just in time for the Candlelight Dance is more than a coincidence. It's a sign. This will be a very special dance for both of you."

Kate took a last sip of her coffee and pushed aside her plate with only a few muffin crumbs remaining. "And that's why I wanted to ask a really big favor of you."

"You know you can ask me for anything. If I can, I'll do it—"

"Good morning." Martha entered the kitchen. "Do I smell coffee?"

"Yes. Let me get you some." Aunt Penney and Kate both started to get up.

"Sit," Martha told them. "I can get it."

"There's still fresh coffee in the pot." Aunt Penney settled back in her chair. "And muffins on the counter."

Kate sat back too. She waited to make her request until everyone had said good morning and Martha got situated at the table. Then Aunt Penney filled in her friend on the latest development.

Martha's face lit up. "I remember that time. Wes had been so resistant to moving. I'd never seen him quite like that. And he wouldn't say why he needed to stay until New Year's. But sadly, my late husband had to start his new job right away. He was forever searching for where he belonged. I don't know if he ever did. We kept moving right up until the end."

Kate couldn't even imagine what that must have been like, constantly moving from one place to the next. She thought of Wes as a kid, having to move from school to school—making friends, only to lose them. Her heart ached for him. She'd had a hard-enough time moving from Hartford to Bayberry. Getting to know people constantly and never having a place to grow roots—it wasn't for her.

Aunt Penney made another pot of coffee and filled their cups. After she returned to her chair, she asked, "Kate, what was the favor you wanted to ask me?"

"I was wondering if you could help me find something special to wear to the dance."

"I don't think they'll have anything left at the boutique in town," Aunt Penney cautioned.

Her aunt was right. The dance was a huge deal. All the fancy dresses would have been scooped up long ago.

"I know," Martha said. "We can order one over the internet."

Aunt Penney shrugged, but she didn't look convinced.

Kate shook her head. "I checked, and I'm worried that if it doesn't fit properly, I won't have time to exchange it." There was only one way to get the perfect dress, but Kate was hesitant to say anything.

As though reading her mind, Aunt Penney said, "We could make you a dress."

It was just what Kate had been hoping for. "It's a lot of work," she said, feeling guilty. "And there's not much time."

"Nothing we haven't done in the past." Aunt Penney added some more sugar to her coffee. "Remember the dresses we used to make when you were in school?"

Kate nodded. Her aunt could work magic with a needle and thread. Cinderella's fairy godmother had nothing on Aunt Penney when it came to creating beautiful dresses.

"Oh, I haven't made a dress in years." Martha's face lit up at the idea. "I could help."

"What sort of dress did you have in mind?" Aunt Penney looked at her niece expectantly.

Kate pulled out her phone and showed her an image she'd found online.

"That doesn't look too hard," Aunt Penney said. She turned the phone to Martha. "What do you think?"

"I think we have ourselves a project." Martha was beaming. "I'd forgotten how much there is to do in a small town. I really love Bayberry."

"Then stay," Aunt Penney said. "I know I'd love to have you in the same town instead of having to talk on the phone or write notes back and forth."

"I've been considering it."

"What's keeping you in Florida?"

Martha arched a brow. "You mean besides the sunshine and warmth?"

Everyone turned to the window. Outside, snow flurries were gently fluttering to the ground. Bayberry's warmth at this time of the year came from its heart. The town glowed with kindness and compassion despite the frigid weather.

"Okay," Aunt Penney said. "You might have me there. But we have a lot that Florida can't offer you."

"That's true. The thought of moving back here— well, it's so tempting. I've even mentioned it to Wesley."

"Your old house is up for sale," Kate offered.

Martha shook her head. "That Victorian is beautiful. But it's much too big for just me. It needs a young family to move in and fill the hallways with happy voices. I'm thinking about something much smaller for just me."

"I'm sure we could find something suitable," Kate said.

"And if you move back, you'll have to rejoin the quilting group," Aunt Penney urged.

Martha's face lit up. "They're still around?"

Aunt Penney nodded. "We'd love to have you back."

Martha kept smiling. "You know you're making this impossible for me to turn down, don't you?"

"That's what I'm hoping," Aunt Penney said.

Kate sat quietly, listening to the women talk. It was as if they'd been best friends their entire lives. And part of her hoped that if Wes's mother moved back to town, Kate would get to see him after the holidays. Because after all they'd shared, she just couldn't imagine him dropping out of her life.

And then she noticed the time. Kate got to her feet and moved to the sink with her dishes. Once they were rinsed off and placed in the dishwasher, she turned to the two women. "I'm sorry, but I don't have much time for a fitting. I have a meeting with the decorating committee at the community hall at nine."

"So the idea about the town pitching in is working out?" Aunt Penney asked.

Kate nodded. "Everyone seemed eager to help."

And then all three of them got busy taking measurements, comparing the online photo to Aunt Penney's patterns, and deciding what fabrics would work best. The coffee flowed and conversation filled the room. Kate sighed with contentment. Things were working out.

"Look at the time," Aunt Penney said. "Didn't you say you had to leave at nine?"

"Is it that late already?" Kate glanced at the red apple-shaped clock hanging above the kitchen sink. "You're right. I should go."

"It's okay," Aunt Penney said. "Go. We've got this."

"You're sure?" She felt guilty leaving them with so much to do.

"Oh, yes," Martha said. "Don't worry. I'll help your aunt."

"Thank you." Kate beamed at them. "If I can do anything else to help, let me know."

"I will. But you'd better get going. You don't want to be late."

"And don't worry about your dress," Penney said. "We'll come up with something special."

"Yes, we will," Martha said.

Kate thanked them profusely and hugged each of them, before walking out the door with her mind whirling. So much was changing, and all of it for the good. This momentum was just what they needed right now. Kate smiled. She had a feeling that everything was going to work out.

# Chapter Twenty-Two

ONDAY MORNING STARTED WITH A testy email from Mr. Summers.

This was not the way Wes liked his weeks to begin—especially the week before Christmas. This was the last week the candle company would be in operation before it shut down for the holidays. This was supposed to be the season of Christmas spirit, not of "Bah, humbug.

Wes sat at his desk and scowled at the demanding email from his irate boss. The city seemed so far away after a few weeks in Bayberry. The corporate rush and fuss that required a solid string of coffees from start to finish each day was not the way things got done in Bayberry. The constant pressure to hurry, hurry, hurry felt unfamiliar to him now.

Yesterday, after helping to decorate the community hall for the dance, Wes had spent the remainder of the day working in his makeshift office. This town and the candle company had become so important to him that he wanted to know where things stood as soon as possible.

And then there was Kate. Her whole world was Bayberry. She loved this place and the people who lived here. He couldn't blame her. This was a very special town.

He'd revised his initial projections with the numbers from the new supplier quotes, but it hadn't been enough to sway the overall conclusion. In fact, he'd spent Sunday evening trying different scenarios to make the conclusion anything other than what it was: the candle company would need to be sold to a larger entity with the resources to invest in the business.

Wes knew that if a big corporation took over, Bayberry Candles would never be the same. His shoulders drooped under the weight of this knowledge. A corporate parent would outsource jobs, slashing the workforce to a small percentage of what it was now.

Faces of the friendly Bayberry employees flashed in his mind. There weren't many employment opportunities in this small town. They'd have to pack up their families and move. Their houses wouldn't sell, because there wouldn't be anyone to buy them. It would be devastating, like falling dominoes.

But maybe there was another answer. Maybe the buyer didn't have to be a heartless corporation focused on nothing but the bottom line. What if there was a buyer who valued employees and traditions?

He picked up his phone and called Penney. It was time they went over his findings and discussed the future of the Bayberry Candle Company.

The new dress was amazing.

On Sunday afternoon, she'd been thrilled with what Penney and Martha had accomplished in just one week. Now Christmas Eve was just three days away. She smiled as she thought of the dazzling dress. While the two women had marked it for adjustments, Fred had snagged a sneak preview. He'd insisted that Wes would be knocked out when he saw her wearing it.

She hoped Fred was right. After waiting all these years for this date, Wes deserved something extra special. She had picked up new silver heels the other day in town. And that left her hair. She couldn't decide if she should wear it up. Or did it look better down?

Her stomach quivered with nerves. Kate hadn't been this nervous about a date since, well, ever. And she feared she was making too much of it. Or was she?

All day yesterday, the citizens of Bayberry had put the finishing touches on the community hall. And by chance, a last-minute cancellation at a florist meant they could have fresh flowers for the dance instead of the usual silk flowers, which were starting to look their age.

The only catch was that Kate had to pick up the flowers in Burlington before the dance. Somehow, she'd fit it into her hectic schedule. It was the one time of year when she didn't mind being so busy.

Speaking of busy, Wes had worked such long

hours all week that she'd hardly seen him. And since she'd already distracted him so much during his stay, she decided to keep her distance and let him finish his report.

She had her own priority: completing the Christmas baskets. She had already distributed the food donations among them. Her special delivery had just arrived, so now it was time to finish things up.

Kate had wanted to personalize each gift, and she'd had the perfect idea. She just didn't know if she had time to accomplish her goal, but she wouldn't know unless she tried.

She'd just gathered all the supplies and settled at the table when there was a knock at her door. She wasn't expecting anyone, but maybe it was her aunt with a question about the dress.

Kate crossed to the door and swung it open to find Wes standing there. His hair was scattered, as though he'd been raking his fingers through it. And his brow was knit with worry.

Her initial elation dissolved. "Wes, is something wrong?"

He shook his head. "I just needed to get away from the office for a while."

She opened the door wide. "Come in."

He entered, stamping his boots on the doormat. "I hope I'm not bothering you." He glanced toward the table and then back at her. "Maybe I should have called first."

"Nonsense. Take your coat off."

He took off his coat and slipped off his boots, then followed her to the table where she had a pile of craft supplies.

"Looks like you're busy," he said.

"I am. Do you want to help?"

He held up his hands and took a step back. "I don't have an artistic bone in my body."

She looked at him skeptically. "When was the last time you tried a craft?"

"Um, junior high?"

The image of the angel ornament came to her mind, and her heart glowed. "That's right. I have evidence of your artistic ability. Have a seat." She pulled out a chair for him. "You're not getting away."

He snapped his fingers in mock resignation as he gave her a smile that sent her heart tripping over itself. "You can't blame me for trying."

She scrunched up her face, trying to scowl, but she failed and instead ended up smiling. How could she not? He filled her with giddiness. "As long as you help, you're off the hook."

"Okay, just tell me what I'm supposed to do."

"We're going to make Christmas tree and reindeer bookmarks." There was a slight tremble in her hands as she picked up a couple of bookmarks she'd just completed. She hoped he didn't notice her reaction to his nearness.

"Bookmarks?"

She nodded. "It's for the Christmas baskets."

"That's an interesting addition. I take it there are a lot of readers in Bayberry."

"I hope so." She waved for him to follow her down the steps to the garage. Then she pulled back a tarp that covered case after case of boxes. "The bookmarks go with these."

He stared at the boxes. "May I ask what's in them?"

"Books." She had an extra book that hadn't been wrapped. She picked it up and handed it to him.

Their fingers brushed. Neither moved for a moment. Did he feel it too—the electrical charge arcing between them?

And then he pulled away. That wasn't what she'd been hoping for. But he was here with her, so that was a good sign.

Wes glanced at the colorful book cover. "What's it about?"

She swallowed hard, hoping that when she spoke that her voice didn't betray her. "It's a Christmas story about a family finding their holiday spirit. It's for readers of all ages. And I hope everyone enjoys it as much as I did."

"But how did you get all these? I mean, they must have cost you a fortune."

"Actually, when I talked to the publishers about purchasing them wholesale for our Christmas baskets, they offered to donate them."

"You are amazing." He looked truly impressed.

"That's one of the things I love about this time of year. It brings out the very best in people. If only it could be Christmas all year long."

He helped her place the tarp back over the boxes. "So how many bookmarks have you made so far?"

"Um..." She worried her bottom lip. "Well, um, none."

"Kate, Christmas Eve is almost here. How are you going to get them all done in time?"

"With a little help." Her eyes pleaded with him. In truth, she welcomed the excuse for him to stay longer. "Come on."

Once upstairs, Wes volunteered to cut the paper and Kate started gluing the pieces together and adding small googly eyes to the reindeer and sequins to the Christmas trees. Luckily, the patterns she'd picked for the square bookmarks were not that complicated, and they moved through them quickly.

Somewhere along the way, they ordered pizza. She was pleased to learn he liked the same topping she did: pepperoni only. Though she was tempted to see it as a sign that they were destined to be more than friends, she had to laugh at herself. It was pizza. Nothing more.

It was growing close to midnight by the time they called it a night. The table, the kitchen counters and every other surface was covered with bookmarks. On the chairs and the floor were scattered bits of brown, red and green paper, as well as glittery sequins here and there.

As they moved toward the door, Wes yawned. "I hate to leave you with this mess."

She glanced over her shoulder. It was nothing she couldn't deal with herself. "Don't worry. I've got this. And you need some rest."

"What about you? Don't tell me you're going to stay up all night cleaning this up."

"Okay. I won't tell you." She grinned up at him.

"Kate." The deep timbre of his voice caused warm sensations in her chest.

She swallowed. "It won't take me long. The vacuum will pick up most of it. Stop worrying."

After his boots and coat were on, he turned to her. "I had a really marvelous time with you tonight."

Was it her imagination or were they drawing closer together? Because right about now, if she were to lean a little closer and rise up on her tiptoes, their lips would meet. It took everything she had to resist the temptation.

And then, realizing that she was staring at him without saying a word, she blurted, "You never did say why you stopped over this evening."

"I didn't?" He shook his head. "It doesn't matter."

"Are you sure?"

"I'm positive. I can't remember the last time I've had such a wonderful Christmas. And that's all thanks to you. If I were in New York right now, my apartment wouldn't be decorated and all I'd be thinking about is work. But you've got me thinking about reindeer and Christmas trees." His gaze dropped to her lips, causing her heart to pound. "And most of all, you've got me thinking that I so desperately want to do this..."

Was it really going to happen? Anticipation caused Kate's breath to catch. She willed him to her—willed his lips to meet hers.

He stepped forward and lowered his head. He really was going to kiss her. And she couldn't think of anything she wanted more. But she also knew what it was like to put your heart out there and have it broken.

No matter how much she cared about Wes, he was

leaving. Soon. He had never let her believe anything else. She would be foolish to kiss him—to fall for him even more than she already had.

Kate jumped back.

When his eyes met hers and she saw the confusion there, she said, "I'm sorry. I...I just can't. I want to. I really want to. But with you leaving..."

A moment of silence lingered between them. And then Wes looked at her as if he wanted to say something important. What was it? Would it change things?

He looked away, breaking their connection. "I understand. I should go. Thanks for a fun evening." He turned, opened the door and walked out.

Her lips pressed together in a firm line. Kate's stomach clenched in frustration. This wasn't how she wanted the night to end.

Why had she chickened out of letting him kiss her? It was just a kiss, after all—not a commitment. A kiss she could remember for the rest of her life. A moment to treasure.

She drew in a deep breath. She could do this. She could put herself out there, because Wes was worth it.

"Wes! Wait." She rushed out the door without a coat. "Wes!"

In that moment, she barely noticed the cold or the fresh snowflakes at the top of the steps leading down to the driveway. Her whole being was focused on this wonderful man, who had stopped on the first step and turned to her.

She flew to him and wrapped her arms around his

neck. Even on the step above him, she had to rise up on her toes.

For a moment, his eyes flashed with surprise. In the next heartbeat, his hands clasped her waist. He lowered his head.

And they met in the middle.

In that moment, time stood still. His lips caressed hers and her heart pounded with a very distinct *thump-thump, thump-thump*. Everything in the world faded away but the two of them.

His kiss was gentle but firm. He tasted sweet, with a bit of spice, like the gingerbread cookie she'd shared with him. Her heart pounded so loudly, it echoed in her ears. Could he hear it? Did he have any idea how special he made her feel?

As his lips moved over hers, it was though her feet were floating above the ground. Nothing had ever felt so right. And she never wanted this moment to end. Not ever.

And then...the sound of a door opening and closing down the block brought Kate back to reality. With great reluctance, she pulled back. She wasn't sure what to say, and so she settled for, "Goodnight."

Wes smiled. "Goodnight."

Kate stood rooted in place until he was down the steps and around the corner. Once he was out of sight, she realized she was cold—very cold. She ran back inside and danced around trying to warm up.

All the while, she couldn't stop smiling. She refused to let the unknown future steal away her giddy happiness right now.

This night had been perfect. And the dance was

coming up very soon. She imagined how amazing that night would be, whirling around the dance floor in Wes's arms.

Maybe she couldn't have forever with him, but they had the here and now. That had to be enough. Didn't it?

# Chapter Twenty-Three

*H*E COULDN'T STOP THINKING ABOUT that kiss. The stirring, life-altering kiss.

The next morning, Wes was at the work early. The office was quiet and empty. The company had fulfilled all of its last-minute holiday orders and was now closed until after the New Year.

After speaking with Penney the day before, Wes had to hurry to implement their plan. His gut was tied up in knots. Would it all work out?

If the candle company went under, there wouldn't be a town for his mother to move to. Without work, people would move away. Businesses would close. And Kate would be forced to leave her beloved Bayberry.

He had to do something to give Kate the most special Christmas present ever—her home. This place was more than a town—it was a home, with heart—a place that welcomed strays like him—a place where neighbors helped neighbors.

He didn't know how it had become his responsibility to save Bayberry, but he couldn't just turn his back and walk away. He didn't believe in Santa, but someone—or something—had had a hand in bringing him back here. He had the know-how to develop a plan to save this community. And that's exactly what he was working on—

*Buzz. Buzz.*

He glanced down at his phone, hoping it was a business contact returning his early morning call. It wasn't. In fact, it was the last person he wanted to speak to at this point—the big boss. Wes groaned inwardly.

He thought of letting the call go to voicemail, but he knew that sooner or later he'd have to deal with Mr. Summers. And this call might have something to do with the pending promotion.

He grabbed his phone. "Mr. Summers, good morning."

"I need you back in the office." The older man's tone was brusque.

Wes wasn't sure what to make of his boss's request. "I have airline reservations for New Year's Eve."

"That's not soon enough. Reschedule your flight."

Wes's jaw tightened. His molars ground together. They'd previously agreed on this schedule. He didn't like being jerked around. "I haven't completed my work." Mr. Summers didn't need to know that his work now included saving the company. "I just need a little more time." Wes's gaze searched the desk for another convincing excuse. "I don't have the report completed."

"By now, you should have pulled all of the relevant data. You can finish analyzing it here. I expect you in my office with what you have at eight a.m. Wednesday."

"Christmas Eve?" Then, realizing it probably wasn't the best response, Wes added, "I just thought you might have other plans that day."

"I don't. And I know you don't, not if you're still interested in that promotion."

Of course he was. He'd sacrificed a lot over the years in order to meet unrealistic deadlines. How could his boss question his dedication?

"Yes, sir," he said firmly. "I am."

They wrapped up the conversation. Wes leaned back in his chair, knowing that his plan would have to go into overdrive. He had today and tomorrow to lay the groundwork. Luckily, he had Penney's support. She was busy making phone calls. She'd also been willing to keep his plan in confidence. He wasn't going to mention it to Kate and get her hopes up—not until it was a sure thing.

And when his plan worked out, he wanted to give her the most special Christmas ever.

As the candle company was closed from now until the New Year, Kate had thrown herself into her last-minute holiday details—like shopping. She'd invited Aunt Penney to join her, but her aunt had said that she had some business obligations to attend to. Kate had offered to help, but her aunt wouldn't hear of it.

And so Kate set out on the snowy morning alone. She'd put off shopping until the last minute, but it also provided her with an excuse not to rush to Wes.

She didn't want to appear too eager after that spine-tingling kiss.

They had exchanged texts since then, but just friendly notes—things like good morning, how's it going? and other banalities that had absolutely nothing to do with their romantic moment or figuring out where to go from here. There was no point in rushing things. Why ruin this new and exciting turn of events?

Kate had set off down Main Street on a mission. Judging by the large crowd of people hustling down the sidewalk with arms full of packages, she wasn't the only one doing last-minute shopping.

Why did she always put off shopping for gifts? Every year she told herself she'd start early and have it all done by early December. And every year, she found herself rushing around just days before Christmas.

Fortunately, her shopping trip was quite successful. In addition to the coffeemaker, she found a beautiful burgundy scarf and matching gloves for Aunt Penney. As for Fred, it was no secret he had a sweet tooth. So she bought him a huge tin filled on one side with caramel corn, and with kettle corn on the other.

Of her friends, Sadie was the easiest to shop for, as she loved books. Kate had picked out a thriller that looked like a page-turner. For Carrie, she'd picked out a cupcake recipe book, to encourage her to reach for her dreams and open her own bakery. Abby was the hardest to shop for...until Kate spotted a purple sweater in a shop window. It was Abby's favorite color.

From all appearances, Martha would be spending Christmas with them. And though Kate had a lot to learn about Wes's mother, she knew the woman loved chocolate. That left Wes. Nothing like saving the hardest for last.

She wanted just the right gift for Wes. Their time together had meant a lot to her and she wanted to give him something to remember her by. So far, she'd purchased a sweater and black leather gloves, but she had nothing for him that was unique or memorable.

The rest of her shopping would have to wait, though. She and Wes had agreed to deliver the Christmas baskets at lunchtime.

She headed to his B&B, but he wasn't there. Knowing how hard he'd been working, she headed to the candle company. She couldn't wait to see him. She had absolutely no idea how she was going to stand the distance when he returned to New York, but she shoved aside the disturbing thought. She'd deal with it later.

Although she hadn't been able to find anything special for him in the stores, she did have something she'd made him the night before. She hadn't been sure about giving it to him, but in the light of day, she was feeling more courageous. And she didn't want to wait until Christmas Day.

Kate hurried home, picked up the little gift and headed to the office. The building was quiet and dark, but when she made her way to his office, she found the lights on. Wes was nowhere in sight. But he must be around, because his laptop was open on the desk. She moved behind the desk and looked for the right place to leave the heart-shaped bookmark and a copy of *The History of Bayberry*.

When she cleared a space next to his laptop, a folder fell to the floor and papers scattered. She sighed at her clumsiness. She knelt down to pick up the papers. As she did, her gaze skimmed over the sheets.

"Bayberry Candle Company" was printed across the top of each sheet. The breath caught in her throat. This was it—the evaluation of the company.

Kate knew she shouldn't look, but it was like watching a train accident: You just couldn't turn away. As she assembled the pages in numeric order, she noticed on the next-to-last sheet a header that read: "Conclusions."

Her heart clenched. She stared at the words.

*Please let it be a vote to keep the business operating.*

*Please. Please. Please.*

Her gaze skimmed down the page. And then it stopped.

Her heart stopped too.

"Recommendation: sell."

*Sell? No. No. No. That can't be right.*

She read it again. But that was exactly what it said. Her worst nightmare had come to life.

At the sound of footsteps, she hurriedly put everything back as she'd found it. She reached for the book, but she fumbled it, and the book landed on the floor with a loud thud. She leaned over, picked it up and rushed out the door. She couldn't talk to Wes, not right now. A storm of emotions choked up her throat.

Kate blinked repeatedly as she found her way to the back exit. Fortunately, her rubber-soled boots didn't make a sound on the tile floor as she made her escape.

"Kate?" The familiar male voice echoed down the hallway.

She came to a halt. She knew that deep, rich voice could only belong to one person: Wes.

A wave of conflicting feelings washed over her. She was excited to see him after that toe-curling kiss. And yet she was upset with him for recommending the sale of the candle company. The logical part of her brain told her it was just a function of his job—the reason he was in Bayberry. But she couldn't dismiss the disappointment that he'd confirmed the worst possibility.

As Wes approached, Kate stood frozen, torn between throwing her arms around his neck to repeat that unforgettable kiss, and telling him what she thought of his report in no uncertain terms. Instead she did neither, and just stood immobile as he blocked her way out of the building.

"Kate, I was hoping to catch up with you. Today's the Christmas basket thing, isn't it?"

She nodded, not trusting her voice.

He cleared his throat. "Something has come up. I won't be able to go with you. I'm sorry. I hate to leave you shorthanded—"

"It's okay." She hoped her voice sounded normal. She just had to keep her emotions in check for a few more moments. "I should be going. Excuse me."

"What's wrong?"

"I...I have to find someone to help with the baskets. Excuse me."

He moved to the side. "Sorry."

She brushed past him.

"Kate?"

She kept going, forcing herself to walk instead of run, but she didn't want him to see her face. She was losing her tenuous hold on her emotions.

How could he act as if everything was normal? Did he know what he was going to do to this town? Her heart broke, imagining this small community shattering, everyone going in different directions. None of their lives would ever be the same. Her past and future were gone.

# Chapter Twenty-Four

$\mathcal{T}$HE NEXT DAY, KATE STILL couldn't process the news.

The Bayberry Candle Company would not exist in the New Year. The thought hurt her heart. How did one accept that an era was about to end? Her family legacy was over. She thought of going to her aunt, but she wasn't in any frame of mind to talk. Not yet.

Kate hadn't seen Wes since they'd bumped into each other at the office, as she'd been busy well into the evening delivering baskets and spreading Christmas cheer that she no longer felt.

She reached for her phone and saw Wes had texted her: *Can we talk about the other night?* He wanted to talk about the kiss, but right now, her thoughts were on the report. How did he feel about his report? Was it just business as usual? Or was it tearing him up too?

She started to text him back, but then stopped. She backspaced. The things that needed to be said should be done in person. And today there was no time to seek him out. Her holiday obligations kept her busy—kept her from absorbing the full import of the devastation it would wreak on her town, her friends.

She'd borrowed a van from work and had set off with Carrie to pick up the flowers for the dance. It shouldn't have taken them too long to get to Burlington and back—just a few hours at most. But on the way back, it'd started to snow again. This snowstorm had come out of nowhere and was about to bury them—just like the mounting bad news.

Kate turned up the windshield wipers and let up on the accelerator. She just had to stay focused on the road, not the throbbing ache in her chest. Soon they'd be back in Bayberry, where there were more Christmas baskets waiting to be delivered. If this was to be the last Christmas before things changed, she would not let her friends down. She would soldier through, even if it felt as though her heart were breaking.

She could only hope that Wes and Penney would wait until after the holidays to let everyone know that the candle company would be sold, at best, or at worst, closed. Either way, her merry Christmas was ruined.

The hum of the motor and the crunch of the tires on the salted roads was monotonous. It allowed her mind free rein to consider the "what ifs" and "might haves." None of which did anything but make Kate more frustrated that she hadn't been able to do more.

While Carrie texted on her phone, Kate turned on the radio, hoping the music would distract her. But every mention of "making spirits bright" mocked her mood. She turned the radio off.

"What'd you do that for?" Carrie asked. "It was better than your silence."

"I'm sorry. I just have a lot on my mind."

"I thought you'd be excited that we were able to get these flowers for free."

"Only because someone had to cancel a wedding."

"At least they're not going to waste."

Kate peered through the snow hitting the windshield. "I'm beginning to wonder if we'll make it back to town before the storm kicks into full gear."

"Last I checked, we had another couple of hours before the worst of it was supposed to hit." Carrie paused. "I don't think it's the weather that's making you so quiet. You have something on your mind. And I don't think it's the dance."

Kate hadn't mentioned kissing Wes to Carrie or anyone else. She didn't know why. Maybe because it hadn't meant anything. Right?

Carrie stared at her. "Kate? Tell me what's on your mind. After all, we're stuck in this van together."

Kate sighed. "We kissed. Wes and I kissed."

"That's great!"

Kate shook her head as her fingers tightened on the steering wheel. "I don't know. In fact, I'm pretty sure it's the opposite."

"Why? Isn't he a good kisser?"

Kate's mind filled with the memory of being held in Wes's arms. "That's definitely not the problem."

"So what's bothering you?"

The problem was that he'd done his job, like he said he would do—fair and impartial. What had she wanted him to do? Lie? That wouldn't have helped anyone.

Now that she'd had time to calm down, she realized that Wes hadn't done anything wrong. It wasn't his fault the candle company had fallen on hard times. And that's what she'd tell him when they got back to town—

There was a blur of movement on the road ahead. A deer?

Kate stomped on the brakes.

The van started to fishtail. Her heart leapt into her throat. She eased up on the brakes. They were in trouble. She pumped the brakes. The van continued to slide.

With her fingers in a death grip on the steering wheel, her whole focus was on the blur of road whirling by them. She cut the wheel to one side and then the other, steering into the skid.

She felt a bump as the tires went over the berm. The van slid off the road and rolled to a stop in a snowdrift. For a moment, Kate didn't move. She continued to cling to the steering wheel as her heart pounded in her chest.

Then she turned to her friend, and was shocked to see how pale Carrie looked.

"Carrie, are you okay?"

Her friend nodded, staring straight ahead.

"Carrie, say something. Please."

Carrie turned to her, eyes wide and mouth open. It took a moment, and then she said, "What happened?"

"There was something in the road. A deer, I think. It all happened so fast."

"That was scary. Are you okay?"

Kate nodded. "Let's see if we can get out of here."

She put the van in reverse and pressed lightly on

the gas. The engine revved. The tires spun. But the van didn't budge. She tried again. And again.

She gave up and put the van in park. "We're not getting out of here without some help."

Carrie tapped at her phone. "I'm not getting a signal."

"Let me try." Kate picked up her phone. "Me neither. So much for calling for help."

"I saw a farm a ways back," Carrie said. "They might have a tractor to pull us out."

Kate smiled with relief. "I like the way you think."

She pushed her door open and hopped out, and promptly sank up to her knees in the deep snow. This just wasn't her week.

Everything was set.

The plan was in motion.

The decisions were made.

And now, Wes had one more important thing to do: speak to Kate. He dialed her cell. It went straight to voicemail. Frustration churned in his gut.

This wasn't how he wanted to leave things between them. He couldn't leave town without letting her know that he'd be back. So he left her a message.

He'd been so busy wrapping up things with the candle company that he hadn't had any spare time to spend with her. He'd literally lived at the office for the last two days. He recalled the disappointment in Kate's eyes when he'd told her he couldn't accompany her to hand out the Christmas baskets. And for that, he felt bad. He felt bad about a lot of things lately, but if his plan worked out, everything would be different. Better. And he hoped she'd forgive him.

Once he returned to the New York office and took care of business, he hoped he'd be able to return to Bayberry and stay until the New Year. He couldn't think of any place he'd rather spend the holidays. And then there was the person he wanted to spend those holidays with—Kate.

Wait. He was supposed to stay in New York, awaiting the announcement of the promotion. Wasn't that where his thoughts should be? How had he forgotten what was most important to him?

For so long now, he'd made his career the sole focus of everything he did. His drive to live and work in one spot had been all he'd thought of in college. He'd sworn that he wouldn't move around from job to job like his father. And here he was, thinking that Bayberry was the place to be—where he wanted to live. But what would that mean for his career?

It was too late now. He had too much invested in his job in the city. He had to keep climbing that corporate ladder...didn't he?

And if he did, what did that mean for him and Kate? He already knew how much she loved this town. There was no way she would leave it. And he couldn't ask her to. He knew what Bayberry meant to her—that's why he'd been doing everything he could to save her family's business and her town.

Conflicting thoughts raced through his mind as he made his way through the empty offices of the candle company. The only thing he could do now was to pack up and make his way to the airport. He needed to be at that important meeting with his boss first thing in the morning.

Wes packed his laptop. And then he gathered his files. In his rush, he knocked a pen off the desk. He bent over to retrieve it. It was then that a piece of red paper under the desk caught his attention.

He reached out and picked it up. It was in the shape of a heart, and it glittered with sequins. He knew those sequins. He'd glued hundreds of them to the Christmas tree bookmarks. This heart-shaped bookmark was from Kate. It was why she'd visited him yesterday.

A smile pulled at his lips. He turned over the book-mark and found writing on the backside:

*To the most amazing man—*
*You made this Christmas sparkle.*
*Love, Kate*

In that moment, it felt as though his heart grew three sizes. He read the short message again. And again. And again.

He had to get back to Bayberry soon—to get back to Kate. He couldn't wait to escort her to the Candle-light Dance. He had a very special Christmas present to give her there. He couldn't wait.

Thanks to the kindness of strangers, the day was saved.

Sort of.

After the farmer used his tractor to pull the van

out of the ditch, Kate and Carrie made it safely back to Bayberry. But it didn't change the candle company's dire fate. For the rest of the drive home, Kate kept thinking "This can't be happening." Wes was recommending the end of Bayberry Candles as she'd always known it. Tears stung her eyes. She blinked them away.

Of course, she'd always known that selling the company was a possibility, but she didn't think it would actually happen. Her heart felt as though it'd been torn in half.

And to make matters worse, when they got back, she overheard MaryJane telling someone that Wes had returned to New York. Her tattered heart was dealt another blow. No date for the Candlelight Dance. Not even so much as a goodbye.

And yet she forced a smile to her lips and shared holiday greetings with her neighbors and friends as people arrived to help with the finishing touches for the dance. All the while, she felt like such a liar. Inside she knew that this was the last happy Christmas they would spend together, because come the New Year, their entire lives would change. Some huge faceless corporation would swoop in and change absolutely everything. She blamed herself. If only she'd acted sooner. Done more.

The cloudy skies had brought on the December evening even earlier than usual, but Kate didn't care. The darkness fit her mood as she walked home. The long shadows shielded her sadness from passersby.

The only reason she'd been able to put on a show of cheerfulness that day was because she'd wanted all her friends to have one last merry Christmas together.

This town, like a family, had stuck together over the decades through every imaginable event, both good and bad. Bonds had been formed that were stronger than steel. And Christmas was the most special time of the year.

"Kate!" An unfamiliar male voice called her name.

She didn't want to talk to anyone. She was tempted to keep walking, but she hadn't been raised to be rude. With great reluctance, she paused and turned back. There stood Santa in his red costume. This time he wasn't ringing a bell or standing next to a red kettle. His piercing gaze connected with hers. Sympathy shone in his eyes as he approached her.

"Cheer up, Kate."

The fact that Santa felt sorry for her made her feel even worse. She shook her head. "Not today."

"Kate, remember your Christmas wish. Don't give up. Just believe."

She didn't know what he was talking about. She started walking away. Still, she couldn't help but think back to the tree-lighting ceremony with Wes. She'd wished for a miracle to save Bayberry.

But how would this guy dressed as Santa know what she'd wished for? She hadn't mentioned it to anyone. She stopped and turned to ask him, but he was gone.

She scanned both sides of the street. No one dressed up as Santa was anywhere in sight. How did he keep disappearing in the blink of an eye?

She continued walking down the sidewalk. Then she heard his voice again. "Just believe."

Kate glanced all around. He was nowhere to be seen. It must have been her imagination. Her mind was working overtime. She pulled her hood low and kept walking.

At last, she reached her aunt's driveway. Just a few more steps and she'd be in her garage apartment, away from prying eyes. And she wouldn't have to put on a show any longer. She could curl up on her couch and maybe lose herself in a movie and a bowl of rocky road ice cream—

"Kate? Is that you?" Aunt Penney stepped outside with a bag of trash in her hand.

Kate crossed to her. "Here. Let me take that for you."

Her aunt handed over the bag. "Thank you."

"Of course." Kate carried the bag to the trash bin and dropped it in. Not wanting to face her aunt's all-knowing stare, she turned toward her apartment and called over her shoulder, "Let me know if you need anything else."

Aunt Penney appeared to be in her usual good mood. Wes obviously hadn't shared his ominous conclusion about the candle company with her. Kate thought about mentioning it. After all, her aunt still owned the company. She should know. But the words tasted bitter in the back of her mouth. She wasn't sure she could actually get them out without losing her tentative hold on her emotions.

And her aunt seemed so happy now that she was spending so much time with Fred. They might not want to admit that they were a couple, but everyone in town knew there was love between those two. Why ruin her aunt's first Christmas with Fred?

Kate choked down the dismal news about the company. It would be her secret for Christmas—her gift to those she loved. Her feet felt weighted as she took another step.

"Kate, were you able to get the flowers for the dance?"

On the bottom step, Kate paused and turned to her aunt, hoping the light between the house and garage wasn't bright enough for her aunt to see the misery on her face. "Uh, yes. It just took a little longer than I expected."

Her aunt nodded. "Would you like to come inside? I have some fresh-baked banana bread. And there's a pot of coffee—it's that new roast you love."

"Thanks, but I have some stuff I need to do." Kate hurried up the steps, knowing that if she lingered, her aunt would continue to press her until the whole sad tale came spilling out.

Once inside, Kate slipped off her boots and coat. She moved to the couch, not bothering to turn on the overhead lights or the television. She considered watching a movie, then dismissed the thought. In the glow of the Christmas tree lights, she kept thinking that if she'd done something different, things would never have reached this point.

And why had she ever thought Wes was on her side in this fight to save the candle company? He hadn't come to Bayberry to save it. He'd come to do his job. And he'd done it. Now he'd gone back to the city to present his findings—far away from her and the damage left behind.

*Tap. Tap.*

The door creaked open. "Kate?" Penney sounded concerned. The overhead light flicked on. "Oh, there you are."

Kate didn't trust her voice in that moment. A lump of emotions clogged her throat. She swiped at her eyes.

Aunt Penney gave her a look. "What's wrong?"

Where could she even begin? Kate's mind raced with thoughts of everything that had happened in the last two days. And then she settled on the least of the problems.

"Everything is okay. But Carrie and I slid into a ditch on the way home from Burlington."

"Oh dear." Aunt Penney's face creased with worry. "Are you sure you're both all right?"

Kate nodded. Then she proceeded to tell her aunt how the very kind farmer had helped them out.

"You must be tired after that big day."

"I'm fine. We were a little late putting up the remaining decorations for the dance, but a lot of people showed up and we got it done in no time."

"Good. This town is known for pulling together." Aunt Penney sat down in the chair opposite the couch. "But that's not what's bothering you, is it?"

Kate knew that eventually her aunt would get it out of her. Her aunt always had a way of reading her.

Kate shook her head.

"Is it Wes?"

Kate swallowed hard. "In a way."

"Do you want to talk about it? It might help."

"Not really." But maybe it was best if her aunt heard the bad news from her.

"I kissed him," Kate began. She told her aunt about the romantic moment she'd shared with Wes, and how she'd imagined it was the start of something real. And then she told Aunt Penney about the special bookmark she'd made for Wes. "When I went to give it to him at the office, I accidentally saw his report about the company. I didn't mean to read it, but now I can't unsee it." Her eyes met her aunt's. "And I think you should know, it isn't good. His recommendation is to sell."

Her aunt didn't say anything for a moment. Maybe she was in shock too. It was a lot to take in. After all, Bayberry Candles had been around for generations. It was part of their past, but it would no longer be part of their future.

"I know," Aunt Penney said.

"You know?" Kate wasn't sure she'd heard her correctly.

Her aunt nodded. "He came to me already and shared the results of his analysis."

"Really? Why didn't you tell me? What are you going to do? Maybe we don't have to sell. He could be wrong." But Kate didn't really believe it. This was Wes's area of expertise. Her gut told her that he'd provided a completely honest and unbiased recommendation.

"It's the right thing to do." Aunt Penney's voice was calm. "I know it's going to take some adjusting—"

"How can you say this?" Pain ripped Kate inside. "It doesn't matter who buys it, it'll never be the same."

"Aren't you the one who tells me that sometimes change is for the best?"

She couldn't believe her aunt was using her own words against her. "But they'll automate things, outsource other things and lay off our employees."

"Stop. Nothing like that is going to happen, or I wouldn't have agreed to the sale." Aunt Penney reached out and took Kate's hand in hers, giving it a reassuring squeeze. "I need you to trust me. You do trust me, don't you?"

Kate trusted her aunt more than anyone in the world. She considered her aunt's words and calm demeanor. If Aunt Penney believed this was going to work out, she must have something really special planned.

"Of course I trust you." Kate squeezed her hand. "But what's the plan?"

"All will be revealed tomorrow." Aunt Penney smiled—not a little smile. but one that lit up her whole face and made her eyes twinkle. "And I have a sneaking suspicion this will be the very best Christmas ever."

Kate wished it were possible, but she didn't believe it. Wes's image flashed in her mind. And then she thought of going to the dance alone. This felt like the worst Christmas ever.

After her aunt left, Kate glanced at her phone and found a voicemail from Wes. She was torn between hearing what he had to say and just ignoring it. At last, her willpower failed and she played the message.

"Kate, I tried catching up with you, but you must be out running errands. I wish I was with you. Right now, I'm on my way to the airport. I have a mandatory meeting in the morning, so I had to return to New York. I'm really sorry to skip out on you..."

There was some static on the line. He said something else that she couldn't make out before the line went dead.

This evening required ice cream. Lots of ice cream. Kate grabbed the rocky road from the freezer and a large spoon. Not bothering with a bowl, she moved to the couch. She sank down, threw a blanket over her legs and turned on the television. *It's A Wonderful Life* was just starting. Somehow that seemed fitting. She just wished there was an angel in her life.

# *Chapter Twenty-Five*

CHRISTMAS EVE HAD ARRIVED AT Watson & Summers.

But it was far from merry.

Wes sat in his boss's office, where the silence was deafening. Mr. Summers sat behind his desk, paging through Wes's report. Christmas here at the office just wasn't the same as what Wes had come to expect in his few weeks in Bayberry. How had he forgotten what a real Christmas was like?

Christmas wasn't about trying to get a jump on the New Year. It wasn't about setting outrageous work-related goals for the next 365 days. It wasn't about chasing after a promotion. Christmas was about so much more.

It was about taking time to appreciate the many blessings in his life, both big and small. It was about spreading holiday cheer to old friends and new ones. Christmas was Bayberry. That small town emanated the spirit of the holiday.

He just hoped that some of its residents were able

to keep a secret—a Christmas secret—for a little while longer. He knew it was a lot to ask, but they'd all been willing to help him with a special surprise for Kate. Everyone loved Kate. How could they not?

"Wes, I've gone over your report and I must say you've done a thorough job." Mr. Summer's eyes met his across the desk. "And the recommendation to sell—I agree with it."

"Thank you, sir." Wes resisted the urge to tug at his shirt collar. It'd been weeks since he wore a tie, and now it felt too tight, too stifling. Or maybe it was his job that was making him feel this way. "I've been doing some thinking—"

"As have I since I received your initial report. I know of a national candle company that's looking to expand. They have the capital to invest in new equipment, and they'd consolidate their operations at their headquarters. This would be an ideal solution for everyone." Mr. Summers leaned back in his chair, looking pleased with himself.

Wes rolled the idea around in his head. He had an uneasy feeling in his gut. He knew about takeovers and buyouts. The acquired entities rarely stayed the same. In some instances, the products and/or recipes were moved to a new location. The original building was put up for sale. In other cases, there was just one thing the buyer wanted, and the rest of the business was broken up and sold off. And where would that leave Kate and the citizens of Bayberry?

Kate would be devastated. He would be devastated. The one thing he knew about Bayberry was that it was the perfect small town. And having big business swoop in was not going to be good for the town or its residents. Fortunately, he had an alternative.

Mr. Summers had been talking, but Wes had been distracted, missing most of what he'd said. Wes forced his concentration back to his. "And so I need you to take this proposal to Bayberry." Mr. Summers handed a red folder across the desk. "I'll need you to leave right away. I know it's not where you were planning to spend Christmas, but sometimes sacrifices must be made."

Wes's lips curved in a smile. He'd been planning to return to Bayberry before the dance anyway, but he wouldn't be taking Mr. Summers' red folder. "I'm sorry, sir, but the owner of the candle company has already agreed to a sale."

Mr. Summers' gray brows drew together into a formidable line. "Why am I just hearing about this? When did it happen?"

"It's very recent. The details are still being ironed out."

"Are you sure Ms. Taylor won't change her mind?"

"I'm sure, Mr. Summers."

The older man's frown deepened. "I was counting on making this sale for my client, but I must commend you for being proactive. You beat me to the punch. I like that. I've come to realize that you take each and every task seriously. It doesn't matter if it's a big account or a small one, you give your all. And that's what we need around here."

Wes couldn't believe it. After all this time wishing, hoping and waiting for a promotion, he was about to get it. Not so long ago, this would have made his Christmas perfect. But now, the excitement was lacking. The thought of staying here and fighting the hustle and bustle of city life on his own didn't have the same draw.

"Wes, did you hear me? I'm promoting you to assistant vice president. I'll have your things moved to a windowed office after the first of the year. For some reason, maintenance takes time off between Christmas and New Year's." Mr. Summers pursed his lips and shook his head. "Come the beginning of the year, we'll meet again. I have a lot of new projects for you. There's no time to waste."

New projects meant more overtime—weekends spent in the office. The prestige of working in Manhattan had lost its luster. Wes's thoughts returned to Bayberry, where work was balanced with life. And overtime at the candle company was sporadic, not a regular occurrence. And then there was Kate—beautiful Kate.

Wes cleared his throat. "Sir, I want to thank you for your faith in me and my abilities."

Mr. Summers smiled as he crossed his arms over his chest. "I know you can handle whatever's thrown at you. If you want, I can give you some of the projects I need you to jump on now."

"Thank you, sir, but that won't be necessary."

Mr. Summers was confused. "What won't be necessary?"

"I learned a lot while I was in Bayberry. I realized I don't have to sacrifice my life just to have the stability I always wanted. It doesn't have to be a tradeoff. Sometimes you really can have it all."

"What?" Mr. Summers leaned forward with a concerned look. "Wes, are you feeling all right?"

"I've never felt better." And he meant it. This decision was the right one for him. "Mr. Summers, I'm sorry, but I can't accept your promotion. In fact, I'm resigning."

The man sputtered. It was apparent he wasn't used to people turning him down. "You're making a mistake. Take the holiday and think this over." When Wes shook his head, Mr. Summers said, "You drive a hard bargain, but you're going to go far. I...I'll throw in a corner office."

Wes shook his head and smiled. "My mind is made up. My future is in Bayberry."

Mr. Summers looked utterly perplexed as he stood and shook Wes's extended hand. "All right, then, if you're sure. I wish you all the best."

"Thanks. Merry Christmas." Wes made his way out of the office.

Jan came rushing up to him. "Did I overhear you correctly? Are you really leaving us?"

He nodded. He had thought he'd be a wreck, wondering if he'd done the right thing, but he was calm and certain. He'd made the right decision, and if he had to do it over, the only thing he'd do was follow his heart to Bayberry sooner.

"Oh." Behind the woman's round glasses, there were tears in her eyes. "You're going to be missed."

"I'll miss you too. And your mother's baking."

Jan dabbed at her eyes. "I just can't imagine never seeing you again. You're just like one of my kids, only better behaved."

He knew what a great honor that comparison was, and he didn't take it lightly. "Maybe you and your family could come visit. After all, Bayberry isn't that far away. And they have a wonderful B&B."

Her eyes widened. "I love that idea. So tell me, is there a certain young woman involved in this decision?"

"As a matter of fact, there is." He smiled when he thought of Kate.

Jan clapped her hands together as an answering smile lit up her face. "I knew it. I'll be expecting a wedding invitation—"

"Slow down. It hasn't gotten that far. But when it does, consider yourself invited."

Jan beamed. "I'm so happy for you. Can I give you a hug?"

"Of course. Merry Christmas."

After they embraced, Wes headed for his desk and booked himself on the next available flight back to Vermont. Next, he placed a very important phone call to the Bayberry real estate agent, Mary Trimble. The call didn't take long. And then he set to work cleaning out his desk. It was surprising how little personal stuff he kept there.

Not much longer, and he'd be at the airport waiting to board his flight home. Home. The word sounded good to him. And this time, home meant more than a place to hang his coat and rest his head at night. This time, home meant love and friendship, and so much more.

# Chapter Twenty-Six

$K$ATE SAT ON THE COUCH with a single light on.
There was no Christmas music playing. There were no Christmas movies on the television. And the Christmas tree was darkened.

Her holiday spirit had deserted her.

It was Christmas Eve. The most wonderful, magical time of the holiday, and she was supposed to be getting ready for the dance.

Her gaze moved to her phone. There had been no word from Wes since he'd left town. She told herself not to expect to hear from him again. His life was in the city, and all she'd been was a distraction on a business trip. Nothing more.

Though it had felt like more to her. She couldn't stop thinking about that kiss, and how much fun they'd had. Their time together had meant so much more to her than she thought possible.

There was no point in going to the dance alone. She wouldn't be able to paint a believable smile on her face. And the town had really come together to put on the best dance ever. They deserved to enjoy it.

Her gaze moved to the dress her aunt and Wes's mother had made for her. It was hanging near the front door on the key rack. They'd draped it in plastic to keep it clean until she put it on for the dance. She didn't know where she would wear it, but she promised herself that she wouldn't let their efforts go to waste.

She couldn't just sit here. She needed to do something. Cleaning? Yes, she would clean and work out some of her frustration. And after all the baking she'd done for the holidays, her kitchen could use a good going-over.

She moved to the kitchen and flipped on the lights. Once the water was steaming hot, she filled the sink and added some cleaning fluid. The lemony scent filled the air and gave her a boost of energy. She grabbed a dish cloth and set to work, clearing one countertop at a time, before washing the backsplash and then the counter. The more she thought about Wes leaving, the harder she scrubbed.

She didn't know how long she'd worked at it before there was a knock at the door. She wanted to ignore it, because she knew her aunt would want to know why she wasn't ready for the dance. And Kate didn't want to get into why she wasn't going. She didn't want to discuss Wes.

*Knock knock.*

Whoever it was wasn't going away. Kate tossed the cloth in the sink, wiped off her hands and crossed to the door. When she swung it open, she was surprised.

"Carrie, what are you doing here?"

Carrie, wearing a midnight blue satin dress with crystals embedded on the bodice, ran her gaze over Kate's black yoga pants and sweatshirt. "That's what you're wearing to the dance?"

"Of course not." Kate opened the door wider. "Come in."

Carrie stepped inside and closed the door against the cold winter evening. "A little dark in here, don't you think?"

"I was in the kitchen cleaning."

"And you forgot about the time?" Her friend wore a surprised expression. Everyone knew the Candlelight Dance was the absolute biggest event of the year. No one forgot about the dance.

"I'm not going." Kate turned and returned to the kitchen.

Carrie followed, hot on her heels. "What do you mean you're not going? If it wasn't for you, there wouldn't even be a dance. You have to go."

Kate shook her head as she wrung out the dish cloth to wipe down the stove. "It's not a good idea. I don't want to ruin everyone's good mood."

"Is this about Wes? I heard through the grapevine that he went back to New York."

Kate shrugged. "He completed his work. It was time for him to leave."

"Just like that, he's gone?" When Kate didn't respond, Carrie asked, "He'll be back, right?"

Kate shrugged again. She didn't want to have this discussion. Not at all. "I don't know."

"Didn't you ask him?"

She lowered her gaze as she tried to keep her emotions in check. She swallowed hard. "I didn't talk to him. He left me a voicemail. He sounded like he was in a big hurry."

"Did you tell him you wanted him to stay?"

Kate scrubbed extra hard, making the stovetop gleam. "I don't want to talk about him."

Carrie sighed. "Hiding from your feelings isn't going to help."

Kate stopped cleaning and turned to her friend. "I'm not hiding. He's the one who left."

"Yes, but did you ask him to stay?"

"No. His career is in New York. He's going to be an assistant vice president. How could he skip out on that? I knew what I was getting into. He never said he'd stay."

"But things have changed between you two. You love him. And he loves you." When Kate started to protest, her friend held up her hand. "You can't deny it, because it's obvious to anyone who sees you two together."

Did everyone think that? Was her love for Wes that obvious? For so long, she'd been denying it to herself. Had she denied it so thoroughly that Wes couldn't see it either? Did she need to tell him?

Kate worried her bottom lip as she considered what her friend had said.

"Kate, you need to call him. Tell him."

"I don't know." Would it change anything? "I need time to think."

"You two belong together. You're just fighting the inevitable. He'll be back. Just wait and see."

Her friend was so confident that it made Kate want to believe her. Maybe she should call him. It wasn't as if they'd parted on bad terms. If nothing else, they could catch up on what was going on with each other—his work and her...her dance. He was bound to ask how it had gone. What would she tell him?

"I'll call," she said. "But not yet."

"Okay. Have it your way, but you still have a dance to go to."

"Carrie, I can't."

"Yes, you can. Everyone adores you. We need you there. And tonight is about Christmas, community and love. Please come."

Kate's gaze moved to the dress still hanging by the door. Carrie followed her eyes. She rushed over to the dress and took it off the hook.

"You have to go, if nothing else to wear the dress that your aunt and Wes's mother took time to make just for you. The whole town is waiting to see you in it. You don't want to disappoint them, do you?"

Kate shook her head. She'd already disappointed enough people.

"Good." Carrie gently propelled Kate toward the bedroom. "Go get changed. I'll wait."

Kate took the dress and headed for the bedroom. She couldn't believe Carrie had talked her into going. But it would certainly beat staying home, thinking about the candle company and mourning Wes's absence.

She was soon dressed. She did her makeup, and then Carrie fixed her hair in a festive style that included long barrel roll curls. She finished her outfit with earrings made of red bows and jingle bells.

Kate moved to the mirror. Aunt Penney and Martha had outdone themselves. Kate's gaze moved down over the simple white bodice with short sleeves. She'd added a sterling silver locket she'd inherited from her mother. Inside was a picture of her as a baby and one of her father as a young man. Kate's fingers touched the pendant as a wave of love and loss, in equal parts, washed over her. It didn't matter how many Christmases came and went, she still missed her parents.

She lowered her hand, smoothing it down over the high-waisted band of satin. It transitioned into a pleated full navy blue and bronze-striped midi skirt. And when she twirled in front of the mirror, it fluffed out just a bit. She laughed when she realized that after all these years, she loved it when her skirts fluffed up like a princess gown. Maybe there was still some childhood wonder left in her, but was it enough to believe in miracles? Was her aunt right? Would this be a great Christmas? Or was it just wishful thinking on her aunt's part?

"Wow! You look amazing." Carrie's voice drew Kate from her thoughts.

"It's all thanks to Aunt Penney and Martha. They did an incredible job. It fits perfectly." And then, just because she could, she twirled in front of the mirror once more.

Carrie smiled at her. "It's good to see you enjoying the moment."

"I'm trying." Inside, her heart ached for what might have been if Wes hadn't left. But for tonight, she would put on a happy face. "We'd better go, or we'll be late."

"Agreed."

They rushed out the door. Since the hall was close by, they opted to walk, as parking would be absolutely impossible. They decided to carry their heels and change into them at the dance. And so in her red coat and snow boots, Kate followed Carrie down the apartment steps.

They walked up Moose Way, where the sidewalks had been shoveled. They cut across on Valley Lane. At the intersection of Flatlander Way sat the old Victorian house where Wes had grown up. It was when they neared the For Sale sign that Kate came to a stop. There was a "Sold" banner on the sign.

For just a moment—a very brief moment—she wondered if Wes had bought the house. She knew how much he loved the place. He would be so happy living there.

In the next moment, she dismissed the idea. She was being utterly foolish. He was gone. His home—his future was in New York. Kate's vision blurred. She blinked repeatedly.

"What's the matter?" Carrie asked.

Kate swallowed the lump in her throat. "The house." Her heart sank down to her fuzzy-lined snow boots. "It's been sold."

"Must have just happened. I didn't hear anyone mention it at the diner. I wonder who bought it?"

Kate's eyes stung. It was the final sign that Wes wouldn't be back. Her hope that he'd return to Bayberry was slipping away with each passing moment.

"Kate, are you all right?" It took Carrie a moment to put it together. "Wait. This is Wes's childhood home, isn't it?"

Kate nodded and then started walking again. It wouldn't help to linger. She was sure that whoever had bought the house would be happy there. It just wouldn't be Wes.

# Chapter Twenty-Seven

*C*OULD THIS REALLY BE THE last Candlelight Dance? An arrow of sorrow pierced Kate's heart.

And as much as she admired her aunt's brave and optimistic attitude, she couldn't help but worry. Kate looked around the room. So many people worked at the candle company. Would the buyer spare their jobs?

"You look like you lost your best friend." Worry reflected in Carrie's eyes.

That's how she felt. Still, Kate forced a smile. "I'm fine. Go ahead in. I'll be right there."

As she hung up her coat and slipped on her silver heels, she sighed. She had to do better than this. She'd told Aunt Penney she would trust her. After all, Aunt Penney cared about these people as much as she did. Her aunt would do what was best for Bayberry.

With an effort, Kate shoved her worries to the back of her mind. If tonight was to be Bayberry's final dance, she wanted to make it the best. And so she decided to concentrate on the here and now. Not the past and not the future, but this dance, and all the wonderful people who'd made it possible.

As she moved further into the great hall, she automatically starting searching the crowd for Wes's face. It took her a moment to realize what she was doing. She gave herself a mental shake. He had done his job and returned to New York City.

The hall was full of townspeople, young and old alike. Compliments abounded over Kate's new dress. And she gave full credit to her aunt and Martha. They were so talented, they could actually go into business together.

The dinner went smoothly, and everything tasted amazing. The covered dish idea had worked out after all. Everyone had brought their favorites, and there were smiles on every face.

Aunt Penney's gaze caught hers from across the room. Her aunt smiled, and then winked. It was the reassurance Kate needed.

Still, her thoughts turned to Wes. He should be here. He'd helped create this special evening. The ache in her heart was still so fresh, so raw. Her eyes stung with unshed tears. She blinked them away.

Just then "Rockin' Around The Christmas Tree" finished playing and the DJ took a break. Aunt Penney, in a festive red dress, and Fred, in a dark suit, red tie and Santa hat, moved to the podium. As they stood side by side, Kate thought fondly that they looked awfully cute together.

Kate was happy to see Fred moving without a limp, though she suspected he hadn't been as injured as her aunt had let on. Aunt Penney had been doing some matchmaking with her niece and Wes. But even with her best efforts, it hadn't worked out for them.

Fred took the mic. "Welcome to this year's Candlelight Dance. I know it's a bit different than it's been in the past, but I think this year is the best. What do you think?"

There was a round of applause.

Fred cupped his ear. "I can't hear you."

The applause grew louder, and there was some cheering. Kate couldn't help but smile. Wes's idea to take the dance back to the community and let them participate in the preparations had worked out so well. She wished he were here to see it. He would have been proud.

"Thank you for coming," Fred continued. "This is a very special year, as the whole town came together to make this tradition a reality, and you all did a mighty fine job. Give yourselves a round of applause." Thunderous applause reverberated off the walls. Once the clapping died down, Fred said, "And now Penney would like to say a few words."

Aunt Penney stepped up to the podium. "Merry Christmas. I'm so glad you all could make it. It just wouldn't be Christmas without everyone in Bayberry coming together. My family, well, they started this town. And I'm so grateful they did. I couldn't imagine living anywhere else. You all are the best." Aunt Penney swiped at her eyes and took a deep breath. "Look at me, getting all weepy. Anyway, I know there's been a rumor going around town about the candle company being in financial trouble." She paused. "It's true." A gasp went over the crowd, then Aunt Penney continued. "But I want to assure you all that we are not closing. I think the man who saved Bayberry should tell you more." Aunt Penney pointed toward the back of the room. "Could you make room for him?"

Kate, standing near the podium, turned as the crowd parted, and there at the back of the room stood Wes. Her heart launched into her throat. *He's back. He's back.* It was all she could think. But what did this mean?

Wes immediately sought out Kate in the crowd.

She looked absolutely stunning. Her long red-brown hair was curled and hung around her slim shoulders. Around her neck hung a silver locket that glinted beneath the lights. The white bodice of her dress fit her curves and connected to a knee-length skirt showing off her legs. And on her feet were delicate silver heels.

*Wow.* She took his breath away.

Kate was all he wanted for Christmas—if she would forgive him for slipping away to New York without speaking to her face to face. He had a good excuse. But would she hear him out?

When his eyes met hers once more, his heart beat erratically. She stared back at him with confusion.

Just seeing her, he knew he'd made the right decision. He'd never been more certain of anything in his life. The next thing would be to convince Kate that they belonged together.

He started for the podium, but he couldn't resist stopping beside Kate. Their eyes met again and held. "I was right," he murmured.

"Right about what?"

"You are the most beautiful woman in the room." He loved how the color rushed to her cheeks.

"Wes—"

"I know you have questions, and I promise to answer all of them. Just let me do this one thing first."

She hesitated, then nodded.

No one said a word as he stepped up to the mic. In fact, the room was so quiet you could hear a candle drop. He had a feeling there were going to be a lot of candles and references to candles in his future. And he couldn't think of anything he'd like more.

He cleared his throat. On the flight back to Vermont, he'd thought about what to say, but now all of those carefully planned words deserted him. He would have to go with what was in his heart.

"First off, Merry Christmas. It's a very special one, and my first, of what I hope to be many, in Bayberry." He knew he had to get to the point, as curious faces were watching him and waiting for the news. He shifted his weight from one foot to the other. "With Penney Taylor's permission, I have worked this past week to put together an offer to buy the Bayberry Candle Company. I think it's going to be a good thing for everyone—"

"Stop stalling," called out Mr. Plummer, the newspaper editor. "Who bought it?"

Fred, who was usually quiet, spoke up. "Let Wes speak. This is important."

Silence once again fell over the room.

Wes continued. "As I've already discussed with many of you, I believe the candle company can be updated and competitive once more. We have identified many cost-cutting opportunities and have already had some discussions regarding ways to expand revenues. In addition, Penney has agreed to sell a portion of the company and roll the proceeds back into the business to replace machinery and update other areas. In return, she'll be paid back with a portion of the sales. And to answer Mr. Plummer's question, the buyer is you. The employees of the historic Bayberry Candle Company."

A cheer went up in the crowd. Everyone started talking at once, making it impossible for Wes to finish what he was going to say.

His gaze zeroed in on Kate, whose mouth fell open.

Wes motioned unsuccessfully for people to quiet down. He turned to Kate and motioned for her to join him at the podium. She hesitated at first but then stepped up next to him.

As the crowd continued to cheer, Kate leaned toward Wes. "How is this possible?"

"After learning how important the candle company is to you and to the town, I started to think of ways to save it. I approached your aunt about selling a portion of the company to the employees. In turn, your aunt can take the proceeds and reinvest it in the company, making the necessary repairs and upgrades." Kate's beautiful eyes widened as he continued to explain. "Your aunt liked the idea enough to propose it to the employees. Everyone's agreed to invest a little in the company. We'll work out the details and sign the papers after the New Year."

Kate's mouth gaped. "Thank you. It's an amazing idea." A smile lifted her glossy lips as tears of joy shimmered in her eyes. "I can't believe it's all going to work out."

"Kate, all of these people," he gestured toward the excited crowd, "they believe in Bayberry—and they believe in you. And so do I." He turned back to the mic. "There's one employee with whom I haven't discussed this idea—and that person is Kate." He turned back to her. "Will you join the employees in the new candle company?"

She didn't even hesitate. "I will." That dazzling smile spread across her face.

Another cheer filled the room.

Wes was thrilled to be the bearer of good news. But the truth was, he couldn't have done any of this alone. He'd had the idea, but it was the people of Bayberry who were going to save their town. And he was happy about it, because he was planning to grow old here—with Kate, if she'd have him. But he was getting ahead of himself.

# Chapter Twenty-Eight

*W*AS THIS REALLY HAPPENING?
Had the company and its town really been saved?

Kate watched as Wes spoke to Aunt Penney and his mother. He was back. He was really here.

Kate's heart swelled with love. Love for this town, which had pulled together to save the Bayberry Candle Company. And love for Wes, the man she'd been waiting for all her life.

Aunt Penney had been right. This was the best Christmas ever. Relief washed over Kate. Her lips lifted into a huge smile as her happiness—the love she felt for everyone in the room—radiated from the inside out.

She realized that instead of trying to save the town single-handedly, it was going to take an entire village. And Bayberry was the best village ever.

Wes turned from Penney and Martha and came over to Kate. His eyes met and held hers. Her heart started to pound. Without evaluating her actions, she reached forward and hugged him.

When his arms wrapped around her waist, she relaxed against him. This was like coming home. She was still smiling. She couldn't stop. Not that she wanted to. Things were going to work out. She was sure of it now.

And then she whispered in his ear, "You are the best Santa ever."

His voice was deep and full of emotion. "I had a lot of help."

"But without you, none of this would have been possible."

With great reluctance, she pulled back, the smile still on her lips. Wes took her hand in his and led her away from the podium.

"Wait, everyone." Fred stepped back up to the mic. "Before we get to celebrating, I have something to say." He looked around for Penney, who was chatting with Martha off to the side of the podium. "Penney, could you join me?"

Aunt Penney looked confused, but stepped up next to him. "Fred, what are you up to?"

He took her hands in his. "I've been meaning to say this for a very long time, but it was never the right time. I've already waited too long, and I can't put it off a minute longer."

Kate stifled a gasp, pressing a hand to her mouth. This was it. He was going to do it. Happy tears blurred her vision and she blinked repeatedly.

Fred dropped to his knee and held up a red velvet box. "Penney, I've loved you for as long as I can remember. I'd love to spend the rest of my life with you. Will you marry me?"

All eyes turned to Penney, who had tears of joy in her eyes too. "Yes. Yes, I'll marry you."

Fred stood and swept her up in his arms and kissed her. All the while, the crowd clapped and cheered, Kate more loudly than anyone. This had been so long coming, and she couldn't be happier for them. She rushed forward and congratulated both of them.

When things calmed down, Wes leaned toward her. "May I have this dance?"

Kate couldn't think of anything she'd like better. "Yes."

On the way to the dance floor, Mrs. Johnson came up to Wes and clasped his hands in gratitude. "Thank you for all you've done."

"You're very welcome," Wes said. "Hey, I was wondering. Do you still have Rascal?"

"We do! I was hoping you'd want him. You two were meant to be together."

"Wonderful," Wes grinned. "I'll come find you later. We were just about to dance."

"Oh certainly. Go. Go." She shooed them away. "Merry Christmas."

As Wes led Kate to the dance floor, she just couldn't help thinking Wes had more up his sleeve. If he was adopting Rascal, it meant he was moving.

Her heart leapt with joy. But she immediately doused the excitement. His moving didn't mean that his destination was Bayberry. It just might be an apartment in New York that allowed pets. Inwardly she groaned. He was so close, and yet he might be so far away tomorrow.

Part of her longed to ask him his plans. But another part didn't want to ruin this magical evening. Torn between knowing and not knowing, she decided to broach the subject later.

In the background, "All I Want for Christmas is You" started to play. Wes held his hand out to her. Wordlessly, she stepped into his arms. If they only had tonight, she wanted to make the most of it. Their bodies swayed to the music. It felt so right to have her hand resting on his shoulder and his arm wrapped around her waist. She was so thankful for all of the blessings of Christmas, both big and small.

As they danced, Kate said, "Thank you so much for going out on a limb for me—for the company—for Bayberry."

"My boss wasn't too happy about it. He had someone else in mind to buy the company."

"I'm sorry. I hope it didn't hurt your chances with the promotion."

"Well, that's the thing. It took all this for me to figure out that I'm not cut out for a lifetime of climbing the corporate ladder. I turned down the promotion."

Kate stopped in the middle of the dance floor and stared at him as couples twirled all around them. "I don't understand. You wanted that promotion so much. You wanted to stay with Watson & Summers for the rest of your career."

"I was wrong. There's only one place I want to spend the rest of my life, and it's right here in Bayberry. I flew back to New York to turn in my last report and resign."

Her heart beat so loud that it was hard to hear over it. "Really?"

Wes stared into her eyes. "Really. I'm here to stay."

This was so much information to take in at once, but she reveled in it. But then a bothersome thought intruded. "I hate to tell you this, but on the way to the dance I saw that your old house was sold. I'm sorry."

He pulled a keyring from his pocket. "I know."

She stared openmouthed at the keys, then at Wes. "What? How did that happen so fast?"

"As soon as I came to my senses and realized that Bayberry is where I want to live, I called the real estate agent and put in an offer. Mrs. Harding accepted, and agreed to rent me the house until we officially close. We met before I came to the dance and she gave me the keys. She told me I could start moving in right away."

"That's wonderful!" This evening just kept getting better and better.

Holding her close, he stared deep into her eyes. "I knew there was something special about you all those years ago in junior high. I just didn't know quite how special. And then I saw you sitting on your backside on the floor of the Steaming Brew—"

"You mean when you knocked me over?" She sent him a teasing grin.

"When I saw you again, you reminded me of all the things I was missing in my life. I don't want to miss any more special moments. I want to share the good and the bad with you. I want to share everything with you. I love you."

Happy tears blurred her vision. "I love you, too."

He got a serious look on his face. "And there's one more thing you should know."

The excited rhythm of her heart slowed. She braced herself for bad news. "What is it?

"Your aunt and the employees have asked me to join the management team of the new candle company. I hope you don't mind working side by side with me."

No words would do for this moment. Kate had to show him how she felt. Their eyes met before her gaze strayed to his mouth. She lifted up on her tiptoes and leaned toward him. All the while her heart was pounding in her chest. If this was a dream, she didn't want to wake up.

And then her lips found his. This was definitely no dream. It was so much better.

# *Epilogue*

*Christmas morning*

 T DIDN'T GET ANY BETTER than this.

Christmas in Bayberry. And there were going to be many more.

The sun wasn't even up, but Kate was awake. She lay in the dark, reliving the events of the Candlelight Dance, from Wes's surprise return to the town rallying to save their company, to being held in Wes's arms.

*I love you.* His words echoed in her mind as her heart soared.

Last night just couldn't have been a dream, right? She resisted the urge to pinch herself. If this was a dream, she didn't want to wake up.

She recalled being guided around the dance floor in Wes's strong, capable arms. And there had been that kiss. Oh, that kiss. She smiled and hugged her pillow.

She rolled over to look at the clock beside her bed.

The glowing green numbers read ten after six. And there was no way she'd be able to go back to sleep. She was too excited. The last time she'd been this keyed up on Christmas morning, she'd been a young child waiting for Santa to bring her a mini bake oven. This Christmas was so much better—so much sweeter.

And then she thought of the mysterious Santa who'd been popping up around town—the Santa whom none of her friends or family had seen. She thought back over what he'd told her, and realized he'd been right. In the end, it had all worked out. Was it possible he really was Santa?

As fast as the thought came to her, she dismissed it. He was just some good-hearted man, trying to make the holidays better for people—Kate included. That was all. Nothing more.

Kate slipped out of bed. Her feet landed on the cold hardwood floor. She hurried to flip on the overhead light, then blinked, giving her eyes a chance to adjust to the bright light. If she couldn't sleep, she could at least do something productive until everyone was up and ready for the gift exchange. She rushed to pull on sweatpants and a coordinating shirt. Casual wear was the only acceptable dress code in the Taylor house on Christmas morning.

Her phone dinged with a text message. Who in the world would be up at this hour after such a late, amazing night?

It was Wes. *What are you doing up so early?*

*How did you know?* she texted back.

*Your light is on.*

Last night, after they'd finished cleaning up the

community hall, since everyone in their group had agreed to spend Christmas morning at Aunt Penney's, Wes had been invited to spend the night in one of her guest rooms. Apparently, his bedroom was the one across from Kate's garage apartment.

Kate texted, *I couldn't sleep.*

*Neither could I.*

*I'm headed over to start a breakfast feast,* she told him.

*Sounds amazing. I'll help.*

*You don't have to.*

*I want to,* Wes texted. *See you in a few.*

She swept her hair back in a ponytail and brushed her teeth. She grabbed the presents she had for Wes, pulled on her boots, shrugged on her coat and rushed out the door. By the time she stepped into her aunt's kitchen, Wes already had the coffeemaker going. He was a man after her own heart. She had a feeling a very happy future awaited them, especially if he remembered that she didn't function in the mornings without caffeine.

She approached him, noticing that he had on jeans, a Bayberry sweatshirt and bare feet. His hair was a bit mussed up. And he'd never looked cuter. Her heart pitter-pattered. She rose up on her tiptoes and placed a feathery kiss upon his cheek.

He turned to her. "What was that for?"

"You started the coffee."

His blue eyes twinkled as a smile pulled at his lips. "I think I'll be making a lot more coffee in the future if that's the sort of payment I get."

She laughed. He was definitely a keeper.

He peered under her arm at the wrapped packages. "Who are those for?"

"You'll have to wait and see." She smiled as she walked into the living room, where the white lights on the tree were already glowing. She placed them among the other colorful parcels.

This Christmas, she had learned that the greatest gifts couldn't be wrapped up in fancy metallic papers or decorated with delicate satin bows. The best presents came from the heart. And this year, her rapidly expanding family had an abundance of blessings.

Kate turned to Wes. "I got you a few things. But nothing special."

He stepped up to her and gazed deeply into her eyes. "You already gave me the most special present of all."

"I did?"

He nodded and then reached into his back pocket. He pulled out the heart bookmark she'd made for him. She thought she'd lost it for good.

"But where did you find it?"

"You must have dropped it when you were in my office. Your office, I mean. I found it under the desk." He held it up to her. "It's the best Christmas present ever."

She shook her head as heat flushed her cheeks. "It's just a silly little bookmark."

"No, it's more than that. It's your heart. And that's the most precious present of all. Merry Christmas, Kate."

"Merry Christmas, Wes."

His head lowered as she rose up on her tiptoes. Once again, they met in the middle, his arms circling her waist and his lips joining hers. Kate's heart fluttered in her chest. This was the best Christmas ever. And it was only the beginning.

## The End

# Cast Iron Beef Stew

*A Hallmark Original Recipe*

In *Christmas in Bayberry*, Wes is in town to make a financial assessment of the Bayberry Candle Company. Kate, who works at the family business, isn't sure she'll like his report. But over a meal at Mel's Grille—beef stew, the Tuesday special—the two get to know each other a little better. Our Cast Iron Beef Stew is a wonderful, old-fashioned winter classic.

Be sure to properly season your skillet by coating the interior with a thin layer of vegetable oil or solid shortening, then placing the skillet upside down in the oven turned to about 325 degrees, for about one hour. Place aluminum foil under the skillet to catch the oil drips–no need to clean the oven afterwards! Once your skillet is seasoned, cooking in it regularly will keep it seasoned so you shouldn't have to go through those steps again. Don't put your skillet in the dishwasher.

## Ingredients
- 1/4 cup plus 1 tablespoon all-purpose flour
- 2 teaspoons kosher salt, plus more for seasoning
- 1 teaspoon freshly ground black pepper, plus more for seasoning
- 1 (1 1/2 to 2 lbs) boneless chuck roast
- 3 tablespoons vegetable oil
- 1 medium yellow onion, medium dice
- 2 tablespoons tomato paste or 1/2 cup tomato sauce
- 3 cups beef broth (or 3 cups water and 4 bouillon cubes)
- 2 bay leaves
- 4 fresh thyme sprigs or 1/2 teaspoon dried thyme
- 2 to 3 medium carrots
- 2 medium celery stalks
- 2 medium Yukon Gold potatoes (about 1 1/2 pounds)
- Optional: 1 cup frozen peas

Note: You can substitute 1 cup red wine for 1 cup of the broth.

## Preparation
1.  Place 1/4 cup of the flour and the measured salt and pepper in a large bowl and whisk to combine; set aside.

2.  Trim the beef and cut it into 1- to 1-1/2-inch cubes.

3.  Toss meat to coat in flour mixture.

4.  Heat the oil in a deep cast iron skillet or Dutch oven over medium heat.

5.  Shake off the excess flour from about one-third of the meat and add it to the cast iron.

6.  Stirring rarely, fry until browned all over, about 4 to 5 minutes.

7.  Remove meat and set aside.

8.  Add the onion to the pot and season with salt and pepper.

9.  Cook, stirring occasionally, until softened and just starting to brown, about 5 minutes.

10. Add the tomato paste, stir to coat the onion, and cook for about 1 to 2 minutes more.

11. Sprinkle in the remaining tablespoon of flour and cook, stirring occasionally, about 1 minute.

12. Pour in the broth, scraping the bottom of the pot as you stir to loosen remnants of beef coating.

13. Cook until the mixture has thickened, about 3 minutes.

14. Return the meat and any accumulated juices back to the cast iron skillet.

15. Add the broth, bay leaves, and thyme and stir to combine.

16. Increase the heat to high and bring to a boil.

17. Immediately reduce the heat to low and simmer uncovered for 1 hour.

18. While it's simmering, cut the carrots, celery, and potatoes into large dice and, when it's time, add them to the pot.

19. If adding peas, put them in at the same time.

20. Stir to combine, cover with a tight-fitting lid, and simmer, stirring occasionally, until the vegetables and meat are knife tender, about 1 hour more.

Thanks so much for reading *Christmas in Bayberry*. We hope you enjoyed it!

You might like these other books from Hallmark Publishing:

*An Unforgettable Christmas*
*Wrapped Up in Christmas*
*A Royal Christmas Wish*
*A Gingerbread Romance*
*Christmas in Evergreen*
*Christmas in Evergreen: Letters to Santa*

For information about our new releases and exclusive offers, sign up for our free newsletter at hallmarkchannel.com/hallmark-publishing-newsletter

You can also connect with us here:

Facebook.com/HallmarkPublishing

Twitter.com/HallmarkPublish

# About The Author

Award-winning author Jennifer Faye pens fun, heartwarming contemporary romances. Internationally published with books translated into more than a dozen languages. She is a two-time winner of the *RT Book Reviews* Reviewers' Choice Award and a winner of the CataRomance Reviewers' Choice Award.

Now living her dream, she resides with her very patient husband and two spoiled cats. When she's not plotting out her next romance, you can find her curled up with a mug of tea and a book. You can learn more about Jennifer at https://jenniferfaye.com/.

*Turn the page for a sneak peek of*

# ℱ COTTAGE
# *Wedding*

A HEART'S LANDING NOVEL
FROM HALLMARK PUBLISHING

# LEIGH DUNCAN

# Chapter One

*J*ASON HEART TUGGED ON THE door of I Do Cakes and stepped into the bakery. A sea of voices rolled over him like a wave, drowning the merry tinkle of the bell that announced his arrival. He brushed an unseen fleck from his starched white shirt while he took a second to regroup. The noisy crowd had thrown him off-stride. Even though he was right on time, owners and managers of the town's businesses already crowded the dining area. Chairs at the small tables were filled. Along the back wall, people had already laid claim to the best spots for leaning against the pink-and-white striped wallpaper. No matter. Unlike previous meetings that had gone on for hours, this one was just a formality—a final review of the agenda in preparation for the arrival of the Executive Editor for *Weddings Today*. He headed for the closest empty space.

"Jason. Here. Sit by me." Mildred Morrey beckoned with an age-spotted hand. "It's about time you got here," she groused, though the lines in her face softened into a smile. The owner of Forget Me Knot Flowers removed a gargantuan purse from the chair beside her. "I've had to fight off three people who wanted this seat. One more, and you were out of luck."

"Sorry. I meant to get here earlier. I was waylaid by an anxious bride on my way out the door." Jason bent his long frame into a pretzel and squeezed in between the woman who'd taken him under her wings ages ago and Cheri Clark, the owner of the area's premier bridal salon.

"Are you ready for all the chaos?" Mildred asked once he'd gotten settled.

"You don't really expect it to be as bad as everyone says, do you? After all these months of preparation, I'd expect everything to go pretty smoothly." For a town that put on more than two hundred weddings each year without a hitch, playing host to one woman ought to be a snap, even if she was one of the most influential people in the industry.

"I keep forgetting that you've never been through one of these."

Jason's throat tightened with a familiar ache. He coughed dryly. During the last review, his dad had still been in charge of the Captain's Cottage. At fifty-five and otherwise healthy, David Thaddeus Heart had complained of indigestion in the weeks leading up to the editor's visit. The diagnosis—pancreatic cancer—had been handed down at a doctor's appointment shortly after Heart's Landing had once again been named American's Top Wedding Destination. Over the course of the last two years, Jason had learned a lot about running one of the country's busiest wedding venues, but every once in a while, something came up that he'd never handled, like the magazine's biannual competition.

"We all miss your dad." Mildred played with an earring that dangled among her silvery curls and cleared her throat.

"He was a good man," added Cheri.

"Thanks. He was always sprucing up something. I bet he'd have enjoyed all the changes we made this spring." Jason glanced out the bakery's front window. With the magazine's evaluation looming, practically every storefront in town had been treated to a facelift. But the heart of Heart's Landing was, as always, the Captain's Cottage.

Jason's mouth tugged to the side in a wry grin. "Cottage" was hardly the word for a house the size of the one his great-great-great-grandfather and the town's founder, Captain Thaddeus Heart, had built. Fourteen bedrooms and two enormous ballrooms took up only a small portion of the home a scant hour southeast of Newport, where wealthy families like the Astors and Vanderbilts had once vacationed on their own enormous estates. Many of those mansions had fallen into disrepair, but the Captain's Cottage looked better than it ever had. Working around a schedule crowded with weddings and celebrations, the house-keeping staff had polished the one hundred twenty-five-year-old hardwood floors, carefully dusted every globe in chandeliers the size of small cars, vigorously shaken out rugs, and repaired even the tiniest nicks and smudges. Outside, white masonry walls gleamed in stark contrast to black shutters and trim. The season's roses had been trellised along the veranda, and every plant on the acres surrounding his family's ancestral home had been carefully manicured.

Mildred nudged his shoulder. "The pressure to retain our number one ranking is intense. Then, there's the fact that Regina Charm is handling the evaluation herself this year. She isn't the most pleasant person to deal with."

"Humph. You can say that again. A cold fish, that's what she is."

Jason smiled at Cheri. "Don't hold back, now. Tell me what you really feel."

The woman's face colored. "Oh, I shouldn't talk about our clients like that. But Regina pushed all my buttons."

"Mine, too." Mildred's voice dropped to a whisper. "She has that whole New York vibe working for her—aloof, snooty. Nothing was good enough for her when she was planning to get married here. And once her dreams of having a Heart's Landing wedding hit a snag—"

"When did that happen?" And why was he just hearing about it now? Jason threaded his fingers through hair that brushed his collar. It sounded like Regina Charm was a real piece of work. No wonder everyone in town was on edge.

"A year ago this spring. Remember the leak at your place?"

How could he forget? He'd taken a rare weekend away from his responsibilities at the Captain's Cottage last April. While he was in Boston, a bad storm had taken out one of the estate's massive oaks. To make matters worse, the uprooted tree had broken a pipe. Water had backed up into the Blue Room, causing severe damage. Among the many phone calls he'd swapped with Alicia, the venue's event coordinator, he seemed to recall a vague reference to a bride who'd been less than pleased that her ceremony had been shifted to the larger, more beautiful Green Room. But by the time he'd arrived back in town, Alicia had worked everything out. Or at least, he'd thought she had. "You're saying that was Regina's wedding?"

"It would have been. She and her fiancé called the whole thing off." Mildred sighed heavily. Though the breakup had nothing to do with Heart's Landing, the town prided itself on delivering a perfect wedding to every bride. On those rare occasions when they weren't able to meet that goal, it hurt. Even a year later. "Let's just say, I don't think she'll be looking at us through rose-colored glasses."

Jason stifled a groan. "I hope we're up to this."

Thank goodness repairs to the Blue Room had finally been completed. He'd hired Ryan Court, the best restoration contractor in the business, and had personally overseen every detail. Not that he'd needed to. Ryan had done an excellent job of painstakingly restoring the wainscoting to its original beauty. Refurbished with new drapes and paint, the second-largest ballroom had once again become a popular spot with the brides who chose the Cottage for their ceremonies and receptions.

"You'll do fine." Mildred patted his hand. "I'm sure you dealt with your fair share of CEOs and celebrities in Boston."

She had a point. He'd started out as the booking agent for a small comedy club and moved up to manager of one of the area's largest convention centers.

Over a span of ten years, he'd worked with the most popular bands and artists on the music scene. But all of that paled in comparison to the importance of the next ten days. Placing second or third in the *Weddings Today* competition was not an option. Maintaining their spot as the first choice for brides from one end of the country to the other was critical to the success of every business in town.

At the front of the room, Mayor Greg Thomas rapped firmly on the hostess stand. The low buzz of conversation died down.

"If I can have everyone's attention." Greg hitched a pair of khakis higher on his round belly. "We'll run through the agenda, item by item, and get this over with. I know you all want to get home to your families, and I don't want to keep you a minute longer than necessary. Let's dive right in, shall we?" He glanced at the notes he'd spread across the makeshift podium. "Regina Charm is due to arrive at three PM on Friday afternoon. She'll go straight to the Captain's Cottage. Jason, why don't you take it from there?"

"Yes, sir." Jason unfolded his legs and stood. Around him, the familiar faces of people he'd known his entire life nodded their encouragement. Everyone in the room shared one thing in common. Their livelihoods depended on a perfect score from *Weddings Today*. Determined to do his part, he cleared his throat.

"Much like it was done in the Captain's day, the entire household will turn out to greet Ms. Charm. I'll assume Thaddeus's role, as usual, but I've asked my girlfriend Clarissa to fill in for Evelyn." Well, not exactly. He and his cousin Evelyn had appeared at quite a few weddings and receptions dressed as the Captain and his wife, Mary. But when Clarissa had heard that the Executive Editor for *Weddings Today* would be in town, she'd begged to play a leading role. Which reminded him, he needed to confirm Clarissa's travel plans. He jotted a mental note and continued. "We've set aside the Azalea Suite for Ms. Charm's use while she's in town. It's the largest of our bridal apartments and has been recently updated. Once she's settled in, we'll turn her over to you, Mr. Mayor, and get ready for the meet-and-greet at six that evening. It'll be in the Green Room. You're all invited, of course."

He took his seat as the mayor nodded. "That's good. My only concern is in the timing. Since Ms. Charm opted to drive up from New York, rather than take the train, I'd be watching for her to arrive any time after noon. She's known to throw things off schedule a bit. Shows up early for interviews. That sort of thing. She likes to test people's reactions."

When a murmur of agreement passed through the room, Jason nodded. So, Regina Charm liked to spring surprises on her hosts, huh? Well, she wouldn't catch him napping. He'd post one of the house staff on the widow's walk bright and early Friday morning. They'd sound the alarm the moment a car turned onto the long, curving driveway that led to the Captain's Cottage.

Greg cleared his throat. "Everyone should have Ms. Charm's agenda." From a list that included practically every business in town, the editor had selected the places she'd like to see, as well as events she wanted to attend. It was more than enough to fill a crowded schedule. "Like I told Jason, Regina is prone to surprises. If your shop isn't on her list, she still might pop in for a quick visit. Stay on your toes."

One by one, the mayor called for brief reports on the plans to entertain the editor. From Something Old, Something New on Bridal Carriage Way to the bed and breakfast on Union Street, owners had arranged for tours of their businesses. Restaurants in the area had signed up to host Ms. Charm and her party at so many breakfasts, lunches, and dinners that the woman was in danger of needing an entire new wardrobe before she headed back to the city. Invitations to several weddings had been issued by brides who were eager for the opportunity to have their special day mentioned in *Weddings Today*. Plus, plenty of leisure activities had been planned in case the editor wanted to take advantage of the warmth of early summer. Last, but certainly not least, Regina would be the guest of honor at a special presentation of the Heart's Landing pageant. Usually performed in the fall, the play portrayed the time Captain Thaddeus had braved a hurricane in order to make port in time for his wife's birthday.

"I guess that sums it up." Mayor Thomas rubbed his hands together. "I'll be on call to serve as Ms. Charm's escort and answer any questions she might have throughout her visit here. One final word. I don't have to tell you how important this competition is for our town. With ceremonies taking place 365 days a year here in Heart's Landing, we pride ourselves on delivering the perfect wedding to every bride. But hard times lay ahead if we lose the designation of America's Top Wedding Destination. If anything goes awry, and I mean even the smallest hiccup, I'll expect to hear from you right away."

Greg scanned the room, his blue eyes meeting and registering agreement everywhere. Satisfied that his team knew what to do, he grinned. "All right now, we've got this. Let me hear that good old Heart's Landing spirit. What do you say?"

Jason, along with everyone else in the room, lifted an imaginary glass of champagne. He chimed in with the rest in the familiar toast. "The best is yet to be!"

"Yes, it will." Greg ran a hand over his bald pate. "Okay, folks. Time to head home now and get some rest."

Jason couldn't agree more. If Regina Charm was half as difficult to deal with as Mildred and Cheri said she was, everyone in town would need to keep their wits about them during her visit.

Read the book! *A Cottage Wedding* is available now!